DESTINY
MADE THEM
BROTHERS

ANDREW J. FENADY

PINNACLE BOOKS
Kensington Publishing Corp.
www.kensingtonbooks.com

PINNACLE BOOKS are published by

Kensington Publishing Corp.
119 West 40th Street
New York, NY 10018

All Kensington titles, imprints, and distributed lines are available at special quantity discounts for bulk purchases for sales promotions, premiums, fund-raising, educational, or institutional use. Special book excerpts or customized printings can also be created to fit specific needs. For details, write or phone the office of the Kensington special sales manager: Kensington Publishing Corp., 119 West 40th Street, New York, NY 10018, attn: Special Sales Department; phone 1-800-221-2647.

PINNACLE BOOKS and the Pinnacle logo are Reg. U.S. Pat. & TM Off.

ISBN-13: 978-0-7860-3069-9
ISBN-10: 0-7860-3069-0

First printing: February 2013

10 9 8 7 6 5 4 3 2 1

Printed in the United States of America

for our son
DUKE—
without whom this
novel would not
be what it is
and for **MARY FRANCES**
without whom . . .

NOTE

The events that follow, might, or might not, have occurred *exactly* as recorded here. They were compiled from accounts by historians—and by the author.

But as someone once said:

"When the truth becomes legend—print the legend."

PROLOGUE

There is a destiny which makes us brothers;
None goes his way alone:
All that we send into the lives of others
Comes back into our own.
　　　　　　—EDWIN MARKHAM

Those lines had not yet been written when the ordained paths of three men converged. The paths of two Yanks and one Rebel, but with an impact on events that changed the history of the United States—and even the world.

Events determined by Destiny? Fate? Providence? Some might shrug and call it Chance.

Events pieced together in a narrative never before told.

The lives and loves of three soldiers of fortune.

The ending for two of the men is known by nearly all. As for the third, the ending is more obscure, as is his life. His sojourn might never have been recorded except for parts of a recently discovered journal he kept, and for which he never wrote the final chapter . . . as far as we know.

Every story has a beginning, a middle, and an end.

This account begins at the middle—nearly a decade since the height of the war between North and South, but at the height of the war to win the West—May 16, 1873, as a man and a woman are in each other's arms in the act of love.

CHAPTER 1

Entwined, the naked bodies that knew each other so well since their marriage eleven years ago, he a flamboyant, heroic figure of the Civil War and scores of Indian campaigns, and she, one of the most beautiful women in America, together in triumph and disgrace, and even more in love for having tasted both.

The bedroom dark, except for a slanting colonnade of moonlight. Silent, but for the soft, sibilant ticking of the timepiece on the bed stand—and the murmurs of rapture, until:

The persistent rapping on the downstairs door, and becoming even more persistent and intense.

"George," she whispered.

"Whoever it is, he'll go away."

"It doesn't sound like it."

"No, it doesn't."

"What time is it?"

"I don't know, and I don't care."

"George . . ."

"All right."

He sat up in the bed, reached for the gold watch and chain, and held it up to catch the moonlight.

"Can't quite tell . . . After two."

"It must be important."

"I can think of something more important." He smiled in the dark.

"George . . ."

"All right, all right. But I'd better put on my pants—and I'll be right back unless the house is on fire, in which case . . ."

"George . . ."

The rapping became even more relentless.

"Have a little mercy on that door, you bastard!"

"The bastard can't hear you." She smiled.

"He will—and then some." Shirtless, he made his way down the stairs, stuffing the gold watch and chain into a pocket.

The knocking stopped only as he opened the door and a big man in civilian clothes stepped in, followed by two bigger men in uniform.

Without hesitation he clipped the first man with his right fist, backhanded the uniformed sergeant, and caught the other soldier with a swift left hook.

"I don't remember inviting you in."

"Sorry, sir. We were just following orders." The man in mufti rubbed his ample chin.

"Whose orders?"

"Not at liberty to say."

"What *are* you at liberty to say?"

"We're special couriers."

"What's so special?"

"Before two thirty a.m., the morning of May 16, 1873—in Monroe, Michigan, to be delivered by hand, General Custer."

"I'm not a general anymore, not even a colonel. Maybe not even in the army. I've been suspended for a year without pay—or haven't you heard?"

"I've heard. Everybody has, but you'll always be the general I followed on the charge at Yellow Tavern, sir."

"What?"

"I was Lieutenant Gary Aikins then, sir."

"Oh, I'm . . . I'm sorry. Didn't recognize you out of uniform, Lieutenant."

"I'd recognize you, sir, in or out of uniform." Aikins smiled.

George Armstrong Custer grinned. "Been a little out of sorts lately."

"Don't blame you, sir. You've got good reason to be."

"There's diverse opinion about that, Lieutenant."

"Not with me, or any of us who know you. And I'm out of the army, too, sir. As I said, special courier now, from Washington."

"What're you couriering?"

"Don't know. Just following orders, General."

"So did I . . . sometimes."

Special Courier Gary Aikins reached into his coat pocket and handed Custer a letter and a package.

"Hope it's good news, General."

"Not likely, not lately. And I apologize to all three of you for my . . . my . . ."

"Not necessary, sir. It's been an honor to be . . ."

"Be whacked?"

"That, too, sir. Good night . . . and good luck, General."

"Thank you, gentlemen, and . . . 'pearls in your oysters.'"

Gary Aikins smiled and saluted. So did the two soldiers as they turned and walked out.

Custer closed the door, looked at the letter and package in his hand, and whispered, "Custer's Luck."

He remembered the story about Napoleon. One of Bonaparte's generals had recommended a young officer for promotion, saying that the officer was intelligent, loyal, and brave. "Yes," Napoleon responded, "but is he *lucky*?"

Napoleon believed in luck. So did Custer—in spite of recent events.

"George."

It was Libbie's voice, Elizabeth Bacon Custer, as she walked down the stairs, in her robe, carrying a small lamp.

"Who were they? What was all that about?"

"They were old acquaintances, Libbie. And it was about this."

He held out the letter and package.

CHAPTER 2

After receiving the telegraph from Mr. Dodson—and the long journey home—Yuma had been back in Mason City only a matter of days. But during that time he once again realized how much he loved Rosemary, now a widow, and her son, who was his son, too.

He also realized, that more often than not, he gravitated toward trouble, or else trouble gravitated toward him. This time another gunfight, right here in the newspaper pressroom where he and Sheriff Jess Evans shot it out with Jim Gettings and a passel of his henchmen, killing Gettings and two of his gang, while the rest of them fled, a couple with bullets embedded in their bodies.

But several bullets that the attackers had fired were now embedded in Mr. Dodson's printing press, rendering it inoperative.

It was past midnight and he was doing his best to fix the *Mason City Bulletin*'s press so he and Elmer

Dodson, who was now upstairs asleep, could print the story and meet the weekly's deadline.

Not yet twenty, he had run away to join the 3rd Texas and fought valiantly until his brigade suffered overwhelming losses at Vicksburg in May of 1863, ten years ago—a lot of dead men ago, both gray and blue.

The events before and after Vicksburg he recorded in a journal he had sent back to Elmer Dodson, a journal that one day he hoped would be part of his dream to be a writer.

And now he and Dodson would write about the gunfight with Gettings—if he could repair the press. There were broken windows and other damage to the room, but his present concern and task was the press.

He wiped at the ink smeared on his face and spun toward the sound at the door—the sound of knocking, then rattling.

His immediate thought was of some of Gettings' survivors back to finish the job—a thought he quickly dismissed. They wouldn't have knocked.

He could make out the silhouettes of three figures in the darkness as he approached the front entrance. "Okay, hold on. I'm coming." He unlocked and opened the door with his left hand. His right hand hovered just above the holstered Colt at his side.

Three men in uniforms of the United States Army. A captain, a sergeant, and a private. All three looked as if they had ridden hard and far. He could hear the snorting of their sweated mounts hitched to the rail in front.

"Good morning, gentlemen. What can I do for you?"

"All depends," the percussive voice responded. "Is your name Yuma?"

"It is, Captain."

"Late of the Third Texas?"

"And other outfits."

"Then can we come in?"

"Come ahead."

They entered.

"You were at Vicksburg?" the captain asked.

"And other places."

"My brother died at Vicksburg."

"So did a lot of other brothers. Is that why you're here?"

"You weren't easy to find, but we did and just in time."

"In time for what?"

"To make a delivery. I'm Captain Robert Bixby."

"Captains make deliveries these days?"

"Captains follow orders—in the United States Army."

"Whose orders?"

"You'll find out before we do—if we ever do. All we know it's from one of our superior officers, to be delivered before two thirty a.m. the morning of May 16, 1873."

"What's the delivery?"

Captain Bixby reached into the pocket of his

tunic and produced a letter and package and handed them to Johnny Yuma.

"Well, I guess your mission is completed, Captain. Anything else?"

"Not as far as I'm concerned, Reb."

"At Appomattox General Grant said to General Lee, 'We are all countrymen again.'"

"Not as far as I'm concerned, Reb."

"Sorry to hear that. Good night . . . gentlemen."

As the three turned and left, a beautiful, but apprehensive, young woman entered through the open door.

"Johnny."

"Hello, Rosemary. You just missed a little get-together."

"They came to my place first. What is it? Is anything wrong?"

"What could be wrong? The war's over. Least I thought it was, 'til this came."

"What is it?"

"What the hell is going on?" Dodson's croaking voice called out as he came down the stairs.

"Special delivery," Yuma smiled, "from the U.S. Army."

"At this time of night? What's so important that it couldn't wait until daylight?"

"There's only one way to find out," Yuma said.

CHAPTER 3

"George, do you think this has anything to do with . . . with . . ."

"Say it, Libbie. Go ahead and say it. It's been said before and it'll be said again . . . The term is *court-martial*."

"I've got another term for it and it isn't ladylike."

"Libbie there's never been any other lady like you."

"And there's never been any man like my 'Custer Boy.' Remember?"

"How could I forget that pert, dimpled and beautiful eight-year-old girl swinging on the front gate? 'Hey you, Custer Boy,' she blurted and ran into the house leaving me dead in my tracks."

"Not for long. You knew how to take command even at the age of ten."

"Eleven . . . and now I'm in command of what? Not even . . ."

"George, are we going to stand here all night?

Or are we going to find out what's in that letter and package? Usually you're a lot more curious and impetuous."

"Me, impetuous?!"

"You. My 'Custer Boy.'"

"Libbie." He held out the letter and package. "No matter what's in here, good or bad, I'm the luckiest man on the face of the earth."

"Married to the luckiest lady."

He set the package on the table and opened the letter.

"Turn up the lamp, will you, please?"

"Who's it from?"

"An old comrade. Listen, Libbie."

"I'm listening."

CHAPTER 4

"Well, we're going to find out right now," Yuma said.

"Johnny." Rosemary looked at the letter. "Whatever it is, maybe you'd like to read it alone."

"Alone? You and Mr. Dodson are part of me . . . and so is the boy. Where is he?"

"At the house sleeping. Jed's more than ten years old, Johnny, and a lot older than his age."

"He sure is."

"If I'm going to lose my sleep, I damn well want to know why," Dodson said. "Open the damn thing."

"What is this?" Sheriff Jess Evans opened the door with his left hand. His right arm was in a sling. "A convention?"

"Come in, Jess. That'll make a quorum. How's the arm?"

"Just creased. Doc Barnes fixed it up fine. What did those dirty blueshirts want? Rode in and out like their britches were burnin'. Blue's never been my favorite color."

"Never mind the rhetoric," Dodson bellowed, "I repeat, open the damn thing!"

"I'm opening it." Yuma smiled, "But what about that press?"

"The press can wait, I can't—except for some coffee."

"There's a pot on the stove." Yuma pointed.

"I'll get it." Rosemary started to move.

"Good," Dodson nodded, "and get a bottle of rye to keep it company. This might call for a bracer. Most people my age don't get to be my age."

Rosemary poured the coffee as Johnny Yuma unfolded the pages of the letter and began to read softly in a voice of almost reverent remembrance at the words on the first page.

CHAPTER 5

George Armstrong Custer also read the letter in his hand as the woman he loved listened.

On the eve of any battle there is a destiny which makes some men enemies and some men brothers. And so, ten years ago tonight, destiny made a choice for the three of us—at Vicksburg . . .

Both Yuma and Custer paused and recalled what happened to the three of them at Vicksburg.

CHAPTER 6

Vicksburg—disputed passage of North and South.

Whoever held Vicksburg controlled the Mississippi and the Mississippi bisected the South—east and west.

Vicksburg, the most strategic geographic prize of the war.

And General Grant had been ordered by President Lincoln to siege and seize the guardian gate of the Confederacy—at any cost.

The South ultimately would stand or fall with the outcome at Vicksburg.

And so would Grant.

There were those, those in great number, who shook their heads in dismay at the appointment of Grant to command the Army of the Tennessee, a man who had been a flat-out failure at the age of thirty-nine, less than two years ago when the war began.

And it was rumored around that Grant had fallen back on his old weakness—whiskey.

But Lincoln had put his faith in nearly a dozen other generals, including McDowell, McClellan, Lyon, Scott, Fremont, Hooker, and Meade. They had all been out-generaled and suffered defeat at the hands of the Southern commanders, most of whom had graduated from West Point, as did Grant, but unlike them, near the bottom of his class. One achievement few could dispute: U.S. Grant was the best horseman in his or any other class, with the possible exception of George Armstrong Custer a few years later.

Lieutenant Grant had served with distinction and valor in the Mexican War in 1846 under command of General Zachary Taylor. He was at the front of the charge at Buena Vista, led by a colonel named Jefferson Davis—along with other comrades, including West Point graduates Robert E. Lee and George McClellan. Grant fought at Monterrey and at the fall of Veracruz and marched with General Winfield Scott into Mexico City.

After that campaign Captain Grant married Julia Boggs Dent. Never before or since had Grant been with another woman. There were few married couples as suited to each other as Ulysses Grant and Julia Dent—from the time they met through their lifetime together. She was the sister of Fredrick T. Dent, Grant's roommate at West Point. Julia and Grant became acquainted while he was on leave, and the mutual attraction was immediate and permanent.

Julia was somewhat less than beautiful, with one eye slightly askew, but winsome, with a ready smile which widened at the sight, even the mention, of her husband. What her countenance lacked in outright beauty, Julia more than made up for in grace and sparkle.

It was a cool cloud-free February evening with a silver ring of moon. They sat on the steps of the Dent family plantation, White Haven, just west of St. Louis, Missouri:

"Julia, do you know the date today?"

"February 14, eighteen forty . . ."

"The year doesn't matter."

"It doesn't?"

"No . . . well, I mean . . ."

"What do you mean, Ulysses?" She smiled.

"Well . . ." He cleared his throat. "This sounds sort of . . . juvenile, coming from an army man, but . . ."

"Charge ahead, Lieutenant."

"Will you be . . . my valentine?"

"Juvenile or no, the answer is 'yes'—or as you say in the army—'affirmative.'"

"Will you be my wife?" he blurted.

"You do know how to charge ahead, Ulysses. Do you want the answer in army triplicate? The answer is 'yes' . . . 'yes' . . ."

"That won't be necessary!" He leaped to his feet, grinning, and brought her closer. "Besides, I won't always be in the army . . ."

"But I'll always be your wife."

"Then we're engaged?!"

"Unofficially." She took his hand. "Meanwhile, I'll wear your West Point ring."

It remained "unofficially" for four years, including the Mexican War, during which Grant saw Julia only once—until their marriage on August 22, 1848, at White Haven. And after that Julia mostly called him "Ulys."

Grant had remained in the army, with Julia never far away, until he was sent to Humboldt, a remote outpost in California—without her.

That was the beginning of heavy drinking and led to the end of his military career—and failure after failure in civilian life—until the North–South hostilities.

The armies of both North and South needed soldiers, and soldiers needed to be led by officers, especially officers with battlefield experience. Grant reentered service at the outbreak of the Civil War as a colonel of an Illinois volunteer regiment. In August of 1861, he was appointed brigadier general and found his destiny—or destiny found him.

There was never a more tenacious, aggressive, defiant, and determined officer, and his men loved him, because inevitably, he led them to victory, from Fort Henry to Fort Donaldson, to Shiloh, and that led Lincoln to put him in command at the siege of Vicksburg, where it was his mission to divide the Confederacy in two—a mission that put a visible strain on Grant as never before.

By the time of Vicksburg, Grant and Julia had three sons, Fredrick Dent Grant, Ulysses S. Grant, Jr., Jesse Root Grant, and a daughter, Ellen Wrenshall Grant.

Major General Ulysses S. Grant—commanding the frontline hammers of his Army of the Tennessee, Generals William T. Sherman, Phil Sheridan, James B. McPherson, and Lew Wallace—had crossed the Mississippi River, then drove back the Confederate army of Lieutenant General John C. Pemberton, but into strong defensive lines circling the fortress city of Vicksburg.

Union assault after assault against the determined Confederate defenders were repulsed and Grant's army suffered severe casualties. Pemberton had the advantage of terrain and fortifications.

Heavy artillery bombardment, laced with torrential spring rain, bolts of thunder and lightning, along with creeping fog, had rendered the area miles around Vicksburg a moat-like no-man's-land.

Corporal Johnny Yuma and a tattered 3rd Texas Brigade had suffered the worst casualties from Grant's attacks, and the remnants of what was once a proud fighting force were scattered and dug in somewhere in that midnight no-man's-land.

It was Yuma's misfortune to be isolated with two of the worst remnants, brothers Joe and Jim Darcy. If this was to be Yuma's last night of the war he would have preferred to die in better company, or alone. Both Darcys were possessed of porcine features: piggish eyes, ears, and noses. The only reason they were with the 3rd Texas was that a Houston judge gave them a choice after they were convicted of assault and robbery, the choice of spending five years in prison or enlisting in the Confederate Army. It was either iron bars or stars and bars. They chose the Confederate battle flag until they could make an escape. The Darcys were known among the rebels as the "gray vultures," a sobriquet due to their habit of stripping dead soldiers, blue and gray, of everything—boots, watches, rings, money, and anything they could carry away. But now Johnny Yuma found himself in the company of the scavengers, Privates Joe and Jim Darcy, amid shellfire exploding closer and closer.

"It's hard to tell," Yuma said, "but . . ."

"It ain't hard to tell," Joe Darcy interrupted, "that if we stay here we'll be buzzard feed by mornin'."

"I was going to say that it's hard to tell, but it seems like most of those shells are coming from the west."

"So?" Jim Darcy shrugged.

"We're heading east toward our brigade."

"You mean," Joe smirked, "what's left of it."

"So long as there's any of us left, we fight."

"You fight, soldier boy." Jim grinned. "Us Darcys are leggin' it in the opposite direction."

"You mean deserting?"

"We mean keepin' alive, right, brother Jim?"

"That's it, brother Joe. So long, soldier boy, say hello to the buzzards. We're quittin'."

Both Darcys lifted themselves from the shell hole, turned, and started to move.

"Just a minute, scum." Yuma's pistol was aimed in their direction. "Lay down your rifles and side-arms."

"Like hell we will!" Joe said.

"Like hell you won't, or you'll both die right here. Either that or I'm taking you back as deserters. I've got no compunction about doing it either way."

"'Compunction'?" Joe said. "What's that mean, brother Jim?"

"Don't know."

"You'll find out if those guns don't hit the ground, slow and easy, right now."

"What chance you got," Jim Darcy said through his crooked teeth, "of gettin' us back to anywhere through this hellfire?"

"I'll take that chance and so will you, unless you want some hellfire from this." Yuma pointed his gun. "Now drop those weapons—like I said, slow and easy."

"Sure, soldier boy." Joe Darcy shrugged. "But it's your funeral."

Both Darcys did as they were told—for the time being.

Johnny Yuma had run away from his home, Mason City, from his father, Sheriff Ned Yuma, and even from the girl he loved more than anything in the world, Rosemary Cutler.

But this was one thing he could not run away from.

CHAPTER 7

Captain George Armstrong Custer and a young, frightened Union lieutenant, Gregg Palmer, were crouched against the stump of an oak tree, amid a curling, patchy mist. The captain wiped at his face with his red scarf.

Custer's eyes tried to penetrate the fog and midnight darkness. He motioned for the lieutenant to follow him. They advanced cautiously from tree to rock, looking for any familiar landmark and looking for anything that moved, blue or gray. The area was wracked with bursts of blossoming explosions and shrapnel that rained down around them.

Custer made out a large shell hole, which might mean temporary safety. He tapped the lieutenant and pointed.

The two of them made their way toward it, dove in, and flattened against the ground.

"Load up," Custer whispered.

Both started to pump shells into their pistols.

"Captain, you got any idea where we are?"

"In hell's front yard, I'd say."

"Well, Captain, I'll say this. There's nobody I'd rather be with, Captain . . ."

"Quiet."

But the night was anything but quiet, and George Armstrong Custer's life had been anything but quiet.

He was born in New Rumley, Ohio, December 5, 1839, and born to be a soldier, his childhood ambition. As a young boy he moved to Monroe, Michigan, to be with his only sister, Lydia, and go to school.

When little more than a baby he had had difficulty pronouncing his name. Instead of Armstrong it came out "Autie." As often as not, the nickname stuck to him through his teens and beyond—but not with Elizabeth Bacon, better known as Libbie. To her he was Custer Boy or George. Some considered him "wild"; others settled for "spirited" as he set a new record for outlandish pranks and after-school punishments. Autie loved to hunt, fish, hike, and ride his sister's horses.

Libbie's father, Judge Daniel Stanton Bacon, glowered with disfavor and admonished his beloved daughter to keep away from such riffraff. She did, but only when the judge was in the vicinity.

At the age of sixteen, Autie moved back to New Rumley and even became substitute principal and teacher in a one-room schoolhouse. But not for long. Back in Monroe, Custer petitioned Senator John A. Bingham for an appointment to West Point.

Custer passed the exams, barely, but barely was good enough for Autie. With the pending war he reckoned this was his path to glory, a glory he would someday share with Libbie.

Lieutenant George Armstrong Custer graduated last in the West Point class of 1861—last in academic subjects and first in demerits. Many of those demerits were due to pranks; however, one went undetected and unpunished. It involved a superior officer who took great pride in a flock of prize hens and a buff cock he had dubbed "Mister Chanticleer," which kept Custer and other cadets awake with his boastful crowing until cadet Custer took it upon himself to kidnap "Mister Chanticleer," dispatch and pluck him, prepare the un-feathered remains in a stew pan, and, sharing his bounty with a couple other cadets, devour the result—and henceforth he enjoyed the uninterrupted sleep of satisfaction, if not innocence. The superior officer had his suspicions as to the identity of the culprit, but lacked sufficient evidence of proof.

But what Custer lacked in academic achievement, he made up by being first in what he considered more important military achievements, marksmanship and horsemanship. And by then the war was no longer pending. It was a reality and the army was less in need of scholars and more in demand of soldiers, leaders who could shoot straight, ride hard, and inspire their troops.

Custer filled the bill.

But so did another West Pointer—James Ewell Brown (JEB) Stuart—a charismatic cavalier from Virginia, who came close and sometimes even tied Custer in the soldiery fields of rifle, saber, and horsemanship.

They became friendly competitors and rode together under Robert E. Lee in the attack against John Brown's uprising at Harpers Ferry and raced to get to Brown, where Custer saved Stuart's life in the assault as one of Brown's sons aimed a pistol point-blank at Stuart's back.

But Custer shot first.

Later, the two of them were among those who watched the abolitionist hang after delivering an impassioned speech against slavery—but John Brown's cause would live on and separate the North and South.

Custer and JEB Stuart would also be separated, as Custer had chosen the Union and Stuart's loyalty remained with his native state.

Now Stuart was already Lee's right hand as brigadier general and the boldest, most beloved cavalry commander, whose Black Horse Raiders hit like bolts of lightning into the blue ranks of Northern infantry and cavalry alike, while Custer was not yet a captain.

It was inevitable that the two would meet

again—and not in friendly competition but deadly combat.

First attached to General McDowell's 2nd Cavalry Brigade, Custer led a decisive charge at Bull Run; then he was assigned to General George B. McClellen, who desperately needed a victory to maintain command of the Grand Army of the Potomac.

The opportunity came at Chickahominy, for General McClellen and Lieutenant Custer. McClellen ordered Custer to lead the attack at dawn.

"Cross that river and you'll come out a captain. Good luck, Lieutenant."

"Luck's my guiding star," Custer replied and rode off.

That's when he came across the Monroe men of the red-scarfed 2nd Michigan Brigade, many of them familiar.

Custer waved his hat, spurred his horse, and hollered.

"Come on, Monroe. Follow me. Ride, you Wolverines! Charge!"

And charge they did, with Custer in the lead, into the erupting Rebel rifles, across the swamp and into flashes of smoke and a fusillade of bullets. But Custer's charge succeeded and McClellan had his victory and Custer his captaincy. That was not the last of many more charges. From then on Custer wore a uniform that included a red scarf. So did his men.

But now, Custer, who would much rather have

been on a horse leading another charge, found himself away from his regiment in response to a summons from General Phil Sheridan to join him at Vicksburg. Sheridan was anticipating and preparing for a future campaign and wanted Custer with him. That would be up to Grant, but at present the primary objective was Vicksburg, and Custer lay in a shell hole with young Lieutenant Gregg Palmer somewhere in hell's front yard.

"Captain . . ." Palmer blurted.

"What?"

"We gotta find our company, we gotta get back . . ."

"Quiet, Lieutenant. There's some of them still around. I . . ."

Before Custer finished, two shrill Rebel yells tore the night and two gray-clad soldiers sprang into the shell hole screaming and shooting. Their long rifles exploded, as did Custer's and Palmer's pistols.

The fiery exchange was blinding but brief, and when it was done, two Rebels were down and still— a broken pattern of what held life a moment ago— the lieutenant badly hit and bleeding. Custer cradled the dying young officer.

"Lieutenant . . ."

"I'll . . . be quiet, Captain . . . forever quiet . . ."

Custer released the lifeless body and slowly climbed out, looked in all directions, hesitated for just an instant, then moved away, leaving behind three dead men—all three born in the United States of America, but in states no longer united, now consisting of two countries, two enemies—and thousands upon thousands of lifeless bodies in what had become hundreds and hundreds of battlefields north and south of the Mason-Dixon Line.

CHAPTER 8

The war became inevitable with the election of Abraham Lincoln in 1860. Lincoln stood against slavery and for a strong Union—and the country stood with Lincoln. Half the country. The other half stood for states' rights, which included the right to slavery.

Faint rumblings had been heard at first in the distance for more than a century—rumblings that had their origins as early as 1619 when a Dutch ship with twenty African slaves aboard arrived at the English colony of Jamestown, Virginia.

But even a century before that black plantation slavery had begun in the New World when Spaniards started importing slaves from Africa to take the place of American Indians who had died of overwork and exposure to disease.

After the Revolutionary War, according to the U.S. Constitution all men were created equal—but not all free. The tolerance of slavery was part of the glue that allowed the states to remain united. It made for an uneasy and temporary unity.

By mid-nineteenth century, abolitionists vowed to awaken the conscience of the entire nation.

The swelling rumble of discontent erupted into gunfire at Fort Sumter on April 12, 1861—Confederate gunfire aimed at the heart of the Union. South Carolina had been the first state to secede, followed on January 10, 1861, by Florida and on January 19, by Georgia. Texas, along with nine other states, would not be far behind.

Graduate officers and even cadets of West Point had to make a choice—their native country or their native state.

One who chose his native Virginia was Robert E. Lee, who had graduated at the head of his class in 1829, served with honor and glory in the Mexican War, became superintendant of West Point, and saw frontier duty in Texas.

It was Lee who commanded the detachment that suppressed the uprising led by John Brown at Harpers Ferry—and was first offered command of the U.S. Army at the outbreak of the Civil War. He wrote to his sister, "With all my devotion to the Union and feeling of loyalty and duty of an American citizen I can not raise my hand against my relatives. My children, my home. My Virginia.

"I hope I may never be called upon to raise my sword."

But he was called, and did so reluctantly but effectively.

Other Union officers born in the South joined with Lee, including Joseph E. Johnston, JEB Stuart, P.G.T. Beauregard, T.J. Jackson, Jubal Early, and Sidney Johnston, for the cause of states' rights—and dealt defeat after defeat at Fort Sumter, Lexington, Belmont, Shiloh, Fort Royal, Bull Run—until U.S. Grant and his generals began to turn the tide. The high-water mark of that tide—and the blow that would split the Confederacy and drain its resources—would be at Vicksburg.

If that blow could be delivered.

Providence? Fate? Chance? Destiny?—something was drawing three of the thousands of soldiers in the field closer and closer together toward a pivotal point in the clash that was to come.

It was not only graduate officers and cadets from West Point who had to make the choice between Union and the Southern causes.

Hundreds of thousands of civilians from cities, villages, and farms—from northern, southern, and border states had to decide—blue or gray. And there were those who chose to buy their way out of the carnage.

Johnny Yuma was not one of those. Texas had seceded from the Union months ago. Exactly what tipped the balance, he was not quite sure. He would not fight for slavery. He had never even seen a slave. But at his age he had become a rebel in more ways than one.

His father, Sheriff Ned Yuma, was a better lawman than husband. Then, after Johnny's mother died, a better lawman than father. He wanted Johnny to grow up and be a lawman. But Johnny wanted to be a writer and was encouraged by Elmer Dodson, publisher and editor of the local newspaper. His father believed in the Union, so Johnny tilted toward Texas and the Confederacy. And when Ned Yuma entrusted his young son with the responsibility of guarding a prisoner, and in the sheriff's eyes his son had violated that trust, Johnny could no longer stay in Mason City—in spite of his love for Rosemary Cutler. He joined the Third Texas and took part in victory after victory—until Vicksburg— and the Darcys. He could have let them desert, but something inside him would not allow that violation of duty to the Third Texas.

And now he was trying to find his way back to his brigade while pointing his gun toward the two "gray vultures."

"It might be days and nights—if ever—that we get back to our lines," Joe Darcy smirked, "and even with them explosions you got to fall asleep sometime. Now me and ol' Jimmy here can take turns—and when you do fall asleep, soldier boy, you're gonna wake up dead. Ain't that so, Jimmy?"

"It's so, brother Joe."

"And so is this," Yuma said, "we're going to keep

on moving, nights and days, all three of us, and if either one, or both of you, do anything sudden you'll both wake up in burning hell and that's a promise. Move!"

Captain George Armstrong Custer moved through the starless blanket of night with only his instinct to guide him. He had always moved toward the sound of guns, but the sound of guns seemed to come from every direction. This was one time when caution appeared to be the wiser strategy.

Custer was not used to caution, not at Bull Run, the Peninsular Campaign, and not at Chickahominy and the red scarf he still wore. Something inside told him that there had to be other charges on other occasions, with other victories and promotions. But that something was tempered by the knowledge that now there might be unseen enemies with every step of the way. If there were to be other victories, other promotions and glory to share with Libbie, Custer would have to survive unseen enemies somewhere around Vicksburg. He stopped in midstep.

Up ahead the outline of a shack, dimly lighted. He took a deep breath and moved toward it.

Custer paused at the entrance, then kicked the door open. Gun drawn and ready, he stepped inside.

There wasn't much to the wooden structure, and what there was of it seemed to be canting slightly from the punishment of time, weather, and the multiple shocks of nearby exploded shells. It was sparsely furnished with scarred tables, chairs, and bunk on a damp earthen floor, beneath a leaky roof.

In the shadows, a figure stood near a table on the other side of the room. The figure leaned on a makeshift cane, in front of him on the table an unopened bottle of whiskey . . . and a pistol.

"Just stand there!" Custer ordered.

The figure did as he was ordered.

"All right now . . . slow . . . Come out of the dark so I can see you."

The figure turned, using the cane with one hand and holding a freshly lit cigar in the other. He took a step forward, then spoke in a voice of gravel.

"You're just in time."

George Armstrong Custer stood thunderstruck.

"General Grant!"

General Ulysses Simpson Grant's face was weary, pain-riddled, but almost calm.

"Sir," Custer managed, "I'm Captain Custer . . ."

"Yes, Captain, I've heard about you. You're just in time, Captain Custer, in time to have a drink with me."

CHAPTER 9

Custer had never before met, or even seen, General Grant. From the descriptions he had heard, he had imagined a smaller, shorter, less-imposing man. But even as he leaned on the cane, Grant was at least of average build and height. And even with all the stress and strain of dozens of campaigns and untold responsibilities heaped on the shoulders of this one man, there was something still smoldering in the tired, tender eyes that gazed at Custer. But Captain Custer was alarmed at what the commander of the Army of the Tennessee had said.

". . . You're just in time, Captain Custer, to have a drink with me."

Custer glanced at the bottle on the table, unopened, and back at Grant as the general put the cigar between his lips, breathed deeply, and exhaled a patternless cloud of smoke.

Was Ulysses Simpson Grant, on the eve of what

would be the most telling battle of the war, about to fall back into his legendary whiskey ways?

It certainly seemed so.

But even though Grant had not yet taken that first drink, he appeared to be in no condition to design and execute the strategy necessary to win a major battle.

In an instant a flurry of thoughts of what he had heard about Grant flooded across Custer's mind. In the heat of battle, when his staff officers were visibly affected by anxiety and doubt, Grant smoked his cigar and calmly issued orders in a clear, composed manner. Often he wrote dispatches as enemy shells burst around him as if he were sitting safely at headquarters a hundred miles away.

On certain other occasions it would have been a pleasure, no, an honor, to have a social drink with the man many considered to be the hope of the North—or perhaps a toast after a victorious battle, but on this occasion, prelude to the most decisive battle yet to be fought, with thousands of lives at stake on both sides, there was the notion in Custer that one drink, maybe one bottle, would not be enough for the "Whiskey General."

Even at Grant's clearest and brightest, the outcome of the siege of Vicksburg would be in doubt. But within that bottle, defeat and disgrace were certain.

In that instant Custer decided to ignore Grant's precipitous invitation while thinking of something to say.

But Grant spoke first.

"Are you alone, Captain?"

"Yes, sir."

"So am I . . . alone . . . except for the dead piled on dead . . . and those who will be . . . I've got to talk to somebody. So . . . put that pistol away and tell me the time."

Custer gladly complied.

He holstered his gun and removed the watch from his pocket, flipping open the lid while trying not to look at the bottle of whiskey on the table.

"It's two thirty, sir."

Grant glanced at the bottle, then looked back at Custer as the sounds of bursting shells echoed in the distance.

General Grant looked upward.

"Those aren't flights of angels, Captain—or are they? Angels of death . . . singing us to our rest . . ."

"I don't think so, sir. Not yet. There's a lot to be done, sir . . . especially by you."

"Hmph . . . a lot to be done . . . but what're you doing way out here, Captain?"

"We . . . I'm cut off from my company, sir. I was trying to get back. There's a rumor we're to attack this morning . . ."

Catching himself, Custer stopped.

"There is, huh? Well, in every war there's as many rumors as rifle shots."

Grant took a step and even though he tried not to show it, there was pain.

"Excuse me, sir," Custer leaned forward, "are you hit?"

"Hit?" Grant paused. "I presume you mean wounded . . . There are different kinds of wounds . . . but the answer is no." He held up the cane. "I also presume you refer to this . . ."

Confused, Custer nodded slightly. "Sir, can I help you get back to headquarters?"

Grant took a deep draw from the cigar.

"What makes you think I want to get back . . . to headquarters?"

"I . . ."

"Never mind."

Grant's answer and attitude only added to Custer's confusion.

"I said I had to talk to somebody, and since you're the only somebody around, sent by fate, or I don't know what . . . do you want to hear?"

"Yess . . ." Custer stammered, ". . . yes, sir."

Grant nodded and took and another deep draw from his cigar.

It seemed to Custer that Grant's head had cleared somewhat, from the effect of the inhaled cigar—or the opportunity to talk to somebody.

"I heard some things about you, Custer—particularly from Phil Sheridan—among other things, that you were an outstanding horseman at the Point. That true?"

Custer managed an embarrassed shrug.

"No need to be modest, I was a pretty damn

good horseman myself—at the Point, the Mexican Campaign, and before we were married, with Julia . . . I rode a bony brown steed—called him Fashion. Her horse was a beauty, part Arabian, she named her Psyche, and . . . but I'm commencing to ramble . . . Well, a couple of days ago I fell from a horse, sprained an ankle." Grant tapped the tip of the cane on the floor of the shack. "The rumor, yes, the *rumor* is, I was drunk . . ."

Grant drew again from the cigar.

". . . The *truth* is I hadn't slept in three days and was suffering a blinding headache. Do you think Halleck will believe it? He's looking for an excuse to relieve me."

Grant breathed deeply, this time without drawing from the cigar, and his voice softened.

"I know someone who will believe me—you a married man, Captain Custer?"

"No . . . no, sir."

"No sweetheart back home? Where is home?"

"Monroe, Michigan, and . . . well . . ."

"Ah ha, there is someone. Marry her, Custer, soon as you can. Don't wait like I did . . . between wars. How old are you?"

"Twenty-two, sir."

"I was twenty-seven. What's her name?"

"Libbie, Elizabeth Bacon, sir."

"Libbie, that's a sweet-sounding name. My wife's name is Julia and . . . the truth is I haven't had a drink since . . . a lot of dead men ago . . .

good men . . ." Grant looked at Custer, ". . . Men twenty-two years old, and a lot younger. Do you believe that, Captain?"

Again Custer tried to avoid looking at the whiskey bottle on the table.

"I believe it, General."

"But you can't help wondering what I'm doing here with that bottle . . . and that, Captain Custer, is the question . . ."

Custer made no reply. He stiffened, almost at attention.

"Relax, soldier . . . Maybe we'll both find the answer."

Grant drew again from the cigar. This time not as deep.

The sounds of bursting shells reverberated anew. Grant reacted. "But I don't know how much time we have to find out . . ."

"Not if we stay here. Don't you think, sir, we ought to . . ."

"I think . . . if one of those shells has our names on it, it'll find us . . . here, or someplace else. Something tells me we still have time."

Custer remembered the young lieutenant's words, and thought to himself if he had to die, there was no one he'd rather die with . . . but he also thought that he'd rather not die.

"Do you know what's in that bottle, Captain? Sure you do. But there's something else. Failure."

"Sir . . ."

"Do you know how to spell failure? With a G . . . G-R-A-N-T.

Custer mustered his courage. This time a different sort of courage—to confront the commanding general at Vicksburg.

"Permission to speak freely, General?"

"I don't think the lack of permission would stop you, Custer, but, permission granted."

"Belmont. Fort Henry. Fort Donelson. Shiloh. They weren't failures. They were victories. Grant's victories."

"Shiloh. There's a rumor about that one, too. They say if Johnston hadn't been killed, the army under me would have been annihilated or captured."

"I've studied your battle plan for that campaign, sir. We all have. It's considered a classic blueprint of modern warfare. If the Rebs had ten Johnstons in the field, it still would have been your day, and your men still say they'd ride to hell and back with you, and I've heard them say it. That doesn't spell failure, General Grant."

"A general is as good as his last battle—or his next one. And for this general, that's Vicksburg."

"All the more reason we need you . . ."

"Oh, I can lead them to hell, all right, but as far as Vicksburg is concerned, I'm not so sure about the *back* part."

"Your men are sure . . . in spite of what you've gone through, and the pain you're going through now and are trying to hide."

"Pain."

Grant set the cane on the table and reached for the bottle.

"They call this painkiller."

"They also call it brave maker. You don't need any of that, sir, in spite of your leg."

"Leg . . . no, not the leg—and not the fever from Panama—nor the ague, but this headache—this thundering headache . . . the pounding boots of a thousand ghostly battalions, battering at this brain—my orders, to men I've sent to die, and those I will send."

Grant looked at the bottle in his hand. "Do you know what it is to bury four thousand men in one grave? I do."

"General, someone has to give those orders. If it weren't for you a lot more men would have been buried—and will be."

Grant slammed the bottle on the table, hard, almost hard enough to break it, but the bottle was still intact, and still unopened. He picked up the cane and limped a few steps around the room.

"Custer, nearly all my life I've had a severe schooling in disappointment—never known flush times— drummed out of the army at Fort Humboldt—a bust at farming—at real estate. When the war broke out I was a clerk in my father's store. Not like those dashing Rebel generals."

"You're the only one who's made them run, sir. Outfought and out-strategized all of 'em."

"Lee—Stuart—Beauregard—Jackson—Longstreet—each one, the stuff of success—brilliant . . ."

"Not successful and brilliant enough to beat you and the generals you lead—Sherman, Sheridan, McPherson, Wallace . . ."

"How far can I lead them? How long before I fail again? I've got a feeling, Custer . . ."

"You're tired, sir. All you've been through . . ."

"Yes, tired. Vicksburg. I've got a feeling Vicksburg will be my biggest failure, taking the lives of tens of thousands of men down with me. Do you know what it will cost to take Vicksburg?"

"I know what it will cost if we don't."

Grant stopped moving around the room. His shoulders squared, he rolled the butt end of the cigar around in his mouth, took a draw, and spit out a tidbit of leaf.

"You're right. Take Vicksburg and we take back the Mississippi and split the Confederacy. Without it the war goes on for years."

"And countless more soldiers die during those years. Soldiers and even civilians on both sides."

"Damn! This cigar's gone out. You got a match, Custer?"

"Don't smoke, sir. Gave it up some time ago."

"You did, huh?! Well, you'll take it up again. They say that smoking serves to steady nerves. But your nerves seem steady enough. Well, never mind, I've got some matches here . . . somewhere."

Grant fumbled around his tunic, pulled out a box of matches, and relit the cigar. "Now, then, if

I can hit Pemberton where and when he least expects it—you mentioned my battle plan for Shiloh, well, I've worked out a battle plan for Vicksburg."

He reached inside his tunic again and withdrew a small folded map. He unfolded and studied it.

"A battle plan. But if it fails it's a death warrant, one common graveyard for the Armies of the Tennessee and Ohio."

Suddenly his shoulders slumped, the light that shone in his eyes a moment ago suddenly dimmed; his fingers trembled. It was as if he were undergoing a seizure, consumed by the ghosts of battles from the past and even the ghosts of battles to come. He seemed to shrink in size physically. He was no longer the commander of the siege of Vicksburg. No longer in complete command of himself.

If the Rebel army could see him now, they would rally around their battle flag and the Confederate leaders defending Vicksburg would take heart and not only defend their positions, but counterattack and drive back the bluecoats.

And just as bad and even worse, if his own generals, Sherman, Sheridan, McPherson, and Wallace, were witness to Grant's dissolution, they would lose heart, unity, and without a master plan and planner, lose the will and wherewithal to win.

Grant was the glue that kept them and the Union forces together. And without that glue and guidance the outcome would no longer be in doubt. It would be inevitable. Defeat for the Union, disgrace, and discharge—failure once again for Ulysses Simpson Grant.

Still shaking, Grant folded the map, let it drop on the table, and put the pistol on top of it.

He lifted the bottle and took a few steps away from the table. In so doing the cane fell to the floor. Grant looked at the bottle.

". . . I'm out of steam, Custer, and that's why I turned and walked away from it all tonight."

"General . . ." Custer stooped, reached for, picked up the fallen cane and was handing it to Grant.

Abruptly the door burst open.

Three men in gray were suddenly in the room.

A corporal, Johnny Yuma, a gun drawn—and the brothers Jim and Joe Darcy, unarmed, begrimed, and not looking anything like the pride of the Confederacy.

"All right, Yankees," Yuma barked, "Hold! Or be shot right now!"

Custer had no chance to go for his gun. Grant was too far from the table to reach for the pistol there.

"Captain"—Yuma aimed at Custer—"you're a prisoner of war." Then at Grant. "And you . . ."

Grant took a step forward and dropped his cigar to the floor.

Yuma and the Darcys were even more surprised than Custer had been.

"Well, hell." Joe Darcy grinned. "Lookit what you bagged, Yuma!"

"Yeah, bo!" Jim Darcy grinned even broader. "Ol' Whiskers hisself!"

"Sir . . ." Yuma almost stammered, ". . . are you . . ."

"That's right, Corporal, I'm . . . a prisoner of war."

CHAPTER 10

Grant's headquarters on the eve of what was to be the climactic battle of Vicksburg was without U.S. Grant, its commanding general.

Four other generals were there in quiet, but deeply concerned, conference: William Tecumseh Sherman, Philip Henry Sheridan, James Birdseye McPherson, and Lew Wallace.

There was another presence there at Vicksburg, though not in person, still, very much in evidence— Major General Henry Wagner Halleck, the nominal commander of the Department of Missouri, which included western Kentucky, Illinois, Wisconsin, Minnesota, Iowa, Missouri, and Arkansas.

Halleck was a competent administrator, but seldom present, or near, the field of battle. While he was Grant's superior officer, it was common knowledge Halleck also was envious of Grant's successes and spectacular career rise. Halleck himself coveted credit and public acclaim for Grant's field operations, and sought any excuse to discredit and relieve him of command.

As on the eve of any climactic battle an eerie silence had fallen on the battleground area. The shellfire had virtually ceased in, and around, the camps.

In no place were the lines more than six hundred yards from the enemy.

And in some places the picket lines were so close to each other—where there was space enough between the lines to post pickets—that the men could converse.

But tonight there was no conversing, no taunting, no boasting between the enemies. Both sides were saving their breath and energy for the coming confrontation.

But on both sides no one knew exactly where or when that confrontation would come.

In an earlier report Grant had written:

My line was more than fifteen miles long extending from Haines' Bluff to Vicksburg, thence to Warrenton. The line of the enemy was about seven. In addition to this, having an enemy at Canton and Jackson, in our rear, who was being constantly reinforced, we required a second line of defense facing the other way. The ground around Vicksburg is admirable for defense. On the north it is about two hundred feet above the Mississippi

*River at the highest point and very much cut up by
the washing rains; the ravines are grown up with
cane and underbrush, while the sides and tops are
covered with a dense forest. The enemy's line of
defense follows the crest of a ridge from the river
north of the city eastward, then southerly around
to the Jackson road full three miles back of the city.*

General Ulysses Simpson Grant had worked out
a plan to storm the city's defenses at crucial points
and take Vicksburg.

But both Grant and his plan were absent from
headquarters just hours before that plan was to be
implemented.

Somewhere along those lines, two Yankee soldiers, silhouettes against the chocolate night, sat
leaning back-to-back against each other, rifles at
the ready. Soldiers as different as night and day,
with only one thing in common—dirty blue uniforms: Taylor Hampton, from the city of New York.
Tom Hawks from the farmlands of Kansas.

It had become a silent night except for the oc-
casional soft crack of a sniper's rifle or the shattered blossom of a distant cannon shell.

"Tay," Tom Hawks whispered. "What're you
thinking?"

"What the hell do you think I'm thinking? Probably the same as you."

"Yeah? Well, what's that?"

"Oh, life and death—and what happens in between."

"Yeah . . ."

"Tom, ol' chum, can you say something besides 'yeah'?"

"Sure . . . I did ask you a question, didn't I?"

"Yeah . . . you did. And I did answer it, didn't I?"

"Well . . . sort of."

"That's the only answer I've got . . . so far."

"Tay, do you think there's an . . . afterlife? You're educated . . . rich."

"My father's rich, not me—but the bastard wouldn't buy me out of the army. Said it would make a man out of me if it didn't kill me, and I was too proud or embarrassed to call upon my so-called friends."

"Fort Donelson, Shiloh, you didn't fight like you wanted to stay out of the army. You fought like . . ."

"Like I wanted to stay alive. Figured I'd be less of a target if I kept moving. It was either move ahead or face the old man."

"You mean General Grant?"

"Who else?"

"He ain't that much older than us."

"He is, in some ways."

There was a brief silence, then.

"Tay . . ."

"What?"

"We been together through a lot. You never told me."

"About what?"

"About wanting to get out of the army."

"I never told you about a lot of things . . ."

"But . . ."

"But what?"

"Didn't you want to fight against slavery?"

"Never thought about it much, did you?"

"Sure, that's why I joined up—to fight against slavery."

"Well, come to think about it, there's something to be said for slavery . . ."

"Tay, I never know when you're joshin' me."

"You don't?"

"No. Like now. What do you mean—about slavery, I mean?"

"Well, boy, there's always been slavery. All the great civilizations were built by slavery. From Mesopotamia, to Egypt, to Greece. The Hanging Gardens, the Pyramids, the Parthenon, even the British Empire."

"But it was wrong."

"I didn't say it wasn't. But there it was—and here it is."

"Not for long—not in this country."

"Well, you're right about that—not if Grant's got anything to do with it."

"Oh damn!!!"

"What?"

"My finger hurts again. Damn!"

"How can a finger that's been shot off hurt?"

"Don't rightly know, but it does . . . right up to the knuckle—the ring finger."

"If you say so."

"Tay . . ."

"What?"

"If I get married, you think I can wear the wedding ring on some other finger?"

"Sure you can, son. You're just lucky it wasn't your tallywhacker that got shot off."

"My what? Oh, I see what you mean . . ."

The rain had stopped. But the stubborn dankness still clung to the night and the skeletal ruins that rimmed the terrain around Vicksburg.

Within Grant's headquarters the four generals' muted conversation was growing more desperate.

William Tecumseh Sherman was the wildest, most erratic of U.S. Grant's generals—and the closest to him. Time and again, in battle after battle, he had proven himself to Grant, and was instrumental in persuading Grant to stay in the army during his clash with Halleck, while advancing on Corinth, Mississippi. Before that, he had been with Grant at Pittsburg Landing. At the battle of Shiloh, Sherman's gallantry led to his promotion by Grant to major-general. At Vicksburg he was in command of 15th Corps.

Philip Henry Sheridan. In size not a big man, with the largest part of his head forward of his ears—restless of sprit, not politic in language. His black-Irish bloodline evident in his long, mobile face. He had a reputation of being sharp and peppery—it took him five years to graduate from West Point due to an altercation with a fellow cadet.

Sheridan was a self-reliant man of courage and decision, a tactician—quick to advance in rank. While a colonel, 2nd Michigan Cavalry, Sheridan took note of Lt. George Armstrong Custer's leadership and made plans for Custer to be transferred to his command in the near future.

James Birdseye McPherson. Graduated first in his class from West Point, 1853, and joined the Corps of the Engineers. With the outbreak of war he quickly distinguished himself. McPherson was the chief engineer to Grant and responsible for selecting deployment positions for Grant's troops on their attacks at Fort Donelson, Fort Henry, and the battle of Shiloh.

Lew Wallace. Born in Indiana, 1827, not a West Pointer, studied law and volunteered for service in the Mexican War, rose to second lieutenant, then back to Indiana, practicing law until the war. Rejoined and rose to rank of colonel of the 11th Indiana Regiment, successfully leading his troops to victories in western Virginia. Promoted to major-general, youngest at that time in the Union Army, Wallace played an important role in Grant's capture of Fort Donelson. During all his life Lew Wallace harbored literary aspirations, hoping someday to become a novelist.

But on that fateful night near Vicksburg, Wallace, along with Sherman, Sheridan, and McPherson, had other aspirations—and worries—due to the disappearance of their commander, Ulysses Simpson Grant.

A disappearance only they were aware of.

"It'll be a sorry sunrise for the Union"—Wallace gritted his teeth—"if we don't find him."

"Or a sorrier sunset if we do," McPherson added, "depending on his condition."

"Damn it to hell!" Sherman growled.

"He's damned us all to hell," Sheridan muttered, "us and the rest of his army if we don't do something fast."

"What do you suggest, Phil?" Wallace took a step.

"I suggest you shut up unless you've got a suggestion that makes sense!" Sheridan caught himself. "I . . . I'm sorry Lew, that remark was uncalled for."

"Maybe not," Wallace said. "Let's go over it. When was the last time any of us saw him?"

"I guess that would be me." McPherson wiped at what was left of his hair. "He was working at that desk, making notes on a map, I think it was. He looked tired—actually beat . . ."

"I wish you wouldn't use that word, Jim." Wallace almost smiled.

"Well, that's the word, beat! And that's the way he looked. Bleary and in pain."

"What did he *say*?" Sherman asked.

"Didn't say a damn thing. He was just making notes, barely able to write . . . or even concentrate. He began to nod off. I just stood there for a while, until I couldn't take it anymore—and knew he couldn't either. I finally suggested he get some rest—as emphatically as I could to a superior officer, especially to him."

"Get to the point, Jim!" Sherman blurted. "What did he *do*?"

"He finally took my advice, he had to, just couldn't go on. Said he'd go to his room, get some sleep. Looked at his watch, picked up the paper, and told me to come back with the three of you in an hour. Some sleep . . . one hour . . . picked up his cane and practically staggered to his room."

"Staggered?" Sheridan's face turned into a thundercloud. "Jim, I want the truth. Had he been drinking at all?"

"I saw no evidence of that, but it was hard to tell under the circumstances, what with that leg and what he's been through. Bill, you know him better than any of us . . ."

"I know that Grant hasn't taken a drink since . . ." —Sherman hesitated—"a long time ago."

"You mean you haven't *seen* him take a drink," Wallace said.

"I mean he told me so . . . and I believe him, and I believe *in* Grant."

"So do we all," Sheridan added. "The fact remains . . ."

"What fact?" Sherman demanded.

"The fact that he's not here and it's no secret that we were supposed to attack tomorrow—actually today—and if we don't, the whole Union army will know that he's gone—and maybe the Rebs will know—if they don't know already."

"And"—McPherson shook his head—"what about Halleck? If he . . ."

"To hell with Halleck!" Sherman waved.

"Just a minute, Bill," Sheridan said, "suppose he *has* been drinking? What then?"

"Drunk," Sherman answered, "Grant's a better soldier than all of us put together sober."

"Maybe." Wallace shrugged.

"Not maybe," Sherman said, "Fact! I'd follow that man . . ."

"All right! All right!" Sheridan snapped. "But he's not here to follow. Besides, drunk *and* in his condition . . . the leg . . . the pressure . . . no sleep . . . he's only human. How much do you think a man can bear? Where the hell could he have gone? What the hell could he be doing?"

"If I were he," Wallace remarked, "by now I might have blown my brains out."

"You're not that good a shot, Lew," Sherman spouted."

"You're right." Wallace nodded, then smiled.

"And this is no time for jokes," Sheridan broke in. "We haven't much time for anything except a decision."

"You're right, Phil," McPherson said. "The point is what do we *do*, besides wait? Who takes command and responsibility?"

"Responsibility, my ass," Sherman clipped the words. "We *all* lose our stars, and worse, a lot worse, a lot of good men out there—God knows how many—lose their lives. Grant couldn't have got far. With that leg he can't ride."

"What if we go after him?" McPherson said.

"Do we have enough time to go?" Wallace speculated.

"Do we have enough time not to?" Sheridan said.

"And what if he comes back and we're not here?" Wallace asked.

"Suppose *one of* us goes?" McPherson suggested.

"Less chance of finding him," Sherman said, "and convincing—"

"Then I say we stay!" McPherson interrupted. "Besides, Grant ordered the four of us never to ride together. I say we stay!"

"Hold on." Wallace thought for just a second. "Jim, you said he was making notes on a map. Maybe he left that map . . ."

"No good, Lew. I looked all over. Wherever he is, that map's with him."

"Sonofabitch," Sherman almost shouted. "We're generals, not drummer boys. We've each of us gone to battles without him, and we can do it again if we have to."

"But," Wallace countered, "*do* we have to?" He looked at his watch. "Not yet . . ."

"Goddammit it, we're wasting time," Sheridan said, his voice rasping. "We've got to decide what to do—and decide *now*. We all stand with Grant—or fall without him!"

CHAPTER 11

Earlier, during the siege of Vicksburg, Grant had written in his diary:

At this time the North has become very much discouraged. Many strong Union men believe that the war must prove a failure. The elections of 1862 had gone against the party which was for the prosecution of the war to save the Union if it took the last man and the last dollar. Voluntary enlistments had ceased throughout the greater part of the North, and the draft has been resorted to to fill up our ranks. It is my judgment that to make a backward movement as long as that from Vicksburg to Memphis, would be interpreted by many of those yet full of hope for the preservation, as a defeat, and that the draft would be resisted, desertions ensue and power to capture and punish deserters lost. There is nothing to be done but to go FORWARD TO A DECISIVE VICTORY.

But now, even if Grant wanted to go forward, it would be impossible.

General Ulysses Simpson Grant was in a shack—a prisoner of war—with a Rebel gun pointing directly at him.

CHAPTER 12

Thousands of soldiers, tens of thousands, on both sides, blue and gray, some veterans, survivors of preceding battles, others facing the enemy in their first bloody combat, waited through the long night.

A night too long for some, anxious to end the waiting and face the enemy.

A night too short for others, fearful of what must come, the savage bloodletting that must inevitably end in death for some of their comrades and themselves.

Some sworn to fight for the states they were born in and for their country, the Union, and the right to freedom for all who lived in that country.

There were those who didn't know exactly why they were fighting—except that they were told they must fight, told by their fathers, mothers, brothers, sisters, sweethearts, their teachers, ministers, and the politicians who represented them—North and South.

Among them, the mostly brave soldiers, braced and anxious to do battle—and those not as brave, even cowardly, cringing at the thought of what was to come.

And hundreds upon hundreds of officers, blue and gray, ready to receive and carry out orders, to lead their troops to success or slaughter—whether those officers agreed with the given order or not.

This was the duty of warrior soldiers since time immemorial, in battles on land and sea—on freezing mountain peaks and furnace desert sands—recorded battles celebrated in history books and unremembered encounters buried in the forgotten past.

The soldiers' duty, nevertheless: "theirs to do and die."

Many would die that day—some in victory, others in defeat to be buried in nameless graves, but mourned by families and friends miles away.

That night, of all those hundreds of thousands, blue and gray, troopers and officers, none among them was aware that, in the storm to come, their fate was centered in the lone shack that held five soldiers—two Yankee officers, General Ulysses Simpson Grant and Captain George Armstrong Custer, and three Rebel soldiers, Corporal Johnny Yuma and the two Darcy brothers.

* * *

Johnny Yuma's gun hand trembled ever so slightly as his pistol pointed at the heart of Ulysses Simpson Grant, and, in a way, the heart of the Union Army. He thought about what the Darcys had just said—"Well, hell. Lookit what you just bagged, Yuma!"—"Yeah, bo! Ol' Whiskers hisself."

Yuma's mind triggered to a different circumstance. What if a Yankee corporal were in his place, at some other place, and was pointing a gun at General Robert E. Lee, a prisoner of war? How would he want and expect that Yankee corporal to treat the man who was the heart of the Confederate Army?

Was it written anywhere in the book of regulations, or more importantly, in the code of ethics, what the exact procedure should be? Within hours armies would clash and most likely thousands would die, and Yuma held the key to the outcome of that clash at the point of his gun barrel.

Custer knew not what the corporal holding the gun had in mind—nor the other two Confederates, but he knew, by what Grant had said, that he had surrendered himself as their prisoner—and to Custer that was unacceptable—not while there was the slightest chance to do something about it.

"Corporal . . ."

"Yuma, Johnny Yuma. What's your name, Captain?"

"Custer, George Custer."

"Yeah," Joe Darcy grinned, "we heard some about you, too. Didn't we, brother Jim?"

"Yeah, but he's small pataters compared to ol' Brickhead hisself—and with a bottle in his hand, seems like the whiskey general's livin' up to his reputation. Heard he don't waste much time between drinks."

At that Grant set the bottle on the table and leaned on the cane.

"Shut up, Darcy!" Yuma ordered. Then looked at Grant. "I apologize, sir . . . for those two pigs." Then to Custer. "What were you going to say, Captain?"

"Never you mind, Yuma," Joe said, "what small pataters was gonna say. It's what we're gonna do."

"You've got nothing to say about what's going to be done. You're both my prisoners, too."

"Now you just hold steady, soldier boy . . ." Joe Darcy was smiling. "You grabbed a hold of a heap more'n you can handle here."

"That's right, corporal." Jim Darcy nodded.

"Shut up, both of you. I'll decide what's right and what's going to be done here."

"Don't figure you can do what's right," Joe said, "not without some hep from your comrades. The odds are too much against ya."

"Comrades!" Yuma spat out the word.

"Sure enough," Jim pointed to his brother, then to Yuma. "The three of us is on the same side—against them bluebellies—and holdin' the high hand."

"No. *I'm* holding the high hand—with this." Yuma lifted the gun an inch. "And I'm not forgetting what happened with you two out there."

"But things is different now and in here." Joe reasoned, "Let me and Jim take their guns. We'll hep you get 'em back to Pemberton. You'll be the shiniest hero of the South . . ."

"The savior of Vicksburg!" Jim Darcy added. "And then we'll all just forget we was leggin' it tonight. Ol' whiskers," he pointed to Grant, "is what's most important."

Yuma stood silent.

But Custer didn't.

"Are they deserters?"

Yuma remained silent.

"Are they?" Custer persisted.

"They're scum," Yuma said without looking at the Darcys. "They had that notion. I was taking them back to stand trial."

"Some trial." Jim Darcy smirked. "Me and my brother'd just be shot."

"Any soldier who turns from battle," Yuma said, "deserves to be shot."

There was a look from Custer to General Grant at those words.

A distant, dissonant rumble—then another. The shack seemed to vibrate.

"Cannon!" Jim Darcy pointed outside. "Looks like the fightin's already started!"

"No." Custer shook his head. "That was thunder."

"Maybe so." Jim Darcy shrugged. "But it won't be long, and we've got ol' Whiskers—worth more'n ten thousand deserters, so, Yuma, you've got bigger fish to fry . . ."

"You know what it'll mean if the bluebellies lose Grant!?" Joe said.

"Lookit what happened to us when Johnston fell at Shiloh." Jim Darcy pointed to Grant. "Then shoot the sonofabitch and be done with it!"

"I know." Yuma nodded. "But I'm thinking of something else. If we can get General Grant to our lines alive . . ."

"That's a mountain of an if, soldier boy, but what if we could?" Joe Darcy said, "What's the advantage of that?"

"It could be the basis for our negotiating a peace." Yuma looked squarely at Custer. "Captain, will you give me your word that you won't try to escape?"

"No." Custer's reply was firm.

"Nor would I, sir," Yuma took a breath, "if I were in your place."

"Corporal." Grant spoke for the first time in a long while.

"Yes, sir?" Yuma answered.

"You neglected to ask me that question. When you first entered I said I was a prisoner of war. Obviously, I still am. But I've been thinking—about a lot of things—but one thing in particular, and I want to remind you as I've reminded myself . . . the most important duty of a prisoner of war . . . is to try to escape."

"I understand," Yuma said. "And it's my duty, sir, to prevent that escape."

"Then shoot 'em both, Johnny!" Joe Darcy said. "Me and Jim'll swear they was both tryin' to escape."

"Hot damn!" Jim Darcy nodded. "That breaks everythin' to a finish!"

Another dissonant rumble. This time not as distant.

"That one sounded like cannon to me," Joe Darcy said.

"No." Custer shook his head. "Thunder."

"Of all the fine brave men in our regiment . . ." Yuma looked at the Darcys, "I have to be here with you two."

"That's how the cards is dealt," Jim Darcy said. "And cannon or thunder . . . time's awastin'."

"Now you either shoot 'em," Joe Darcy said, "both of 'em, or let us hep you get 'em back . . . but we'll need their guns."

"No," Yuma answered. "You don't get their guns. Captain, place your pistol next to the one on the table and be careful, mine's pointing right at the general."

Slowly, Custer placed his sidearm on the table next to Grant's pistol and the bottle of whiskey.

"General Grant," Yuma spoke in a measured voice, "if you were in my gunsight on the battlefield, I'd pull the trigger without hesitation. But you are a prisoner of war and I don't wish to harm you, sir . . . so long as you don't try to escape . . ."

"I understand," Grant said. "You're a good soldier, Corporal."

"Now, sir. Both you and the captain move away from that table and toward the door."

As both Grant and Custer started toward the entrance, once again the sound of cannon or thunder echoed from outside.

In a whipping fast movement Jim Darcy's arm was around Grant's throat, holding him as a shield, and Joe Darcy had leaped to the table and the guns as Custer raced across to try to help Grant. But Joe Darcy had both pistols, one in each hand.

"Now the cards is dealt different!" Joe Darcy grinned. "Seems like all us Rebs has got guns." He handed his brother Custer's pistol as Jim Darcy turned loose of Grant. "Now it's my gun that's pointed at ol' Whiskers. Now, you, Yuma, drop yours to the ground; go ahead or I'll give it to him right now."

"All right," Yuma said and did.

"Clear thinkin', soldier boy. Clear thinkin'. Now I'm promotin' myself and givin' orders. Right, brother Jim?"

"Right, brother Joe."

"First order is to plug Grant."

"That's a good order." Joe smirked.

"Darcy!" Custer shouted. "Listen, I will give you my word, we won't try to escape, neither of us, will we, General?"

Grant said nothing.

"Too late, Yankee," Joe Darcy said.

"No, listen," Yuma implored, "you can't do this.

I swear to you I'll never bring up the matter of your desertion."

"Not if you're dead, you won't," Joe Darcy said.

"All right, kill me," Yuma went on, "but take General Grant back to our lines. He's worth more to the Confederacy alive."

"Not to us, he ain't," Joe said. "Dead men have no tales."

"Right again, brother Joe. Now, les just go over our report that we're gonna give headquarters after which we'll be proclaimed the heroes of Vicksburg." Jim Darcy waved his gun at Grant, Custer, and Yuma. "Them two Yankees tried to escape. One of 'em, the captain, shot our comrade, Corporal Yuma—and me and brother Joe kilt Custer and had no choice but to drill ol' Whiskers as he turned yellow, but still tried to escape. How does that report sound to you, brother Joe?"

"Mighty fine . . . might-tee fine."

"Do this," Yuma said, "and both your souls will burn in hell."

"We ain't worried about the hereafter," Jim Darcy said. "We're thinkin' about the here and now. You first, General."

"It seems, Captain," Grant looked at Custer, "the battle of Vicksburg, for us . . . is here and now."

"So it seems." Custer's eyes went to Yuma. "And for you too, Corporal."

"I'll drink to that." Joe Darcy grinned, and started moving toward the table.

With unexpected swiftness General Grant's cane

smashed Joe Darcy's gun from his hand onto the floor. Yuma sprang toward the fallen gun as Custer leaped toward Jim Darcy, who fired at Yuma. The bullet grazed Yuma's forehead, but he managed to grip the fallen gun and fire at Joe Darcy.

Custer was locked with Jim Darcy, whose gun went off, but down toward the floor.

Yuma's shot had ripped into Joe Darcy's chest, felling him dead to the ground as Yuma lost consciousness.

Custer and Jim Darcy tangled on the floor, twisting and turning over each other with Custer's grip around Darcy's gun hand until the gun went off.

Both were still for a moment; then Custer pushed Darcy's lifeless body away from him and slowly got to his feet.

"General . . . are you all right?"

"It appears so. Thanks to you and him." He pointed to Yuma, who was unconscious. "How is he?"

Custer moved near to Yuma and knelt to examine the corporal.

"He's passed out but looks like he'll be all right."

"Good. He's . . . well, you know."

Custer nodded. He rose, went to the table with the bottle and map still on top of it.

"You'll be needing this, sir."

Custer reached out and took hold of the folded paper.

"Yes." Grant nodded. "We all will."

Another sound from outside—not thunder—not cannon.

Hoofbeats.

Then men dismounting.

Grant pointed with his cane toward the door.

"More company."

Custer, gun still in hand, went to the door and opened it slightly.

"Gray?" Grant asked. "Or blue?"

"Blue, sir." Custer smiled. "Deep blue!"

Custer opened the door wide and four men entered—Generals William T. Sherman, Philip Sheridan, James B. McPherson, and Lew Wallace.

George Armstrong Custer saluted the generals, who all looked toward Grant.

"General," Sherman asked, "are you all right, sir?"

"I've already answered that question. You fellows weren't around to hear it, but *he* was, Captain George Armstrong Custer. Generals Wallace, McPherson, Sherman—and Phil, you know Custer, of course, but not *all* about him, believe me. Stand at ease, Captain."

Grant reached inside his tunic and pulled out three damaged cigars, too damaged to smoke.

"Say, any you gentlemen bring along a cigar? That skunk," Grant pointed with his cane to Joe Darcy on the floor, "crushed mine when he grabbed hold of me."

The generals shook their heads negatively as they looked around the room.

"What happened, General?" Sherman asked.

"Never mind that now. I'll tell you later. But my orders were that you four were never to ride together."

"You were gone. We decided to look for you. I guess we disobeyed orders."

Grant smiled and the generals were obviously further relieved.

"Uh, huh," Grant grunted. "Well, Custer here tells me there's a rumor we're going to attack this morning."

"According to your plan, sir," McPherson said, "we're waiting for your order to attack Clinton."

"Anytime you say, sir," Wallace nodded, "we're ready."

"Clinton, huh." Grant began to unfold the map. "Well, plans have changed. That's where Pemberton's waiting for us to attack."

It was as if a new, invigorated set of reflexes had infused Grant.

"Custer and I have worked out a better plan. Isn't that so, Custer?"

"Well . . . *you* have, sir."

"You did your part, Custer . . . and it's a plan that's going to *succeed*. We storm Champion Hill!"

The generals, taken by surprise, looked at each other.

"Champion Hill?" Wallace blinked.

"That's right." Grant held up the map. "Jim, you move along the railroad. Bill, you hit the bridges and factories. Lew, to Edwards Station. I'll tell you the rest on the way."

"Yes, sir!" All the generals reacted.

"This army's going to dive in at Vicksburg and come out at salt water on the Atlantic! Custer."

"Yes, sir?"

"I know Sheridan's got plans for you at the Shenandoah, but that comes later. Right now, we'll take Vicksburg, but I hear Lee's in Pennsylvania marching toward Gettysburg, and I'm sending you up there . . . General Custer."

"*General*?! But . . ."

"No *buts*. That's an order. I'll see to your promotion as soon as I can. And"—Grant pointed to Yuma, still unconscious on the floor—"take care of that . . . prisoner."

"Yes, sir."

Grant looked at the bottle on the table.

"The headache's all better now. What time is it, General Custer?"

Custer looked at his watch.

"Three thirty, sir."

"Uh, huh. Well, maybe someday . . . in heaven or hell . . . or somewhere in between, we'll have that drink, *one* drink."

General Ulysses Simpson Grant swung the cane hard against the bottle, smashing it to pieces and spilling the whiskey on the floor.

"Time's awasting, gentlemen. Let's move!"

CHAPTER 13

General Ulysses Simpson Grant's plan succeeded beyond General Henry Halleck's expectations, and much to the relief and pleasure of President Abraham Lincoln.

Lincoln's belief and trust in General Grant was reaffirmed with Pemberton's unconditional surrender to U.S. Grant.

Later, Grant wrote in his report:

At the appointed hour the garrison of Vicksburg marched out of their works and formed a line in front, stacked arms and marched back in good order. Our whole army present witnessed the scene without cheering. Our men had full rations from the time the siege commenced, to the close. The enemy had been suffering, particularly towards the last. Before I gave an order, I myself saw our men taking bread from their haversacks and giving it to

the enemy they had so recently engaged. It was
accepted with avidity and with thanks.

The blow to the Confederacy at Vicksburg was severe, but not conclusive. General Robert E. Lee's Army had invaded Pennsylvania and was approaching Gettysburg.

The other Southern generals, including, James Longstreet, George Pickett, Jubal A. Early, and Edmund Kirby Smith, were determined to go on fighting. So were the thousands and thousands of Confederate soldiers—including Johnny Yuma— now a prisoner of war.

CHAPTER 14

Days after Captain George Armstrong Custer rejoined his brigade he was still Captain George Armstrong Custer.

Still anticipating the unlikely promotion Grant had promised him, Custer did not seem his usual rollicking, braggadocious self and his behavior did not go unnoticed by the rest of his comrades—particularly by his closest comrade, Lieutenant Adam Dawson.

Their friendship dated back to Monroe, when Custer was ten and Dawson a husky eight-year-old.

That friendship was cemented at that time during a school picnic along the Raisin River—and Libbie was among the young picnickers.

It was an ideal opportunity for Autie to show off, and he did, winning all the athletic games and finally the pie-eating contest, and then diving into the river after announcing that he was going to swim across and back.

Twenty yards out his head was swallowed by the river. He bobbed up a few seconds later and gasped. Everybody thought it was another one of his jokes, everybody except Libbie. She screamed.

Adam Dawson dove in as Autie disappeared again. Young Dawson was big for his age, a strong boy and a strong swimmer. Autie went down for the third time as Adam reached the cramped and retching Custer Boy and got hold of his golden locks, then shoulders, and pulled him back against the currents toward the riverbank.

None of the other student-spectators or their teacher, Mrs. Willow, moved. Only Libbie dashed into the water to help Dawson drag the Custer Boy onto dry land, where all three, Custer, Libbie, and Dawson, collapsed, spattered with the mud and dirt of the river Raisin.

Then everyone burst into cheers and applause and rushed to the side of the muculent trio. But it was Dawson who turned Autie over, straddled him, and pumped with both palms into his rib cage. When there was no breath evident, Dawson turned him over again onto his stomach and whacked him as hard as he could between the shoulders. There was a sudden eruption of assorted pie filling, mucky crust, and indeterminate matter from Autie's stomach, followed by deep, if irregular, breath.

More cheers. More applause.

Later, when Autie was fully revived and had been apprised of what happened and properly admonished by Mrs. Willow, he sat against a tree with Adam and Libbie beside him.

"Your name's Adam Dawson, isn't it?"

Dawson nodded.

"I'm George Armstrong Custer. Autie, for short." He grinned and stuck out his hand.

"I know." Dawson took Custer's hand and grinned back. "Everybody knows. At least in Monroe."

"Someday everybody in other places'll know too, thanks to you. You saved my bacon."

"No, Libbie Bacon did. If she hadn't yelled, well, everybody thought you was funnin' . . . again."

"Well, I thank you both. I guess that makes us . . . Three Musketeers of Monroe, Michigan."

And so they were—except when Judge Bacon was around—and until George Armstrong Custer went to West Point.

Custer didn't see Adam Dawson after that until Chickahominy, when Custer's commander spoke the words, "Custer, cross that river and you'll come out a captain. Good luck, Lieutenant."

That's when Custer recognized Adam Dawson among the thirty Monroe men of the 2nd Michigan Brigade. He leaped off his mount and put his arms around his boyhood friend.

"Adam Dawson! you ol' cabin robber! Now we'll give 'em hell. Are you ready to ride to glory?"

"I am if you are, Autie." Dawson smiled. "But you've already had your share."

"I'm just getting started. Ride next to me, Adam. We'll scatter those Rebs."

Custer jumped on his mount, and that's when he gave the command that became his cavalry calling card.

"Come on, Monroe. Follow me. Ride, you Wolverines! Charge!"

Charge they did and scattered the Rebs and he became Captain George Armstrong Custer. But to Dawson, still "Autie."

And now, after what happened at Vicksburg, Dawson was still with Autie and could tell that Autie was not himself.

Something was troubling Captain Custer. Something was amiss.

"What is it, Autie?" Dawson spoke to him when they were alone.

"What is . . . what?"

"Come on, pal. I know you too well. Is it something to do with Libbie? Is she . . ."

"No, not Libbie. Everything's fine with her"—he smiled—"except for her father. It's . . ."

"Get it off that chest of yours, my friend."

"Well, between just the two of us . . ."

"That's the way it'll be."

"I . . . I was sort of . . . expecting something . . . sort of . . ."

"What's this 'sort of' stuff? Has it got anything to do with . . . Gettysburg?"

"Sort of." Custer smiled.

"Well, now I know everything." Dawson smiled back. "And nothing. If you feel like . . . 'confessing,' ol' Reverend Dawson'll be around . . . at least until Gettysburg."

"There's a letter for you." Lieutenant George W. Yates came up and handed it to Custer. "At least I think it's for you."

"From Monroe?"

"Nope. Official. But it's addressed to Brigadier General George A. Custer, U.S. Volunteer."

By then, there were dozens of officers standing next to Yates as he handed the letter to Custer.

George A. Custer was visibly affected. An unopened letter had done what no battlefield encounter had ever done—make him tremble.

"Read it to us!" a chorus of voices shouted. "Read it, General! Read it to us!"

He ripped open the letter, and with a voice that quavered just the slightest, read aloud.

It was official, and George Armstrong Custer was now brigadier general, by order of General Alfred Pleasonton. But Custer knew it was because of General U.S. Grant and what happened at Vicksburg.

Adam Dawson grinned, then laughed, then took Custer's hand and shook it.

"Is this . . . is this what you were expecting, Autie?" Dawson whispered.

Custer answered, also in a whisper. "Sort of."

The first thing General Custer did was send off a letter to Libbie.

Dear Libbie,

*Be first in Monroe to know of my—of our—
good fortune. I have been promoted to a
BRIGADIER GENERAL, the youngest in the
U.S. Army.*

*I hope that this promotion will favorably affect
your father's opinion of me, but truthfully, the
opinion that matters most to me is yours.*

*As always,
Custer Boy*

The promotion of George Armstrong Custer did affect Judge Daniel Stanton Bacon most favorably.

The last time Lieutenant Custer had been on leave in Monroe, Adam Dawson was with him.

Unwelcome at the Bacon residence, Custer and Dawson went on a drinking spree, Custer more than Dawson.

When Custer woke up the next noon, he had no recollection of the events of the prior evening—until Dawson recalled the events to him.

"It was at our last stop, the Sword and Shield Tavern. By then we'd had more than our limit, but didn't know it. I went outside to relieve myself both ways. When I came back the kitchen boy was standing against the wall and you were throwing steak knives too damn close to his skinny body; but I was able to convince you it was time for us to take leave of the premises—and on the way to your sister's house we happened to meet up with your prospective father-in-law, who, busy citizen that he is, just kept on walking straight ahead as if we were invisible."

Custer was penitent.

First he promised himself he would never throw a knife again . . . at any human target. Then later, he promised Libbie he'd never take another drink.

"Custer Boy"—Libbie smiled—"I'm going to ask you to do something even more difficult."

"Whatever it is, I'll promise."

"Not to take more than *one* drink within each twenty-four hours . . . unless it's with me or someone very special."

"Libbie, there is no one more special . . . or ever will be."

And there never had been . . . not even U.S. Grant.

And from the time of General Custer's letter to Libbie and the news of Custer's promotion, Judge Bacon's remarks concerning his future son-in-law, General George Armstrong Custer, were nothing but favorable.

The next thing that Brigadier General Custer did was to have a new uniform tailored for himself, and from then on there could be no mistaking the boy general at the head of his brigade with broad collar of blue sailor's shirt rolled into a black velveteen jacket adorned by rows of brass buttons and gleaming braid. His legs were covered by britches of the same material, seamed by twin gold stripes and tucked into top boots cupped by silver spurs. A heavy sword with Toledo blade, captured from the enemy, hung from his black belt. And, of course, the scarlet scarf flowed from his throat. All this was topped off by a broad-brimmed black hat, the crown rimmed with gold cord and a highly visible star on the forefront of the crown.

If other, more straitlaced officers smirked at Custer's flamboyant uniform and attitude, those smirks soon turned to admiration, envy, and respect in the battles that ensued—beginning two weeks later with Lee's stalwart cavalier, JEB Stuart.

Lee's strategy was inflicting immeasurable effect and casualties on the Union forces.

It was at Gettysburg that Custer's brigade once again encountered Stuart's Invincibles for the first time since Brandy Station. This time, Stuart's overwhelming forces did seem invincible as they tried to outflank the Yankees and hook up with Pickett's valiant charge that would doom the North.

But with fewer troops at his command, and suffering heavy losses, Custer led his Wolverines in charge after charge—until the final "suicide charge" that prevented Stuart's attempt to join Pickett. It seemed there were a hundred red-scarfed Custers that day with a hundred bloody blades striking—in and from—all directions.

Lee's army, in defeat, was forced to retreat.

And once again Custer had ridden to glory.

The war likely would have ended at Gettysburg

were it not for General George Meade's reluctance to chase after Lee and destroy the tired, suffering Confederate ranks. Meade had already been dubbed "The Reluctant General," and his inaction once again earned the title.

But Custer rapidly reaffirmed his newfound glory along with his devoted Michigan brigades with another Union victory at Culpepper, where he was shot off his horse, mounted another, continued the charge, and dispersed the Rebel forces.

Newspapers all over the North hailed the boy general as the shining star and indestructible pride of the Yankee army.

Custer's victories and the leg wound he received at Culpepper merited a leave, enthusiastically granted by General Pleasonton.

The boy general had only one thing in mind: go to Monroe and become the husband general of Elizabeth Bacon.

But it was not to be—not yet. Since Judge Bacon was out of town, Custer had to settle for parades, picnics, and plaudits—and of course the embraces of his loving Libbie.

But Judge Bacon did get back in time to give his blessing for the betrothal of his daughter and the celebrated boy general, who had to leave the same day.

The wedding would have to wait, but the war wouldn't.

More victories, more glory, at Rappahannock

and Buckland Mills, and then for Custer, in his own mind, his greatest personal victory—so far.

Elizabeth Clift Bacon became Mrs. George Armstrong Custer.

War makes for one hell of a honeymoon.

But Custer and Libbie both were in heaven on earth.

CHAPTER 15

As the war flared on, Lincoln, more and more, relied on U.S. Grant. After Vicksburg there could be no doubt in Lincoln's mind that Grant was "his man."

Following Grant's victory at Vicksburg, then Chattanooga, U.S. Grant was made supreme commander of the Federal forces in the West, and then promoted to the rank of lieutenant general, and became general in chief of the armies of the United States.

His every order was carried out by his generals without question in spite of heavy casualties. But the North could suffer such casualties much better than the South.

One person to whom General Grant never gave an order was Julia. She was the wellspring of his being, and as often as possible—and out of harm's way—he wanted her with him, and she wanted to be with him.

"Julia, everything is different when we're together. Even though sometimes I can hear the sounds of war too close, there is a certain tranquility in you being with me."

"Where else would I want to be?"

"But Julia, I can't help thinking of all the officers and men, on both sides, that can't be with their wives—with those they love—during the war—and those who never will be after it's over. Every time I work out a plan and give an order . . ."

"You're doing your duty, and doing it better than anyone can—for your country . . ."

"And for you, Julia. You stuck with me when everybody thought I was a flat-out failure . . ."

"That's because they didn't know you like I do."

"I didn't know myself." Grant smiled.

"I think you always did. It just took . . ."

"A little war? There's no such thing as a little war—at least not this one. And it's far from over. I'm afraid the worst may be yet to come."

"Not for us, Ulys. Not as long as we can be together, like this."

And the worst was yet to come—for the North, and even more so, for the South.

There were over eighteen million people in the North, nine million in the South, a third of whom were slaves. The North had nine-tenths of the nation's manufacturing capacity, two-thirds of the railroads, and most of the country's iron and copper. It controlled the seas.

The South had cotton, and as the war went on, less and less of that.

But if the Confederacy was aware of the odds, it ignored them. Either that, or the South was determined to more than make up for the sum of its disadvantages with grit, gumption, and especially valor, even through thousands of its soldiers were dead, thousands more wounded, and thousands, like Johnny Yuma, in prisons—prisons like Rock Island.

CHAPTER 16

Union and Confederate prisons were scattered across the landscape. Numbered among the Confederate were: Andersonville, Belle Isle, Cahaba Prison, Castle Pinckney, Danville Prison, and Libby Prison.

The Union prisons included: Alton Prison, Camp Chase, Camp Douglas, Point Lookout, and Rock Island.

It was Corporal Johnny Yuma's plight to be incarcerated at Rock Island.

He thought back to the events leading to that incarceration. It was at first difficult to review the circumstances because when he was revived at the battlefield hospital he had all but lost his memory of recent events.

What he didn't know was that Custer had given orders that this prisoner was to be treated as humanely as possible. But those orders, like many other orders during the ongoing conflict, were soon lost, forgotten, or ignored.

His head wound was treated, stitched up, and then he was treated like any other prisoner of war—and like many other prisoners of the Vicksburg campaign, he ended up at Rock Island.

He had a clear recollection of Mason City; his father, Sheriff Ned Yuma; the owner and editor of the *Mason City Bulletin*, Elmer Dodson; his aunt Emmy and her husband, Ainsley Zecker; Deputy Jess Evans; and most of all, the girl he loved, Rosemary Cutler.

He clearly recalled running away from home and joining the 3rd Texas, the battles that led up to Vicksburg, and the decimation of his brigade, then being stranded with the Darcy brothers, the "gray vultures," would-be deserters—and slowly, much more slowly, the confrontation with Captain George Armstrong Custer and, even more unlikely, General U.S. Grant.

As always, it was Yuma's custom to keep a journal of his activities since leaving Mason City, but that journal had been lost somewhere in the no-man's-land of Vicksburg.

It all seemed unreal. At times he thought he might have dreamed it all—could it all have been a hallucination, the strange fruit of a would-be writer's imagination? But no, it was real. It did happen. The scar on his forehead was real. It must have happened. He couldn't have dreamed anything so unimaginable—even as a would-be writer.

And he had remembered that somewhere, probably in or on the way to the hospital, he had heard that there had been two unidentified Confederate bodies, along with his wounded self. Yuma never bothered to identify the traitorous Darcys. They were both a disgrace to the 3rd Texas and to the Confederacy. Let them rot in anonymous graves, their names unworthy to appear with the valiant dead of Yuma's brigade.

In the days and nights during his recovery, the events in the forlorn shack became clarified in his mind—his gun pointing at Grant and Custer, holding both of them at bay as prisoners of war, the dastardly Darcys urging him to kill them both, his refusal to do so, the Darcys' attempt to overpower and kill both Grant and Custer, along with Yuma himself, and escape the charge of desertion and proclaim themselves heroes instead.

Yuma's personal code of ethics would not permit such a cowardly act, and Yuma believed Grant as a prisoner of war was more valuable to the Confederacy. Grant, then, could be the basis of a negotiated peace between North and South.

When the Darcys got hold of guns and started firing, Yuma attempted to stop them and, in the shooting that ensued, suffered a head wound and passed out. What happened after that was still unclear, except he found out that Grant and Custer survived, and Vicksburg was lost to the Confederacy and both Grant and Custer went on to other battles and victories.

If Andersonville was the hell of the Confederacy, then Rock Island was the purgatory of the North. But at Rock Island Yuma met and made friends with another Confederate prisoner, Danny Reese.

Yuma never told Reese or anybody else about the events at the Vicksburg shack—nobody would believe it anyhow.

But Johnny Yuma often thought of two things that transpired there. First, what he had said to General U.S. Grant: "General Grant, if you were in my gunsight on the battlefield, I'd pull the trigger without hesitation. But you are a prisoner of war and I don't wish to harm you, sir . . . so long as you don't try to escape."

Second, what Grant later had said to him: "When you first entered I said I was a prisoner of war. Obviously, I still am. But I've been thinking—about a lot of things—but one thing in particular. I want to remind you as I've reminded myself . . . the most important duty of a prisoner of war . . . is to try to escape."

Escape. Escape. Escape. The words burned into his brain. Into his body and soul. Into every fiber of his being.

And finally, Johnny Yuma and Danny Reese did escape—as no prisoner of Rock Island had done before—surviving the icy waters of Sault Sainte Marie.

CHAPTER 17

Despite Grant's leadership and the advantages in the North's favor, the South's determination, along with Lee and his generals' tenacity—one general in particular, JEB Stuart—the Confederates regrouped time and again, struck back, inflicting heavy losses on the Union forces, so heavy that many, too many citizens and politicians began to consider making peace with the Rebels under less-than-favorable terms for the Union.

Abraham Lincoln had no such notion.

In the office of the president of what remained of the United States of America the tall man stood looking out the window behind his desk. The others in the room, all cabinet officers, were Secretary of the Treasury Salmon P. Chase, Secretary of War Simon Cameron, and Secretary of the Navy Gideon Welles.

The tall man at the window had been heralded and hailed as a Mid-Century Messiah by many and cursed and damned as the Abolitionist Ape by almost as many.

The war had worn on his face and mind and on his soul, but his resolve was as fierce and unbending as it had been at the beginning, no matter what the cost.

Lincoln had called for 300,000 three-year enlistments, but the enlistments were slow to materialize in anywhere near that number, and the antiwar and anti-Lincoln sentiments were materializing faster, too much faster.

"Gentlemen, despite General Grant's successes on the western front, we are losing the will of our people to fight and incur further losses. The Second Battle of Bull Run ended in a Federal rout. Lee has reached Fredrick in Maryland and defeated Burnside at the Battle of Fredericksburg. JEB Stuart has destroyed Chambersburg, and Jackson's captured twelve thousand Union troops at Harpers Ferry.

"The cry for peace from the people we represent is growing louder and louder—and from the Democratic Party—who now refer to themselves as the Peace Party.

"I want to say to you at this moment, you and any of the other members of this administration who harbor such thoughts—get out now!

"Your resignations will be accepted without question, and with alacrity.

"And that goes for any officer of our army.

"As long as I am president of this Union we will

fight on to undisputed victory—not anything that can even be considered near defeat."

But the drumbeat of defeat continued to thunder even louder—Lincoln's defeat at the upcoming elections.

This would involve the decisive and final clash between the president and one of his own generals.

George B. McClellan, dashing, handsome, graduated second in his class at West Point in 1842, an engineer, and an outstanding organizer who wrote several books on military tactics. Was appointed commander of the Army of the Potomac, which he organized and trained into a proud example of what an army should look like. But looks were deceiving.

Soon, too soon, he was dubbed, even by his own men, as "General Caution"—then as "General Retreat."

Again and again, even with overwhelmingly superior forces, when he should have struck, during the Peninsula Campaign and at Richmond against Lee's Army of the Northern Virginia, then at the Second Battle of Bull Run, his strategy was to retreat, handing the South a string of victories.

Abraham Lincoln, in letter after letter and order after order, urged McClellan to attack, and each time the "Reluctant General" found excuse after excuse to ignore President Lincoln.

Finally, and in contrast to U.S. Grant's aggressiveness and successes in the west, the president could bear no more. Shortly before he dismissed McClellan,

Lincoln was heard to say: "General McClellan has only one failing. He can't stand the sight of blood. The blood of his own army—or the blood of his enemies."

But McClellan had another strategy in mind—to defeat Lincoln in the upcoming election—and he succeeded, at least in the first step of his strategy.

At the Democratic National Convention in Chicago, the Democrats, who wanted to sue for peace, nominated George B. McClellan as president and George Pendleton as vice president.

And for a time McClellan and his peace offensive strategy were gaining momentum.

But U.S. Grant had his own strategic plan, a plan that was reinforced after the events at Vicksburg— and after receiving a letter from Abraham Lincoln.

My dear General Grant, I do not remember that you and I ever met personally. I write this now as a grateful acknowledgment for the almost inestimable service you have done the country. I wish to say a word further. When you first reached the vicinity of Vicksburg, I thought you should do what you finally did—march the troops across the neck, run the batteries with the transports, and thus go below; and I never had any faith, except a general hope that you knew better than I, that the Yazoo Pass expedition and the like could succeed. When you got below and took Port Gibson, Grand Gulf, and vicinity, I thought you should go down the river and join General Banks, and when you

*turned northward, east of the Big Black, I feared
it was a mistake. I now wish to make the personal
acknowledgment that you were right and I was
wrong.*

> *Yours very truly,*
> A. LINCOLN

General Grant sent William Tecumseh Sherman
on a scorched-earth march through the South with
orders "to invade and destroy."

And destroy Sherman's Army of the Tennessee
he did—bridges, railroad tracks, mills, crops, and
plantations.

And as the election loomed in dark defeat for
Lincoln, Sherman, on September 2, 1862, sent a
telegraph to his commander in chief.

"Mr. President, I give you Atlanta."

Abraham Lincoln continued his presidency, and
Sherman continued his march toward the Atlantic
salt water—but without General James Birdseye
McPherson, one of the generals who had been in
the shack at Vicksburg and was killed in action
during the bloody siege.

Grant gave no thought to slowing down after
Vicksburg and Chattanooga.

The ensuing part of his strategy was to send
Philip Sheridan into the Shenandoah Valley with
the same orders—"invade and destroy."

And General Philip A. Sheridan's first move was

to make sure General George Armstrong Custer was with him in the campaign.

The Shenandoah Valley. Geography and fate destined the Shenandoah Valley to be among the bloodiest of battlefields. The valley, more than one hundred fifty miles long and ten to twenty miles wide, nourished by the Shenandoah River, was rich in farmlands, orchards, and pastures. Between the Blue Ridge on the east and the Alleghenies on the west, the region was one of varied scenery and natural wonders.

Unfortunately for the valley, it was also the ideal avenue of approach between the forces of the North and South. Both sides considered the Shenandoah Valley the passport to victory or defeat.

General George Armstrong Custer, continuing his ride to glory, was destined to play a vital part in the bloody drama's last act.

CHAPTER 18

With the devastating advance of the Union forces in the Shenandoah, the reputation of General George Armstrong Custer and his red-scarf brigades grew to legendary proportions.

His name and fame spread, then soared with each victory—at Chancellorsville, where in the coarse darkness, Stonewall Jackson lay mortally wounded, and at Cedar Creek, where what was left of General Jubal A. Early's army was overwhelmed and broken by Custer's charges. His cries of "Ride, you Wolverines!," "Follow me!," "Ride!," "Charge!" could be heard as the earth shuddered under the din of hoofbeats, the striking of sword blades, the barking of rifles—across once-fertile vales, through foaming streams, across flaming farmlands and bullet-scarred forests—against the cacophonous chorus of gray-clad troopers screaming their Rebel yells, trying, and dying in vain, to halt the advancing avalanche of the Michigan brigades led by the boy general who made rubble of Shenandoah's principal towns—Winchester, Front Royal, Luray, Stanton, Waynesboro, and Lexington—and laid waste the fertile countryside.

One last impediment stood between Sheridan and Custer's complete victory.

The place—Yellow Tavern.

The opposing commander—General JEB Stuart.

During the course of the war, Stuart's Invincibles were also known as the Black Horse Raiders. Since the conflict began, Stuart had consistently conquered the Yankee cavalry—with two exceptions—the battle of Brandy Station, where the reckless twenty-two-year-old Captain Custer led the 1st Michigan on what everybody else thought was an impossible charge—and at Gettysburg, where General Custer prevented Stuart from hooking up with Pickett, dooming Pickett's valiant charge.

Yellow Tavern loomed as the third, fateful and final, encounter of the two most dramatic and daring cavalry generals of the North and South.

Custer had made arrangements for Libbie to join him at his headquarters as he made ready for what was to come.

The two of them had supper and one drink of brandy before retiring.

"Libbie, no matter what happens, being with you has been the most gracious thing in my life—and made everything worthwhile."

"My Custer Boy, you've done everything and more, than anyone could have done."

"Not without you, Libbie . . ."

"I'll always be with you."

"In a way you always were."

"It won't ever change—not even at Yellow Tavern."

"No, it won't, but at Yellow Tavern there'll be someone else . . . and not with me."

"JEB Stuart?"

Custer nodded and said nothing.

"You've beaten him before."

"But this has to be the last time for one of us—he's a good man—a good friend—and a great general."

"So are you, Custer Boy. But he's the enemy."

"It wasn't always that way. Of all the other West Pointers who joined the Confederacy I always felt closer to . . . JEB. We were on the same side at Harpers Ferry—saved one another's lives . . . We both raced to capture Brown."

"The way I heard it, it was you who saved his life when one of John Brown's sons aimed a pistol at him point-blank, but you shot first."

Custer did not remark on Libbie's comment, but changed the subject somewhat.

"JEB and I were together at John Brown's hanging. I'll never forget what Brown said that day.

"'I, John Brown, am now quite convinced that the crimes of this guilty land can never be purged away but with blood.'

"And later, what JEB said to me—and I to him.

"'Well, Autie, that's the end of that.'

"'No, JEB, that's the prelude, the overture—there's already talk of succession, more than just talk.

The Union will never countenance succession—and where will you stand—you and the other Southerners from the Point?'

"'We won't just stand. We'll fight for states' rights.'

"'You were born in the United States of America.'

"'But those states have the right to become un-united.'

"'I don't think so—neither does the Constitution.'

"'The Constitution? That's just a piece of paper that can be torn.'

"'As Brown said, "not without blood,"—including yours and mine, my friend.'"

"Let's hope it doesn't come to that, Autie."

"But, Libbie, it has. And will again at Yellow Tavern. I don't . . ."

"George, you've come this far in life—in peace and war—by being who you were born to be, George Armstrong Custer. You mustn't be any different, not for me or anyone else. You mustn't change—anytime, or anyplace—including Yellow Tavern."

"I won't Libbie, but . . . I'm going to take you in my arms like it's the last time."

"Take me, Custer Boy."

CHAPTER 19

Yellow Tavern would be the last obstacle on the road to Richmond—but that obstacle consisted mainly of General JEB Stuart and thousands of war-tested cavalry, determined to turn back the equally determined invading blue brigades.

Since Custer had bid good-bye to Libbie, his Wolverines had wrecked Beaver Dam Station, destroyed a half-dozen locomotives, captured piles of munitions and supplies, ruined railroad tracks, and liberated hundreds of Federal prisoners. Still Stuart's Invincibles were firmly lined up, confident, and ready to repel any further advance.

Major General JEB Stuart, chief of cavalry of the Army of Northern Virginia, and his Invincibles were all that stood between the Union brigades and the capture of Richmond, the Confederate capitol.

There was no more respected and beloved officer in gray than Major General JEB Stuart, "Flower of Cavaliers"—"Chevalier Bayard"—"Knight of the Golden Spurs."

As always, he had meticulously planned and deployed his troops, but was always ready and able to quickly readjust, even in the heat of the battle-field with advantage to advance—or to cover a weakness in his line of defense.

And, as always, at Yellow Tavern he would once again carry a photograph of his wife, Flora, near his heart, although he had said "I do not need it, my love, to keep you vividly before me no matter where or when."

On this occasion the *where* would be Yellow Tavern, the *when*—the coming dawn of May 11, 1864.

Custer's boyhood friend and wartime compan-ion, Captain Adam Dawson, was once again beside Autie.

"Adam, you've been with me since we hooked up again at Gettysburg. I've never had a better comrade."

"Autie"—Dawson smiled—"I've never had a better friend or commander, neither has anybody else."

"Adam, that's enough of that, let's not get maudlin. Suffice to say, 'Here we go again.'"

A volley of shots had already torn into the Michi-ganders. Custer withdrew his sword from its scab-bard and gave his familiar command.

"Ride, you Wolverines! Charge! The day is ours! Follow me!"

And follow him again and again they did. The Michigan brigades along with the 1st Vermont. The boy general had noted a slightly vulnerable line in Stuart's left flank and tore at it in the lead of his red-scarf command.

Suddenly, this became the be-all and the end-all of the day's effort. The red-scarf charge into the gray line of defense. This time it was Custer's bolts of lightning flinging all their might and fury at Stuart's bending, then broken, flank.

Gun smoke smeared the air, riders on both sides fell, and the battlefield became hell incarnate.

Stuart, himself, rode into the thick of it to seal the breach.

Both Custer and Dawson spotted General JEB Stuart at the same time.

"Autie!" Dawson shouted.

"I see him!"

Both fired at the same time—one shot just missed, the other found its mark—JEB Stuart's heart.

Stuart fell dead off his horse.

At the sight of their beloved commander on the ground, the die was cast.

Custer had lost a friend—and won the day.

General Sheridan wrote in his report: "Custer's charge was brilliantly executed. The Confederate cavalry was badly broken up. The engagement ended by giving us complete control of the road to Richmond."

Later, after a long silence, Custer and Dawson found words.

"Autie, do you know whose shot it was?"

"I don't know—and I don't want to know."

After Major General JEB Stuart died, the South never smiled again.

CHAPTER 20

A fish don't know it's wet
The South don't know it's beat.
Sherman's on the march, gray boys,
Your only hope's retreat.
The Shenandoah's been split
Phil Sheridan's seen to it.
And Custer's chargin' deep and wide.
The truth is, Rebel lads,
There is no place to hide.
A fish don't know it's wet
The South don't know it's beat.
Grant just lit one more cigar.
The South can feel the heat.

So sang some of the Yankee troops—this, and
other hearty songs.

But they should have known better.

Some Southern lyricist countered with his own

version of "A Fish Don't Know It's Wet" and the Confederate reply was taken up as a rallying chorale among the Rebel forces.

> *A fish don't know it's wet*
> *A fish don't feel the heat.*
> *You'll hear the Rebel Yell, Blue Boys,*
> *On your way to hell, Blue Boys.*
> *On your way to hell, Blue Boys*
> *We'll teach you how to spell retreat.*
> *Sheridan, Custer, Grant,*
> *They'll find out that they can't.*
> *Sherman's hit a wall,*
> *The South'll never fall.*
> *A fish don't know it's wet,*
> *We'll beat you Yankees yet,*
> *We'll beat you Yankees yet.*

The South never smiled again—but, the Confederate brigades fought on with grim determination, and heavy casualties continued to mount on both sides.

The so-called victory celebrations, in anticipation of final peace parties, in New York, Philadelphia, and even Washington, proved disappointingly premature.

For every champagne toast and swallow of bourbon, hundreds, then thousands, of blue- and gray-clad soldiers were falling dead or severely wounded.

Those who had survived in victory or defeat at Shiloh, Antietam, Bull Run, Stone River, Vicksburg, Chattanooga, Gettysburg, Chickamauga, Spotsylvania, Chancellorsville, the Wilderness, Yellow Tavern, and other battlefields were still falling as dead, or dreadfully maimed, as did the soldiers, troopers, and officers in the days, weeks, months, and years past.

Among the Union general officers already dead were Brigadier General Thomas Williams, Brigadier General Robert L. McCook, Major General Philip Kearny, Brigadier General James S. Jackson, Brigadier General Stephen W. Weed, Major General John Sedgwick, Brigadier General James C. Rice, and Brigadier General James Birdseye McPherson—plus twelve other general officers.

And the South had suffered the fatal loss of General Albert Sidney Johnston, Lieutenant General Thomas "Stonewall" Jackson, Major General William D. Pender, Brigadier General Barnard E. Bee, Brigadier General Ben McCulloch, Brigadier General Turner Ashby, Brigadier General James B. Gordon, and Major General JEB Stuart—plus sixty-four other general officers.

And so far, hundreds of thousands of officers and soldiers killed and wounded: of Union forces—more than 660,000—with the South's killed and wounded numbering over 450,000.

In addition, thousands and thousands of Northerners and Confederates were still languishing in wretched enemy prisons.

But there were those, particularly in the North, far from the hue and carnage of battlefields, who were in no hurry to see the South surrender:

The profiteers.

The beneficiaries of U.S. government contracts—contracts awarded not on the best products or fairest price, but on the highest bribe or payback:

Clothing companies whose shoddy goods could neither withstand the sun-drenched heat of summer nor rain- and snow-drenched cold of winter.

Butchers dealing out spoiled meat; horse traders selling old, near blind, and spavined horses delivered to the government at outlandish prices.

Purveyors of faulty ammunition, sometimes killing and maiming nearly as many soldiers, as did the enemy.

All in violation of President Lincoln's rules and regulations but, nevertheless, delivered and paid for at high profit.

No, these Northern profiteers were in no hurry to see the South surrender.

For the South there was no profit, no profiteers.

Only valor in the blood-smeared face of defeat, "A fish don't know it's wet."

Still, the Southern forces vowed to fight on.

Among those forces was an escaped prisoner from Rock Island.

Corporal Johnny Yuma.

CHAPTER 21

Too many Confederate soldiers had died on battlefields and in battlefield hospitals, and others in Yankee prisons.

Johnny Yuma had made a silent vow that he would not die at Rock Island but would fight again. If he had to die it would be not as a prisoner, but as a soldier in the field of battle.

If he had to perish, and leave behind those he loved, and those he hated, it would be with gun in hand firing at the enemy.

He had made good his silent vow to escape. But there was still another part to that vow—to fight again.

Somewhere, somehow, in spite of insuperable losses, the South and General Robert E. Lee would make a stand—a stand that could turn the tide, breathe new life, and reap a final glory and ultimate victory for the South.

"I will be with Lee's Army of the Northern Virginia and, gun in hand, do my part in that fateful fight."

So wrote Johnny Yuma in the journal he had begun to keep again.

CHAPTER 22

The leaves of autumn had begun to fall, and for the Confederacy it would not only be a winter of discontent, but of impending defeat.

The Shenandoah Valley had been *peeled*—devastated and occupied by Sheridan and Custer.

In his report Sheridan stated, "Even a crow flying over the Shenandoah would have to bring his rations with him."

General Philip Henry Sheridan was not prone to exaggeration.

The last faint hope of the South was the remnants of General Robert E. Lee's Army of the Northern Virginia.

And Corporal Johnny Yuma was now an infinitesimal component of that faint hope and army.

CHAPTER 23

*This probably will be the last entry. I am
writing by first light—Saturday, April 8, 1865.
We have been ordered to attack, secure, and hold
the bridge at Three Forks. If this journal is found,
please try to get it to my father, Sheriff Ned Yuma
in Mason City. I am with . . .*

Sniper fire. Two rapid shots. Then a third and
fourth whipped by, inches above the Confederate
contingent dug in near the southern bank of the
Little Dirty.

"Keep your heads down!" Lieutenant Cane
snapped.

"If that's an order, sir, I am happy to obey and
oblige." The voice belonged to Private Danny Reese
of General Robert E. Lee's Army of Northern
Virginia.

Danny smiled from out of the receding darkness

and winked at the Reb next to him, Corporal Johnny Yuma.

Yuma almost smiled back and tucked the diary into his tunic. Johnny Yuma and Danny Reese had met a little less than two years ago in the Yankee prison at Rock Island.

For months Yuma and Reese shared meager rations of bread, beans, and tobacco. Johnny Yuma had never smoked before, but he smoked at Rock Island. The tobacco dulled his appetite. And Yuma, like the other prisoners, was always hungry— hungry, and unlike Danny Reese, always serious. Yuma was most serious about escape, and finally they did, the two of them, surviving the icy waters near Sault Ste. Marie.

Another prisoner, L.Q. Jones, who hadn't long to live due to advanced tuberculosis, helped by sewing Yuma and Reese inside one of the body bags used to dispose of the already dead Rebel prisoners. The two of them, Johnny and Danny, had four corpses as overnight companions before being dumped from a cliff overlooking nearly frozen waters below.

Yuma had what served as a knife he had honed from a purloined spoon, and when the body bag hit the water he managed to cut through the burlap container, freeing four stiffened corpses and the two barely breathing escapees.

Together, Yuma and Reese made their way south as far as Freeport, Illinois, then separated, figuring they had twice the chance split up as they had together.

Danny Reese, who wore a perpetual smile even in the purgatory of Rock Island, grinned as they separated.

"Johnny, if you get to heaven before I do, just bore a hole and pull me through." He slapped Yuma on the shoulder and disappeared through the bramble, heading southeast.

Johnny Yuma made his way due south along the course of the Mississippi to Vicksburg, where he intended to rejoin his brigade, the 3rd Texas. But there was no longer a 3rd Texas. After suffering overwhelming losses inflicted by U.S. Grant's Army of the Tennessee, the 3rd had been broken up, and survivors, few as they were, were attached to other regiments.

Yuma had managed to stay ahead of Sherman's bluebellies on their march toward the sea. In late summer of '64, Johnny Yuma hooked up with General Jubal A. Early at Cold Harbor.

Jubal Anderson Early, a Virginian, graduate of West Point, Indian Fighter against the Seminoles in Florida, and veteran of the Mexican Campaign, had voted against secession at the Virginia Convention in April 1861. But when war broke out he accepted a commission as a colonel in the Virginia troops. He won victories and promotions at Salem Church in the Wilderness Campaign and defeated Lew Wallace in the Battle of Monocacy.

Johnny Yuma was with General Early at Cedar

Creek, where what was left of Early's small force was overwhelmed and broken by General George Custer of Sheridan's army.

After that, Corporal Johnny Yuma became an infantryman in a battalion of General Robert E. Lee's Army of Northern Virginia. As casualties mounted and survivors dwindled, the battalion was reduced to a company, then little more than a platoon under the command of Lieutenant Clayton Cane with orders this Saturday dawn of April 8, 1865, to attack, secure, and hold the bridge across the Little Dirty at Three Forks, Virginia.

The last months had held mostly defeats for the ragged Confederates and Johnny Yuma suffered those defeats along with his comrades, but he had survived in spite of twice inflicted wounds, once from a sniper and again in hand-to-hand combat at Falls Church. The wounds had healed. He was lucky to be alive and he was lucky in two other respects.

First, he had met up again with Danny Reese, who was beside him now, and he had met Douglas Baines, who was also dug in next to him on the other side. Baines had saved Johnny Yuma's life at Falls Church when a Yankee sergeant was about to squeeze the trigger as Yuma, disarmed, wrestled with the enemy on the ground. Baines' bayonet struck the sergeant, who died while Johnny Yuma went on living. Until now.

Baines, a farmer from "bleeding Kansas," was only a few years older than Yuma and Reese, but he became almost a father to both young Rebels in the fading cause of the Confederacy. Every night when there was light to see by, Douglas Baines would read softly from his Bible while Johnny, Danny, and the rest listened. And when there was no light, Baines would recite a passage or two from memory. Last night there was no light. No campfires were allowed. Baines spoke softly. Words from Psalm 91:

"He shall cover thee . . . and under his wings shalt thou trust; his torch will be thy shield and buckler,

"Thou shalt not be afraid for the terror by night; nor for the arrow that flieth by day,

"A thousand shall fall at thy side, and ten thousand at thy right hand; but it shall not come nigh thee.

"He shall raise you up on eagle's wings."

"Amen, brother," Danny Reese had added.

And now, the three of them together, along with the others, waited for the order from Lieutenant Cane. The certain outcome, no matter which side took the bridge, would be more casualties.

The only uncertainty, who would live and who would die.

Night's sorry blue faded into a yellowish dawn creased by the *crack, crack* of intermittent sniper fire.

The Rebels looked toward Lieutenant Cane and

waited for his command. Cane had no resemblance to a fighting officer; his appearance was more like the bookish schoolteacher he had been.

Tall and thin, with an overlarge brow, an unsoldierly stoop, still, he had proved to his men that he was a soldier and a leader. Twice in the last month he had led them against superior odds. They had followed him into hell and victory.

Cane had taught high school English and literature until there was no one left to teach, and then he finally prevailed upon the Confederacy to accept him in spite of his diseased lung. He knew from the beginning that the Confederacy was doomed, but that there would be one last stand, a remembered battle, and most probably, Robert E. Lee would be there. Clayton Cane wanted to be there too, despite the fact that he abhorred slavery. But he loved Virginia.

Now, he realized that no one would remember the battle for this bridge. And Robert E. Lee was nowhere in sight.

But Lieutenant Cane had his orders. He would follow them—and his men would follow him. The ones who were still alive, who were so skeptical of Cane when the rope-thin schoolteacher replaced Dion O'Brien, a barrel-chested, heavy-shouldered, hard-hitting Irishman who could lick any man in the regiment, but not a six-ounce minié ball that went through his heart.

After that first charge Lt. Cane led, one of the

men asked why the frail lieutenant seemed so unafraid. Cane quoted a few lines from one of Shakespeare's plays:

> *It seems to me most strange that men should fear,*
> *Seeing that death, a necessary end, will come when*
> *   it will come.*
> *Cowards die many times before their deaths;*
> *The valiant never taste of death but once.*

Yes, they would follow him, even though they knew that many of them would taste of death that April morning.

The Little Dirty was barely more than a creek, less than thirty yards across and no more than waist deep. But trying to wade across, the Rebels would be easy targets. The only chance, slight at best, was a charge onto and across the wooden structure to the other side.

And now from the other side came the Yankee taunts, along with sporadic rifle shots.

"Hey, you Rebs. You gonna have no more breakfasts!"

"Rebs! You want this bridge?! Come and get it!"

"You're finished, Rebs!"

"We're gonna hang Lee!"

"And Jefferson Crowface Davis!"

"We're gonna hang 'em both from the same tree!"

Shots.

And more taunts.

"You're gonna have to pick your own cotton!"

"If you live!"

"But you ain't gonna!"

"We'll play taps over you, Rebs! All of you!"

Shots.

"What're you waiting for, Lieutenant?" one of the Rebs said. "Give the order. Let's get it over with!"

"Quiet! The order is to wait a half hour after dawn. Wait for reinforcements. If they don't come by then, I'll give the order all right."

"How much longer?" the same man asked.

"Ten minutes."

More bullets whistled among the branches and nipped the trees. The Little Dirty became amber-tinted with sunlight. The Rebs tried to keep hidden from everything but sky.

"Hey, Rebs! This is Bart Vogan! Come ahead! I'll take you on. Just me and my little ol' Yankee sling-shot. Lookee here! I'm standing tall! All in blue!"

Danny Reese raised his rifle and his head just enough to take a shot.

He took it. Simultaneously, another shot rang out.

Danny Reese fell on his back in the mud. Johnny Yuma bent down and grabbed Danny by both shoulders.

He was being looked at by a dead man, eyes still open, a black hole in his brow, and for the first time there was no smile on Danny Reese's face.

Johnny Yuma looked into the vacant eyes for only a second, but for that second he, too, was dead, drained of life, suspended in eternity, without future, without purpose, without feeling—but for only a second. Johnny Yuma had seen other men die, friends and foes—and women, too, nurses in the field blown apart by the bursting blossom of cannon. And he had waited and watched as his mother died in the bed of his father and mother while he was too young to really understand, and while his father, wearing a badge and gun, was away killing someone who had killed someone else.

But seeing, touching, and realizing the death of Danny Reese was like nothing that had ever happened before. Nobody wants to die. Every living thing wants to go on living. But nobody was better suited to go on living more than Danny Reese. When Johnny Yuma's despair had reached its lowest depth at Rock Island, it was Danny Reese's unconquerable spirit, eternal optimism, and sunny face that kept Yuma going. And now the sun had set on that face. There would be no more smile—except for the grave's eternal smile, which creases every skull.

All this in one suspended second and then every fiber and feeling in the body and soul of Johnny Yuma was consumed by a single emotion.

Hate.

The voice came again across the sun-splattered stream.

"Hey, you, Rebs! There's one less of you now! Vogan! Bart Vogan's the name, sharpshootin's my game! Ohio Volunteers! Who's next?!"

Hate. A wild, chaotic hate. A black hate for a man whose face he had never seen. A name he would never forget. Vogan. Bart Vogan. Yankee. Sharpshooter. Killer. And, war or no war—murderer.

In that instant, the barking sound of cannon, or so thought Johnny Yuma and the other Rebs, but only for an instant.

The dawning sun suddenly seemed covered by a purple sheet. Lightning, then thunder, tore that sheet and an April storm exploded out of the sky pouring into the stream and onto the soldiers now lying in muddy rivulets.

"Follow me!" The voice of Cane.

Johnny Yuma looked up from the corpse of Danny Reese to the face of Douglas Baines, whose lips were moving. Curse or prayer, Yuma could not hear, but they all heard Cane's command.

"Charge! Follow me, you valiant Rebs! Valiant Rebels, follow me!"

The rain poured down, as if to wash away the blood that would be shed. A crooked sword of lightning struck the sky and thunder reverberated like a hundred drums.

And then—

The Rebel yell!

It erupted from the throat of a single soldier, and then became a screaming whirlwind, a challenging chorus, searing screams, each out-screaming the other. A terrifying torrent—ghostly, ghastly—a rebellion against reality, against reason; a call to annihilation.

Johnny Yuma tore through his comrades. He would be the first to cross the bridge—or die. Consumed with burning hate. Propelled by rage for revenge. His brain echoing the rasping voice, *"Bart Vogan's the name . . . Bart Vogan's the name . . . Bart Vogan's the name . . . Bart Vogan's the name . . ."* Like the screeching whistle of a speeding train . . . Yuma charged, elbowed, and stumbled past the churning gray tide.

"Bart Vogan, you bastard! Where are you?!" He yelled with all his fury—but his yell was buried in the ringing rifle fire, the clash of wet steel, the screams of zeal, and the tumult of agony and dying.

The bridge over the Little Dirty became hell's own bridge across the Styx. Wet with rain and blood, blood bursting from tunics of blue and gray. Rifles and swords, pistols and bayonets, hand to hammering hand.

The Yanks had risen out of the brush and mud of the northern bank, their dirty blue uniforms steaming from the sun and rain. The valiant Billy Yanks clashed against the screaming, rampaging, valiant Johnny Rebs, fighting and clawing for every yard and foot and inch of a nameless bridge, as if the war and their lives depended on it.

The war did not. But their lives did.

As hard as Johnny Yuma fought through his own ranks and tried to be the first to reach the enemy, he failed.

Lieutenant Clayton Cane was first, and among the first to fall. The shot tore into his throat. He spun with a final grunt and slammed into Johnny Yuma, who held him dead for just a moment, then let him drop.

"Bart Vogan, you craven bastard! Here I am!"

But the challenge went unheeded and unheard. It was impossible to distinguish any single voice out of the thunder and gunfire, the turn and tangle of bodies; bent, broken, and bleeding, cursing and screaming their frenzy and fury through the morning nightmare from which many would not wake.

Johnny Yuma let his empty rifle drop and drew his sidearm, firing into the chest of a Yankee corporal, a lad his own age and rank. Yuma hoped the name was Vogan, Bart Vogan. They were all Bart Vogans, and he fired again and again. Yuma caught a glimpse of Doug Baines and thought he saw him fall.

And then above the hue and din of battle, a slight rending sound—a bugle, bugles. The Rebels caught sight of a mounted column splashing through the stream, men in soaked gray uniforms firing—but something was wrong. The guns and rifles were pointed in the air—and it was not a single line, but twin columns. The other column was wearing blue and the bugles were sounding "Recall."

Battle guidons slanting forward—field trumpets now closer and louder—

"Recall."

And the voices of both captains leading the columns, advancing side by side.

"Cease fire! Cease fire!" came the command again and again.

Those who had fallen and were able, rose slowly, carefully, still dazed and bleeding, but alive. One of those who rose with blood leaking into his eyes was Baines. He made his way toward Yuma. Instinctively, the Yankees slowly gravitated together, just a little closer to the northern section of the bridge, and the Rebels closer to the south, as both captains shouted, "Regroup, men! Regroup!"

"Armistice!" the Yankee captain shrieked as he reined his animal to a stop a few feet from the bridge.

"Truce!" the Rebel captain confirmed and reined up next to the Yank.

"Men," the Yankee captain went on, "Generals Grant and Lee are meeting tomorrow. Until then all activities, all hostilities are suspended!"

Soldiers on the bridge, soldiers on both sides, looked at each other and murmured. The reality still had not sunk into most of them.

"You men of the Ohio Volunteers are to fall back and follow me to Three Forks," the Yankee captain added.

"What do we do, Captain?" one of the Rebs shouted.

"Your orders are to return with me to Appomattox Court House and wait."

"For what?" The voice was Johnny Yuma's.

"For Lee and Grant," the Confederate captain replied.

The rain abated. There was no more lightning or thunder. What remained of the Confederate infantry regrouped with the Confederate cavalry column on the south bank of the bridge.

Johnny Yuma approached the captain who had not dismounted.

"Sir."

"What is it, Corporal?"

"May I have permission to look after a friend of mine who was hit?"

"Wounded?"

"Killed."

"He'll be looked after, Corporal. By a burial detail."

"But . . ."

"That's all, Corporal. Your orders are to return to Appomattox Court House with us, now."

"Sir, General Lee's not going to surrender, is he?"

"Corporal, General Lee does not confide in captains. And captains do not confer with corporals."

"Yes, sir."

Johnny Yuma did not move.

"Is there something else, Corporal?

"Just one thing, sir."

"What?"

"We would have taken that bridge."

"I know that, Corporal." The captain turned his mount and moved south.

Doug Baines' hand touched Johnny Yuma's shoulder. "Johnny, you all right?"

"Yeah. What about you?"

"Just a knock on the head. Nothin' to speak of."

Yuma turned and faced the opposite bank of the Little Dirty, where the Yankee forces were retreating.

"I hope he got his," Johnny Yuma said.

"Who?"

"Bart Vogan."

CHAPTER 24

Palm Sunday. April 9. A nation divided and bleeding. A nation less than a hundred years old. A nation whose sixteenth president, a man who wanted peace, but who led his country into bloodbaths of battle after battle, burying thousands upon thousands of sons and fathers and brothers. And there were thousands more, whose limbs were torn and maimed. Survivors who would never be the same in body and mind and spirit.

The battles on land and sea, in fields and streams, in cities and swamps—conquests and defeats—on horseback and foot, all the dynamite and destruction, fire and devastation—all led to the inevitable end:

Appomattox.

Wilmer McLean had been forced to move twice. First from Manassas Junction, where the war's first fierce battle had occurred in 1861. Then again during the Second Battle of Bull Run. He settled in the quiet little community of Appomattox Court

House—and that is where the conflict would be settled.

Appomattox.

An unreal quiet prevailed outside McLean's house that fateful Sunday. The sky remained melancholy from the recent rain, the ground still April soft.

April. The time of rebirth. Of aspiring life. With spring rain bathing newborn birds and chasing the chill winds of winter. April. The time of seedling hope. Of budding promise.

April at Appomattox. The time for burying yesterday's casualties. The time to pause. The time to listen to the silence of the machinery of war—and wait for the rebirth of a nation.

Outside McLean's house they waited, some of the remnants of General Robert E. Lee's Army of Northern Virginia.

One Confederate soldier stood in front of the steps leading to the porch of McLean's house. The soldier's uniform was dirty and worn, and in the area of the left shoulder there was a wound, slight, but crusted crimson. With his right hand, the soldier held the reins of a magnificent white steed.

Most of the rest stood with a weary rigidness, looking toward the north.

But there were two others in the nearby barn. Johnny Yuma and Douglas Baines. Baines sat on a stool rubbing his forehead. Yuma paced and spoke with a hushed nervousness.

"Doug, we can't let it happen . . ."

"Let what happen?"

"The surrender."

"Johnny . . ."

"It's got to be stopped."

"Johnny, your saddle's slippin'. You're off your feed . . ."

"I'm telling you . . ."

"You think you, a little ol' nubbin of a corporal, is going to tell General Robert E. Lee what to do? It's all over, son!"

"Not yet, it's not."

Baines rose from the stool and faced Yuma.

"Well, it will be and, thank God, in a matter of minutes. No more fear and death every morning. Pretty soon old fuzzy-face Grant and his staff'll ride up to McLean's house outside and Lee'll sign a piece of paper and give him a tin sword and we can go home, son."

"To what?"

"I'll tell you . . ."

"No, I'll tell you. To boot-lickin' shame and sufferin'."

"To life! To my Cora and little Jimmy."

"Not me."

"Well then"—Baines turned away and walked two steps—"you stay and keep playing soljer."

Yuma advanced, grabbed the man, and whirled him so they were face-to-face.

"Don't you fun me, paperback! I fought every day you fought . . ."

"Did you fight as much as Stone Jackson and JEB

Stuart? Hill and Pender? And Rhodes? They're all dead . . . and most of their soljer boys with 'em!"

"Sure they are, all dead. And if we give up now, what'd they all die for—what?"

"Sometimes you lose."

"Well, not yet."

"Yes, yet! Now! Lost! Listen to me. I ain't no general, but I know somethin'. Two weeks ago Gordon had seventy-five hundred men. Now there's less than two thousand, all starved. You listenin'?"

"I'm listening."

"Field's got more men absent than present! All that's left of Pickett's whole army is sixty bone-beaten men! Now what do you expect to fight with?"

"So long as I got a gun, I fight!"

"Johnny . . ."

"If I didn't, I'd be untrue to those screamin' Rebs I charged with at Cedar Creek and Cold Harbor. We vowed together that we'd fight until we were all dead if we had to—and then our ghosts 'ud go right on fighting!"

"Yeah, well that's about all we got left is a phantom army—and as far as I'm concerned, Grant's welcome to the leavins."

"Grant!" Yuma grunted out the name. "Grant!" Johnny Yuma thought back to the shack at Vicksburg when he had the chance to kill Grant, but with his own innate honor had decided to take him as a prisoner of war and bargain for an honorable peace. But then was then, and now was different.

Yuma had a different plan for Grant, and another chance for the South. "I can see him strutting up to General Lee—humiliating a saint—beating him over the head with the bones of the Confederacy!"

"There's nothin' to be done about it, son. So you'd just better be content to witness some history this here Palm Sunday."

"Witness?" Johnny Yuma drew the sidearm from its holster. "Witness? I'm gonna make history—and alone if you're not of a mind to help . . ."

"Johnny . . . what you nurturin' in that hot Texas head of yours?"

Johnny Yuma took a couple of steps toward the door of the barn, then turned back, still gripping the gun in his hand.

"I've been in McLean's house this morning."

"So?"

"So right now General Lee's sitting in the parlor. I'm climbing around back to a room right over that parlor. A room with a vent. It's there all right. I've laid it all out and when Grant walks in that room, he's going to run straight into a head full of lead."

"You're fevered!"

"I sure am. If a Southerner kills Grant, there'll be no peace. We'll have to keep fighting—and you'll see, we'll win."

Doug Baines leaped at Yuma, grabbed him, and tried to get the gun away.

"No, I won't see, you young owl head. Give me that . . ."

Yuma smashed his left fist into Baines' jaw and,

as Baines started to fall, lifted the gun to hit him with the barrel but realized that that would not be necessary. Baines was unconscious as he fell to the floor.

Johnny Yuma looked around. He spotted a length of rope across one of the stalls. He walked over, holstered the gun, took the rope, and started to tie up the unconscious soldier lying on the floor.

"I'm sorry, ol' Doug. But now you know, and I got to make sure you don't spoil it. Four years is nothing. We'll fight forty. And we'll win without them having Grant."

CHAPTER 25

General Ulysses Simpson Grant, mounted on his black stallion Cincinnati, and accompanied by several of his general officers, rode into the clearing where another detachment was mounted and waiting.

Grant's face and uniform were used up and dirty. His eyes told of tired victory and inconsolable sadness. The stub of an unlit cigar stemmed from his thin, creased lips.

"Sheridan!" Grant waved and rode closer. General Philip Henry Sheridan nodded and faintly smiled as Grant approached. Sheridan's uniform was not in much better shape than Grant's.

"Phil, you made good time. But then," Grant added, "you have right along. How are you?"

"First rate, sir."

"Been waiting long?" Grant's voice was raspy and dry.

"Not too long . . . not for this."

Grant looked at the mounted, unmistakable red-scarfed figure of General George Armstrong Custer next to Sheridan.

"Custer." Grant smiled and removed the stub of cigar from his mouth. "Good to see you, *General* Custer. You've more than earned that rank, George."

"Thanks to you, sir."

"No, I thank you for Gettysburg, Culpepper, Yellow Tavern, and all the rest, you and Sheridan." Grant turned to General Sheridan and inquired, "Phil, Lynchburg?"

"All gone our way," Sheridan replied.

"Good. I wanted both of you along for this."

"Thank you." Sheridan nodded. "I hear you've been feeling poorly."

"Phil, I had the damnedest headache . . . for near a week now." He looked at the butt of the cigar he had taken from his mouth. "Pain so fierce it hurt to open my eyes. Hurt worse to close them. No sleep. Couldn't eat. But after I got Lee's letter . . . there was no more pain."

"Was a long time coming," Sheridan affirmed. "Don't know how they held out this long."

"I do. Lee . . . Where is he?"

"At the McLean house . . . just down the way."

"Well, then," Grant nodded, "let's go over and see him."

The road to Appomattox was less than a mile away and level all the way. But the road that

Ulysses Simpson Grant had traveled to get this far was uphill—twisted, strewn with disappointment, danger, drink, disillusionment, depression, and death.

But no road was traveled by a man with more determination, guts, and endeavor.

At Fort Henry. Fort Donaldson. At Shiloh, and at the siege of Vicksburg, where he divided the Confederacy in two. Grant stormed Lookout Mountain, Missionary Ridge, and Chattanooga. He took command of the Army of the Potomac and dogged Robert E. Lee's Army of Northern Virginia, culminating in the Battle of the Wilderness. Lee's army never recovered, and finally Richmond fell. The "U.S." in Grant came to stand for "Unconditional Surrender"—on the part of the enemy.

Sheridan and Custer had routed the Confederate defenders at Five Forks and wiped out Pickett's column, capturing more than 5,000 Rebels. On April 8, Sheridan with Custer reached Appomattox Station, cutting off Lee's retreat.

Lee's men, hungry and worn out, stayed with the colors only because of their unshakable confidence and love for Lee himself.

But Lee realized that confidence and love were not enough. No match for the overwhelming numbers, strength, and power of Grant's army. And so Lee had sent, out of his thin lines, a Confederate horseman with white flag fluttering.

And now, U.S. Grant was on the road to Appomattox where Lee waited.

But at Appomattox someone else was waiting. Waiting with a loaded revolver for Ulysses Simpson Grant.

Someone named Johnny Yuma.

CHAPTER 26

Johnny Yuma had bound Douglas Baines and dragged him out of sight into one of the stalls. For extra good measure, Yuma had piled straw on top of his unconscious friend and comrade. The young corporal could barely keep his hands from trembling.

At first, it had been a wild notion he had thrown out at Baines without even thinking. Something said in a mad moment, as men will, in moments of madness. Something so unlikely, so impossible, so daring as to be dismissed with the passing of that moment of madness.

But Johnny Yuma would not let it pass. He would not dismiss it, or let it be dismissed. He, a lowly corporal, would change the course of history, even though the odds were that he would not live to see the change. The odds were that he would be dead. But he had faced death many times before, for lesser reasons. For a hill, a barn, a bridge. For no good reason except that he was a soldier and a soldier followed orders.

This time he would not follow.

This time he would lead, lead the Confederacy to a new day, a new chapter, a new beginning. He had felt hate for the enemy—all the enemies who took the lives of the men who fought beside him, the lives of his fellow Texans, the sons of the South, from Mississippi, Alabama, Georgia, South Carolina, Virginia, and all the rest who followed the stars and bars.

Still, if he had met those young enemies at other times and at other places, without uniforms, without weapons, the chances were that they would work and laugh, play cards and drink together. They would stand together and fight a foreign enemy as did their fathers and grandfathers before them.

But war had come. A war he never really understood, but a war that had torn him away from Texas, across the Red River and the Mississippi, him and thousands of other young men like him. A war that drained the life out of Texas and drained the blood out of thousands of other Texans. A war that was being waged and won under the leadership of a great general. A general who outfought and outmaneuvered everyone and everything the enemy could throw against him.

Until—

Until U.S. Grant, who was not interested in taking just Confederate territory, but more interested in taking Confederate lives. Grant knew he could sacrifice more soldiers than could the South. And sacrifice he did. The capture of strategic points and occupation of Southern territory were secondary. Grant's primary objective was the destruction of the Southern army. The only way to destroy that army was to kill. And kill he did.

And now Johnny Yuma would kill Grant, even if he had to sacrifice his own life in the killing.

Maybe that sacrifice would spark a new flame, a new fire for those comrades he would leave behind, and maybe the South would reap a second glory.

Unlike the time at the shack near Vicksburg, now there would be no opportunity to take Grant prisoner and negotiate for favorable terms of peace. The only opportunity would be to kill Grant and force the fight to continue. Maybe even to continue in the McLean parlor with Yankee generals shooting at Confederate officers, and that would escalate into a continuation of the war itself, and without Grant the South might rise again and ultimately emerge victorious.

But no matter what else happened, General Ulysses Simpson Grant would not live to see it.

Grant would be dead.

Yuma took a long, deep breath. He looked at both his hands and silently commanded them to stop shaking. They ignored the command.

He took another deep breath, opened the barn door, went out, and closed the door behind him.

Yuma tried not to look at any of the other soldiers, not to meet their eyes. Few were talking to each other. Most stood silently waiting. The few who said anything to the other men spoke in whispers.

Yuma did not want to be whispered to, or even noticed. He would not be one of those who waited.

He made his way from the area of the barn toward the side and then rear of the McLean house. It was a two-story red-brick structure fronted by a four square-columned porch. The porch also had a second story, both stories with wooden railings painted white. Cedar and maple trees, April green, rimmed the house on all sides. Soldiers stood under the shade of the trees and in front of the porch. Their uniforms bespoke time, travel, and defeat. There were no smiles. The faces were grim and there were tears.

Yuma barely glanced at the soldier holding the reins of the white horse, then moved on. There was no one at the rear of the house. Johnny Yuma went to a trellis, took a final look around, and began to climb.

The latticework was covered with vines, slippery, and not meant to support human weight. Slowly he made his way upward, step by tentative step. Four feet upward. Five, six. He had reached the second story, then stopped, frozen by the sound.

A bell tolled in the village. A church bell. Of course. It was Sunday. Palm Sunday at that. Church bells were sounding in all the villages. In all Virginia. In all the cities in all the states. North and

South. In all the country. In all the countries all over the world. Bells were tolling.

On the grounds below, a dog barked. For a terrifying second, Johnny Yuma thought the dog was barking at him. But no, the dog was not in sight. Still, in Johnny Yuma's mind, every sound was magnified. The dog barked again. Dogs don't know it's Sunday, thought Johnny Yuma. Sometimes soldiers don't know either. There were times in the past years when he didn't know what day it was, or care. Calendars didn't count. The machinery of war went on seven days a week, day and night.

There had been no time out from war. No time out from killing.

Wherever Grant was at this time, and he must have been near, he, too, could hear the church bell peal.

The poet was right:

Never send to know for whom the bell tolls.
It tolls for thee.

That's right, General Ulysses Simpson Grant, Unconditional Surrender Grant, Johnny Yuma thought, *it tolls for thee—and maybe it tolls for me. Sunday's as good a day as any to die. Everybody dies. Not everybody can die for a cause and be remembered for the dying.* Yuma was ready to die. Not willing—but ready.

He had already done and experienced more

than his share of almost everything. Of sorrow and pain.

Sorrow at the death of his mother and of all the young men who had died and fought alongside him. Most recently at the bridge without a name. Danny Reese and Lieutenant Cane and all the rest.

Pain. Pain at Rock Island and from the wounds of battle.

And he, too, had inflicted wounds. Often fatal. He would inflict one more and make sure it was fatal.

All this he thought in less than a second. And that's all it took to clear his mind. It seemed that another set of reflexes had taken over. Reflexes honed for revenge and retribution.

He felt a surge of readiness and confidence. His body was prepared. His mind clearer than it had ever been.

Johnny Yuma started to climb again.

The church bell fell silent and there was a different sound.

Hoofbeats.

Generals Grant and Sheridan, Custer, Ord, Parker, and Williams along with the staff that would see to the details of the surrender.

Reflexively the soldiers of the South stood at attention—and clenched their fists.

They were trying to neither look at nor avoid looking at Grant, who was the first to dismount.

One of the Yankee soldiers hurried over to take

the reins from Cincinnati's bridle; Grant, followed by his staff, approached the nine steps that slanted up to the porch, but he paused as he noticed the Confederate soldier standing with his hands on the reins of the majestic white animal.

Grant turned and took a step closer. He gently touched the horse's head. The officers stood by.

Johnny Yuma moved—quiet and quick—across the upstairs room toward the vent that faced the parlor below.

"His name's Traveler, isn't it?" Grant asked.

"Yes, sir," the soldier replied with a soft Southern meter.

"You been tending him long?"

"About a year, sir."

"Looks like a good animal . . . Where you from, soldier?"

"Chattanooga, sir."

"Chattanooga." The campaigns flashed across Grant's mind. Lookout Mountain, the Tennessee River, Moccasin Point, the assault on Missionary Ridge. Stunning victories for Grant. Shattering defeats for the Confederacy.

Grant took note of the Confederate soldier's wound.

"When did you get creased?"

"Yesterday, sir."

"Doctor see it?"

"I guess . . ." The soldier shook his head. "I guess they're all up at the front lines, sir."

"The front lines . . ." Grant removed a handkerchief from an inside pocket of his tunic and awkwardly pressed it to the soldier's wound. The soldier took hold of the handkerchief and Grant touched the soldier's hand.

"You take care," said Grant, "And take care of old Traveler there."

"Yes, sir. Thank you, sir."

Grant turned and walked to the porch steps where Sheridan, Custer, and the others were waiting.

"You know, Phil," Grant spoke just above a whisper, "I met General Lee during the Mexican campaign when we were both in the same army. I was just a captain then. I wonder if he will remember me."

"After today, he'll remember you."

"Yes, I s'pose . . ."

Grant hesitated. Sheridan looked at him as if to say, "There's no putting it off." Grant threw down the butt of his cigar and moved forward. The other officers began to follow. All but Custer.

Grant turned toward the boy general.

"George?"

"I'll wait out here, sir, if you don't mind. There's nothing I can do in there. I just might say or do something that . . . well, I'd better stay out here."

"If that's what you'd prefer, George. You've done more than enough." Then Grant smiled. "I could *order* you in . . ."

Custer inhaled.

". . . but I won't."

Custer exhaled.

"I'll just say thanks again, and see you later."

Grant, Custer, and Yuma didn't know it, but fate, destiny, providence . . . or chance, had just determined that the three of them would meet again that momentous day.

Johnny Yuma knelt by the vent. He had his gun in hand and was checking the cylinder.

CHAPTER 27

Doug Baines rose out of a murky, black pit into consciousness, but his body lay prone. At first his brain could not tell him where he was. He knew he had been hit, hard but not fatally. He was alive. That much he knew.

For a fleeting moment he thought he was on that nameless bridge near Three Forks. But the battle was not raging, except for the battle in his brain.

And he was dry. Then he realized something else. He was bound. Hand and foot. Hog-tied. He could barely move and the gag in his mouth prevented him from crying out.

His eyes were shrouded in darkness. Hay. His face and body were covered with hay. He managed to move, then turn, dislodging the hay that covered his face.

Then it struck him. What had happened. No, he was not on the bridge. That was yesterday. A lifetime ago. He was at Appomattox. In a barn. Bound and gagged. Alone. And Yuma, Johnny Yuma, where was he? What was he doing? Or about to do? Was it too late? How long had Baines been unconscious? He strained to listen, for what he was not sure.

A gunshot? Or gunshots? Footsteps? Voices? Anything that would tell him it was not too late.

And even if it weren't, it soon could be. He remembered the words of Johnny Yuma, ". . . we can't let it happen . . . it's got to be stopped . . . if we give up, what'd they all die for . . . as long as I got a gun, I fight . . . Grant! I can see him strutting up to General Lee . . . humiliating a saint . . . beating him over the head with the bones of the Confederacy . . . a room right over that parlor . . . I've got it all laid out . . . when Grant comes into that room, he's going to run straight into a head full of lead . . ."

Was it possible? Could one lone man with a gun do what the great generals of the South—Lee, Stuart, Beauregard, Jackson, Bragg, Early, Johnston, Longstreet, and the rest, with all their armies could not do—stop Grant?!

Not just stop him—kill him.

Douglas Baines tried to remain calm and think. It could not have happened yet. If it had, there would not be this silence at Appomattox. There would be noise, activity, and, very likely, hostility.

If Grant had been shot, there would be more shooting. First, at Johnny Yuma, then God only knew. The whole village might erupt in gunfire. Neither side had laid down its arms.

So, no, it hadn't happened—yet.

There was still time, but how long? And for what? What could he do, gagged and tied in a barn, while in a house only yards away the great generals of a nation's worst war would meet to make peace, a rendezvous with history . . . ?

CHAPTER 28

Johnny Yuma looked through the vent into the room. There were several Southern officers. But Yuma was looking at only one man.

The imposing, immaculately uniformed figure of General Robert Edward Lee. Commander-in-chief of the Confederate Armies. The heart and soul of the South. And with him in command, at the outset the South had seemed invincible, winning battle after battle . . . Fort Sumter, Lexington, Belmont, Shiloh, Fort Royal, Bull Run.

No one had expected a long war. No one expected half a million casualties. The South had superior tacticians, but the North had superior everything else. It took more than four years, but the culmination was predestined.

There was some slight noise from the hall. Lee did not move, but two of the officers, Babcock and Marshall, reacted. Babcock went to the door and opened it. Framed there was Grant, dressed for the field, tunic, breeches, and mud-bespattered boots. Johnny Yuma started to bring the gun up to aiming position.

Grant stepped inside and offered his hand. The other Northern officers entered. Lee rose. He and Colonel Charles Marshall moved to meet Grant. Johnny Yuma's aim was spoiled.

He knew he would have only one shot. He took a hard look at Grant and remembered again the other time Grant's fate, and maybe the fate of the South, was connected to his own trigger finger— and his own code of honor. But this time it was different, he told himself, and as far as Yuma was concerned this was still a battlefield. The war was not over, nor would it be if one shot could make the difference.

Below in the room there was some awkward hesitation. By now, Lee was seated. Grant moved to the table and sat across from the Southern commander.

Johnny Yuma started to take aim again, but Sheridan leaned down and whispered something to Grant, obscuring Yuma's target. Sheridan, for the time, remained between Grant and Yuma. Grant cleared his throat and smiled toward the elegant man on the other side of the table.

"I met you once before, General Lee . . . while you were serving in Mexico . . . when you came over from General Scott's headquarters to visit Garland's brigade. I have always remembered your appearance and think I would have recognized you anywhere."

"Yes," Lee replied softly. "I know I met you on that occasion . . . and I have often thought of it and tried to recollect how you looked, but . . ."

"I know"—Grant smiled slightly—"you probably couldn't recall a single feature."

"I'm sorry."

The fingers of Lee's right hand touched the edge of the table. His voice tried to disguise what must have been immeasurable anguish.

"I . . . I suppose, General Grant, that the object of our present meeting is fully understood."

Grant nodded.

Johnny Yuma could feel, and almost hear, his heart pounding.

"I asked to see you," Lee continued, "to ascertain on what terms you would receive the surrender of my army."

Yuma's gun was ready. His hand unsteady as he braced himself to squeeze the trigger. Only then did the full import of what he was about to do strike him . . . but he would do it.

General Grant put his hand to his forehead and tried not to look directly at Lee, tried to make the moment easier.

"The terms I propose, General Lee, are those stated in my letter of yesterday. That is, the officers and men surrendered, to be pardoned and properly exchanged . . . and all arms, ammunition, and supplies to be delivered up as captured property."

Lee nodded, not displeased.

"Those are about the conditions I hoped would be proposed."

"And I hope," Grant added, "this will lead to a general suspension of hostilities, sir. And be the means of preventing any further loss of life."

Johnny Yuma shuddered at the words . . . "further loss of life."

"May I suggest, General," Lee said, "that you commit to writing the terms you have proposed so they may be formally acted upon."

"Very well," Grant replied as easily as he could. "I will write them out."

This was not what Johnny Yuma had anticipated. No strutting, commanding, or disrespect. Still his gun was ready. His clear opportunity had not yet presented itself, so he told himself.

Douglas Baines struggled fiercely against the bindings. His wrists were bleeding, but the rope was only tightening deeper into his wrists.

General George Armstrong Custer walked down the steps of McLean's house as he recognized a familiar figure in a Yankee uniform and red scarf of a Michigan brigade, Captain Adam Dawson.

Neither saluted as Custer extended his hand.

"Adam, I've been looking for you . . . knew you'd show up."

"I try not to be too far behind you, Autie." Dawson smiled. "How come you're not in there?"

"Because I'm out here."

Dawson pointed to the McLean doorway.

"Afraid you wouldn't be able to hold on to your temper?"

"Partly that. Partly afraid that I *would* . . . Oh, I don't know, Adam . . . for the first time since this started I'm all jumbled up."

"Well, lad, the war'll soon be over."

"One war just leapfrogs onto another, Adam, but in the meanwhile I won't be General Custer, just one more colonel, unless I can get out west."

"You'll get there, Autie, and meanwhile I've got to get back to the ranks."

"You do that, and I'm going to take a walk." Then Custer whispered, "Truth is, Adam, I've got to take a leak."

Grant was writing rapidly. Sheridan leaned over beside him, impeding Yuma's aim. When Grant was finished, he rose and slowly took the few steps to Lee and handed him the paper.

"I have written that what is to be turned over will not include the sidearms of officers, nor their private horses or baggage."

There were reactions from the Union officers, Sheridan, Ord, Parker, and Williams. And from the Confederates, Marshall and Babcock, and from General Lee.

"This will have a very happy effect on my army."
Lee looked at the paper in his hand.

"Unless you have some suggestions in regard to
the form of the terms as stated, I will have a copy
made in ink and sign it." Grant took a couple of
steps back toward Sheridan as General Lee began
to read.

Baines could feel the blood leaking onto his
hands and sleeves; still the rope was not loosening.

Johnny Yuma now thought of shooting Sheridan,
who stood in front of Grant, then quickly firing
again at Grant, but it was too risky. Grant would
instinctively react and become a moving target.
There was still time.

Lee had finished reading. He hesitated as if embarrassed to speak, but did.

"There is one thing, General, the cavalrymen
and artillerists own their own horses in our army. I
know this differs from the United States Army."

Grant nodded.

"I would like to understand," Lee went on,
"whether these men will be permitted to retain
their horses."

There was a stilted moment.

"The terms do not allow this, General. Only the
officers are allowed their private property."

Yuma's face was grim. He placed the barrel of the gun between the vents.

There was a regretful nod from the Commanding General of the South.

"No." Lee looked back at the paper. "I see the terms do not allow it. That is clear . . ."

General Grant could not fail to recognize Lee's wish and with consideration that prevailed throughout the meeting, would not humiliate the great general by forcing him to make a direct plea for modification of the already generous terms. Grant spoke as gently and respectfully as possible.

"Well, the subject is quite new to me. I didn't know that any private soldiers owned their own horses." Grant paused for just a beat. "I take it that most of your men are small farmers. I know they'll need their horses to put in a crop to carry their families through next winter . . . I'll instruct my officers to allow all men who own a horse or mule to take the animals home to work their little farms."

Lee's face was filled with manifest relief and gratitude. He looked directly into the eyes of the man who had defeated him.

"This will have the best possible effect on the men. It will do much toward conciliating our people."

As he watched and listened, a shadow of confusion fell upon the face of Johnny Yuma, but his finger was still on the trigger.

* * *

Outside the McLean house the pall of silence grew even deeper. Regret, reconciliation, reverence, the feelings of the survivors swelled within them in silence—almost as if the entire outdoor area had been transformed into a church setting, while in the McLean parlor a liturgy of sorts was taking place.

The Yanks avoided the eyes of the Rebels and the Rebel eyes shunned the Union faces.

Palm Sunday, and the palm was a symbol of peace. There would be peace, but at what terms, what price? At what further cost to the South? The South that already had paid a crippling price in human lives and worldly treasure. What further punishment would "Unconditional Surrender" Grant inflict on the enfeebled South?

Would there be reconciliation, or revenge?

Behind the barn, Custer had finished his business and was buttoning the front of his pants when he heard sounds from inside the stable. A soft, then louder banging against the wall.

The sound stopped, started again, stopped and started even louder. Not the sounds of horse's hoofs. He thought of walking away but then thought better of it. Custer made his way around to the front and opened the barn door, stepped in.

Once inside he heard it louder, then spotted the source of the noise.

Within a stable, a man in a Confederate uniform,

bound and gagged, desperately kicking his boots against the wooden wall.

Custer rushed to the soldier, whose jaw bled and eyes implored for help. Custer leaned down, tore away the bandanna that had been tightened across the soldier's mouth, started to untie the knots of the rope that bound his body, but the soldier shook his head and pulled away.

"You've got to stop him," Baines cried out. "He's going to kill Grant!"

"Who is?"

"Johnny Yuma . . . corporal . . . McLean house . . . up in the attic . . . there's a vent . . . he's crazy! Going to kill Grant . . . Hurry!! NOW!!!"

The other copies of the terms were being written by Grant's staff. Lee wished in some way to reciprocate for the kindness shown to him and his army by the victorious general.

"General Grant, I have about a thousand of your men as prisoners. I shall be glad to send them to your lines as soon as possible, for I have no provisions for them. I have, indeed, nothing for my own men."

"Of course," Grant smiled warmly, "I should like to have our men within our lines as soon as possible."

"I've telegraphed to Lynchburg," Lee said, "directing several trainloads of rations to be sent by rail. I should be glad to have the present wants of the men supplied from them."

The Union officers reacted uneasily to this. There was a slightly perceptible movement in their shoulders. Their eyes shifted toward Philip Sheridan.

"I'm sorry"—Grant did his best not to embarrass General Lee—"but those supplies won't be coming, General. Phil . . . I mean, General Sheridan here captured the train from Lynchburg last night."

"I . . . I see . . ." There was a dignified, but final resignation, in the voice of General Robert E. Lee.

U.S. Grant wanted to divert Lee's mind from Lynchburg. It was not easy for him to think of anything to say, but after a brief hesitation he spoke.

"Of how many men does your present force consist, sir?"

"I'm not able to say," Lee replied. "My losses in killed and wounded have been exceedingly heavy." He paused. "Many of our companies are without officers . . . I have no means of ascertaining our present strength."

Yuma's finger started to squeeze the trigger as Grant looked to Sheridan, but something made him pause and listen.

"Suppose I send over twenty-five thousand rations," Grant said. "Do you think that would be a sufficient supply?"

"I think it will be more than enough," Lee replied softly, a soldier doing his best to hold back emotion. "And it will be a great relief, I assure you . . ."

General George Armstrong Custer hurried as fast as possible without drawing attention—through the ranks of Northern and Southern soldiers—up the nine steps of the McLean house where a Yankee captain stood at the doorway.

"Step aside, Captain! I'm going in there!"

"But, sir, I have orders not to . . ."

"General Custer just gave you an order."

"A direct order, sir?"

"Did you ever hear of an *indirect* order?"

Custer brushed briskly past the captain and went in.

Marshall had finished and blotted the inked letter from Lee to Grant accepting the terms. Lee was reading it aloud and preparing to sign.

Grant and the others in the room waited and listened. So did Johnny Yuma.

Lee read aloud in his soft, Southern eloquence. He neither rushed, nor lingered, over the words:

>   *"Lieutenant General U.S. Grant,*
>   *Commanding Armies of the United States,*
>
>   *"General: I have received your letter of this date*
>   *containing the terms of surrender of the Army of*

*Northern Virginia. They are accepted by me and I
will proceed to designate the proper officers to carry
the stipulations into effect.*

> "*Very respectfully,*
> *Your obedient servant,*
> *Robert E. Lee*"

He signed.

For Grant and the other Union officers, the long
bittersweet victory had finally come. But their faces
were not those of brute conquerors, rather of compassionate comrades.

Custer had run up both flights of the McLean
house and was hurrying along the narrow stairway.

General Robert E. Lee stepped closer to Grant,
readying himself for the final gesture of defeat. He
spoke as he moved slightly in anticipation of giving
up his sword.

"Thirty-nine years of devotion to military duty
has come to this . . . and this, too, is my duty . . ."

But Grant gently placed a restraining hand
toward General Lee's gesture.

"General," said Grant, "the war is over. You are
all our countrymen again." And Grant extended
his hand.

Lee did not hesitate. He withdrew his hand from
the hilt of the sword; then, he, too, extended his

hand in a gesture of reconciliation and friendship. Grant took it warmly.

General George Armstrong Custer burst through the door of the upstairs room, gun drawn, ready for anything . . . except for what he saw . . .

Johnny Yuma, with the unfired gun in his hand, and in his eyes, unashamed, tears. Both Lee and Grant had shown Johnny Yuma the ways of defeat and victory. Of grace and generosity. Of pride and privilege. Of endurance and honor.

Johnny Yuma had wanted to make history. But now he was thankful to be alive, and to have watched it. To have seen two of the greatest men one nation had ever produced . . . and, like both of them, to be a part of that nation again.

Custer took a step toward Yuma and spoke just above a whisper.

"Johnny, what stopped you? You could have done it."

"No. I couldn't. Not after I heard and saw what General Grant said—and did."

The war was over. There would be a new beginning, for the country . . . and for Ulysses Simpson Grant, George Armstrong Custer, and Johnny Yuma.

Chapter 29

"Here, Johnny." Custer pulled the red scarf from his throat and handed it to Yuma. "Wipe the . . . sweat off your face."

Johnny Yuma holstered his pistol, took the scarf. It was not sweat, but tears, that he blotted from his cheeks.

"Thanks." He handed the scarf back to Custer.

"Johnny . . . it's best, best all around, that nobody ever knows about you . . . about us . . . being up here today."

Johnny Yuma did not reply.

Both Yuma and Custer went to the stable and released Doug Baines, who was more than just relieved to see the two of them together.

When Baines started to say something, Yuma interrupted.

"Doug, everything is all right. The war's over; I'll see you later."

Smoking a fresh cigar, General Grant, with his staff, was descending the steps of the McLean house as Grant paused and looked at the two men in uniform—one blue, the other gray.

Grant motioned for those on his staff to wait as he approached Custer and Yuma.

"George." Grant nodded, then with near disbelief, gazed at Johnny Yuma.

"I know you . . . Vicksburg."

"You remembered, sir."

"How could I forget? Yuma. What happened to you after Vicksburg?"

"Sent to Rock Island as a prisoner of war . . ."

"But," Custer said, "he escaped."

"I'm not surprised." Grant grinned.

Yuma swallowed, looked at Custer, then back to Grant.

"General, there's something I've got to tell you . . ."

"Johnny, don't . . ." Custer's hand touched Yuma's shoulder.

"I have to . . . sir." Yuma gazed squarely at General Grant, then spoke just above a whisper. "Today I was upstairs in the attic—hiding there with this gun." He touched his holstered sidearm. "This time intending to kill you and keep the war going."

Yuma's voice and body came close to trembling as he took a deep breath.

Grant seemed surprisingly calm.

"What stopped you? Custer?"

"No, sir," said Custer. "I was a little late."

"Then what?" Grant drew smoke from his cigar.

"It was you, sir . . . what you said . . . and did . . . for General Lee. I realized something."

"What?"

"That the war was lost . . ." Again Yuma's eyes began to well. "And you, sir, were the best hope for a new South."

"And so are you, son," Grant said. "I'm glad we met again . . . the three of us."

Grant motioned to his staff and started to walk away. His officers followed.

As Sheridan passed, he paused for just a moment and spoke to Custer.

"George, I have something for you, a memento you deserve. I'll be sending it along."

"Thank you, sir."

Custer and Yuma remained next to each other.

"Well, Johnny, I don't know what's going to happen to me . . . where they'll send me. I hope it's out west."

"So do I, if that's what you want."

"That's what I want. And, Johnny, maybe, just maybe, we'll meet again. If you ever want to wear one of these red scarves . . . I'd be glad to have you join up."

"I don't know what's going to happen to me either, but . . . I'll remember that."

"See that you do, Johnny." Custer smiled. "And that's a direct order."

CHAPTER 30

Johnny Yuma and Doug Baines were now out front waiting with the remnants of the Army of Northern Virginia.

Grant and most of his contingent had gone, but a Yankee regiment had been assigned to stay behind. A newspaper correspondent who was there later wrote:

> As Lee left the house, he found his men waiting outside . . . It was a stark, tragic moment for the tired officers and soldiers who had fought so long and hard . . . As Lee appeared, a shout of welcome instinctively went up from the army. But instantly recollecting the occasion that brought him before them, their shouts sank into silence, every hat was raised and the bronzed faces of grim warriors were bathed in tears.
>
> As he rode slowly along the lines, his devoted veterans pressed around the noble chief, trying to

*take his hand, touch his person, or even lay their
hands upon his horse, thus exhibiting for him
their great affection.*

    *The general then, with head bare, and tears
flowing down his manly cheeks, bade adieu to
the army.*

Douglas Baines turned to Johnny Yuma. Neither
thought he'd live to see this day, whether in victory
or defeat.

"Well, Johnny, I always said the shortest farewells
are the best."

"Yeah, it's best to go easy on the good-byes."

"But this good-bye's not easy."

"Doug. I'm sorry for what I did back there . . ."

"I'm happy for what you *didn't* do."

"There was a crazy man in that barn. I just hope
that he's not crazy anymore."

"He's not. You've got a lot different look in your
eyes than you had in that barn . . . Johnny, what're
you gonna do?"

"Do?"

"I mean you're going home, aren't you?"

"Home? Where's that?"

"Mason City, isn't it? That's what you said."

"It was, home, I mean, but I don't know anymore."

"Why's that?"

"Well, Doug . . . you been like a father to me,
almost . . . what I mean is, well, I didn't leave my
father under the best of circumstances. I guess you

could say it was under the worst. I'm not sure I'd be welcome."

"Didn't you ever write him? Seems like you were always writing something to somebody . . ."

"Yeah, to myself mostly. I figured I'd get killed and never see him again . . . so I wrote a lot of things . . . to him . . . and to a man named Elmer Dodson . . . and to . . ."

"A girl?"

"Her name's Rosemary. I should've written to her, but I didn't."

"Well, since as far as I can tell, you didn't get killed, why don't you go back and . . ."

"And what?"

"I don't know, maybe straighten things out."

"Maybe there's something else I got to straighten out first."

"What's that?"

"Myself."

Over the last part of their conversation a couple of Yankee soldiers had been passing by—a sergeant and private—and heard some of what was said.

First the sergeant stopped, then the private.

"Hear that, Joe?" The sergeant grinned. "That Reb still needs to be straightened out." He turned from the private to Johnny Yuma. "I thought we already did that . . . taught you how it feels to get whipped like you used to whip your slaves."

The sergeant poked the private's shoulder and laughed at his own wit.

Neither Yuma nor Baines was laughing. It was Baines who spoke.

"Neither of us had any slaves," he replied softly.

The sergeant was still smiling.

"You hear that, Joe? Them two never had any slaves—don't you know—*nobody* in the South had any slaves—that was all made up by some dirty, low-down Yankee liars." The sergeant's face turned grim. "Is that what you're calling us, Reb? Low-down Yankee liars?"

"You called it." Yuma spoke for the first time. "I didn't."

"What *are* you calling us?" the sergeant spat out. "Go ahead and put a name to it."

"I'm not calling you anything . . ." But suddenly a strange expression overtook Yuma's face. "Unless . . ."

"Unless what?" the sergeant challenged.

Johnny Yuma's mind had snapped back to the bridge at Little Dirty and Danny Reese, the dead comrade beside him and a sniper's taunting voice.

". . . Unless your name's Vogan. Bart Vogan."

"No, Reb. It ain't. My name's Schmidt. Sergeant Erik B. Schmidt and this is Private Joe Hahn, both of the Pennsylvania Hundred and First. What're you gonna do about it?"

"Nothing today. Yesterday would've been different. Let's just forget about it."

"Let's not! Joe, I think these Rebs still think they can order their betters around. I think . . ."

"I think I've heard enough." A Yankee lieutenant's voice interrupted. "I think you two better move on."

"Yes, sir," Sergeant Erik B. Schmidt replied, as he and Private Joe Hahn moved on.

"I heard part of that exchange," the lieutenant said. "I'm sorry, Corporal, they were out of line. On behalf of our regiment, I'd like to apologize."

"No apology necessary, sir," Yuma said. "And thank you, sir."

The lieutenant nodded, turned, and walked away.

After a pause, Doug Baines looked at Yuma again.

"Johnny, what would you have done if he *was* Bart Vogan?"

"I don't know. That's just one of the things I have to find out about myself. There's other things . . ."

"Look, Johnny, we been pretty close for some time now, haven't we?"

"Yeah, I guess we have."

"Well, I don't see much wrong with you, if anything . . . anymore."

"Maybe you been too close, Doug. And that goes for me, myself, too. You know 'the forest for the trees.' Maybe I've got to step back and get some perspective, or maybe even climb a mountain and get a good look at everything . . . including myself . . . get something done, before I go home . . . Hell, this was supposed to be a short farewell. I haven't talked so much in years."

"Sometimes . . . sometimes it's good to talk . . .

Johnny, you go ahead and climb that mountain. You'll know when it's time to go home, I do. And the time for me is now, right now, and the place is . . ."

"Kansas." They said it at the same time and laughed.

"Lawrence," Baines still smiled. "Easy to find and not much out of your way to Texas. Come visit a contented old farmer and his family. Cora'll cook you up the best beef stew you ever sat down to."

"I just might do that, Doug. And I just might go visit another friend's family. . ."

"Danny's?"

Yuma nodded.

"Sure, Johnny, that'ud be good. Oh, when you do come see us don't be surprised at something else."

"What's that?"

"Well, before I left, our little community was in need of a pastor . . . If the job's still open I just might take it . . . along with farmin'."

"That doesn't surprise me . . . Well . . . take care of yourself . . . Reverend."

"So long . . . Reb."

They shook hands. The two former Confederates.

CHAPTER 31

Champagne. Liquor. Parades. This time the victory celebrations in countless northern cities and villages were in earnest.

Survivors were reunited with loved ones.

Among them were to be George and Libbie Custer.

For weeks and months there had been rumors of impending truce and peace, rumors that had been proved false by the echoing sounds of gunfire and dynamite proclaiming that there was no truce, no peace.

But now the gunfire was aimed in the air, and instead of dynamite, the tattoo of drums and horns sounded ceaselessly through the day and night.

The country was united, at least on paper, if not in spirit.

The dead were buried, and in the southern cities and farmlands the future was uncertain and dependent on the judgment of the northern victors, many of whom wanted to further punish the Rebels and extract every sort of vengeance—financial, social, and spiritual—possible.

But the North reveled in continuous celebrations, and among the most celebrated heroes was George Armstrong Custer, hailed and cheered since his arrival in Washington.

Finally, after dark he managed to break away from the throngs and make his way to the stable behind the Hotel Eden where Libbie was waiting.

Custer had dismounted and the stable owner took the reins from Custer's hand.

"General, it's a privilege to serve you, and you can be assured we'll take the best care of . . ."

"Brawny—he deserves a good rest and the best feed . . ."

"No need to say more, General—nothing but the best for Brawny and the hero of Brandy Station, Gettysburg, Yellow Tavern, of . . ."

"Yes, well, thank you, Mr . . ."

"Tolan, Josh Tolan, General, and it's my honor to . . ."

"Good night, Mr. Josh Tolan. I'll see you and Brawny tomorrow . . . sometime."

"You bet your boots, General, and . . ."

"Good night, Mr. Tolan."

Custer walked away from the stable into the dark pathway that connected to the Hotel Eden.

He had taken only a few steps.

"General Custer." The voice was deep and the figure imposing as it stepped closer through the darkness. The figure wore a heavy coat for such a balmy April night.

"Yes," Custer replied, then stopped directly in front of the broad figure.

"I know. Been watchin' you most of the day. Just wanted you to know who it was that's going to . . ."

"To what?"

A bowie-type knife flashed out of the man's coat pocket and, gripped by an overlarge hand, was pointing too close to Custer's red-scarfed throat.

"Cut your throat like I've done to other pigs like you! I'm a hog butcher by trade."

It took less than a second for Custer to reason that the man had more to say before he carried out his intention.

"Why?"

"General JEB Stuart, that's why . . . you pig!"

"You knew JEB Stuart?"

"Never met General Stuart, but he *was* the South, and you killed him . . . and the South, at Yellow Tavern."

"Well, mister, I *knew* JEB Stuart, and maybe I did kill him, maybe not. But in the honorable field of battle, not some dark alley. We rode together, side by side at Harpers Ferry, drank and sang together and fought against each other where either one of us might have killed the other, as soldiers do in battle. Not in some craven ambush."

"You knew General Stuart?!"

"He was my brother. They were all my brothers at

West Point and even after . . . but we were soldiers, not dastardly assassins like you."

"I *am* a soldier."

"Still wearing your uniform under that coat?"

"And proud of it!"

"You should be . . . up to now. But why is your hand shaking, proud soldier of the South? Look at it."

The man's hand *was* trembling, but the knife came even closer to Custer's throat.

"Is it because you're violating a soldier's code . . . because JEB Stuart's spirit might be watching? Go ahead, butcher boy, go . . ." Custer's left hand smashed into the man's leathery face as his right drew his sidearm and pointed it at the man's heart. Stunned, he had dropped the knife onto the ground as blood leaked out of his nose and mouth from the impact of Custer's blow.

And the man trembled even more.

"Now then, we've talked enough," Custer said.

"Go ahead," the man said. "I've got nothing to live for. Shoot."

"I'm not going to shoot."

"Then turn me in and watch me hang . . . Nothing to live for . . ."

"Yes, you have and so does the South. Pick up that knife."

"What?!"

"Pick it up and go home. Have you got a family?"

"Wife"—the man nodded—"two kids . . ."

"Go home and forget about tonight. Think about tomorrow."

"I . . . I . . ."

"Go home, soldier."

George Armstrong Custer holstered his sidearm and walked toward the Hotel Eden.

Libbie had received the memento Sheridan had spoken of to Custer at Appomattox, along with a letter:

> *My Dear Madam,*
>
> *I respectfully present to you the small writing-table on which the conditions for surrender of the Confederate Army of Northern Virginia was written by Lt. Gen'l Grant: and permit me to say, Madam, that there is scarcely an individual in our service who has contributed more to bring about this desirable result than your very gallant husband.*
>
> > *Very Respectfully,*
> > *Phil H. Sheridan*
> > *Maj-Gen'l*

General Sheridan had paid Mr. McLean twenty dollars for the table. He could have paid no higher praise or compliment to Libbie and her "gallant husband."

Outside, the streets of Washington were still awash with celebrants—songs, parades, and hoop-dee-do, and even into the night the celebrations persisted and could still be heard by both Custers in the dimly gaslit room.

"My Custer Boy," Libbie whispered. "My 'gallant husband.' I can still hear them cheering for you. Listen, George."

"I can't hear anything—or see anything—but you—tonight, or forever."

"Tonight is forever 'Custer Boy' . . . 'gallant husband.'"

CHAPTER 32

During the war years Julia Grant had visited her husband a number of times, but always near, sometimes too near, the battlefields and the echoes of cannon fire.

But now the cannon fire had ceased.

The battle flags were folded.

"Ulys," Julia said. "Do you realize that since you left Galena almost four years ago, whenever and wherever we've met, this is the first time I don't have to pray for you before you go into battle again? The war is won."

"Won . . . and lost."

"Lost?"

"For the South. Lost, just as we could have lost."

"Not with you in command." She smiled.

"There are too many people up here who want to bleed the South even more, instead of help build it, who say I went too easy on the terms of surrender. But thank God for Lincoln. I've spoken to him about it, and he favors reconciliation and reconstruction. So long as he's president . . ."

"But after him, you'll be president and . . ."

"Julia, I'm a long way from ever being . . ."

"You were a long way from being the general in charge of the U.S. Army."

"I've got to think of what's best for our family . . ."

". . . and for our country." Julia smiled again. "I don't want to sound like Lady Macbeth, but it's your destiny, Ulys, I just know it, just as Mrs. Lincoln said she knew the same about him."

"She told you that?"

"No. She never talks to me unless she has to, whenever there are others around. Ulys, I never told you this, but when the president's boat, the *River Queen*, was anchored in the James River near City Point not a hundred yards from the boat where I was living—remember?"

"Of course." Grant nodded.

"The president had lingered there to get the first news from the front. I saw very little of the presidential party at the time, as Mrs. Lincoln had a good deal of company and seemed to have forgotten my friends and me. I felt this deeply and could not understand it, as my regard for the first family was not only of respect but affection."

"I know that, Julia."

"President Lincoln had stood by you when dark clouds were in the sky, and I felt grateful. By then Richmond had fallen, so had Petersburg, thanks to you . . ."

"Julia . . ."

"That's the truth and you know it. All these places were visited by the president and his party, and I, not a hundred yards from them, was not invited by Mrs. Lincoln to join them. For some reason she has a grudge . . ."

"Not against you. She couldn't have. Nobody could, Julia . . ."

"She's heard it said that her husband couldn't have won the war without you and so she takes aim at me, indirectly, but . . ."

"But the war's over, Julia, and we should both . . . we should all, pray for Lincoln.

CHAPTER 33

April 13, 1865

Outside the White House, military and civilian bands and songsters had been serenading President Abraham Lincoln for hours—calling for the president to appear and speak to the throng.

When, at last, they saw the tall, gaunt figure on the balcony, the cheering swelled even louder until he raised both arms.

"Mr. President," the military bandleader shouted, "is there anything we can play for you?"

Without hesitation the president nodded, his weary, war-worn eyes moistened.

"Please play 'Dixie.'"

At first there was a rumble of disbelief, even disfavor among the assembled."

Abraham Lincoln repeated.

"Please play 'Dixie.'"

The bands played, and the songsters, including

the Union Army serenaders, started to sing the
lyrics to "Dixie"—in the beginning almost hesitat-
ingly, but as Lincoln smiled and waved, their voices
swelled, and they waved back in gratitude and joy.

April 14, 1865

In the morning Abraham Lincoln and his wife
were discussing plans for the evening.

Almost from the time they had been married it
was not unusual for the two of them to harbor a difference of opinion on many subjects and people.

And it was not unusual for him to keep those
differences harbored in silence or gentle replies.

For the last few years the conflict was not only
between the North and South, but the patient president had to endure a less than tranquil environ-
ment at home.

Once more Mrs. Lincoln's rankled voice had
risen to a higher pitch and crescendoed.

". . . and what she wants most is to be the First
Lady of the land!"

"Mary, you criticize Mrs. Grant for having the
same ambition for General Grant that you had for
your husband. Remember those times in Illinois?
So why shouldn't she? We're not elected for the rest
of our lives. Somebody has to take our place. Yours
and mine. I'll vote for Grant; too bad you can't
vote, too. You were my biggest booster. Why
shouldn't Mrs. Grant . . ."

"That's different. *We're* different, and, besides, I

think you should run for a third term, there's no law against it."

"No," Lincoln replied calmly, "but President Washington thought it a bad idea."

"Maybe for him—not for you. He was rich; we're not. We'd just be scraping along. Think of the children . . . and me. What're you going to do—go back to being a country lawyer?"

"Better a country lawyer than a city slicker . . ."

"But being the first third-term president of the country you saved is even better, *much* better! Think of your place in history if . . ."

"Mary." Lincoln's voice was still soft and calm, but firm. "Right now I'm thinking about the next couple of years for the Union and the South, not about a third term . . . Oh, and about the theater tonight. I'm inviting General Grant and Mrs. Grant to sit with us this evening . . ."

"And heap more glory on him?!"

"And show a little appreciation for what General Grant has done—and what he can do to help in the future."

"You're a stubborn fool, and don't expect me to . . ."

"Mary, I only expect you to be your usual gracious self."

". . . but Ulys, you know we've made other plans."

"Julia, do you know how many times I've changed plans? Even before, during, and after battle?"

"My dear husband, you're the one who keeps saying the war is over."

"More to my point . . . if plans can be changed under dire circumstances, why not our plans to leave tonight? We can leave tomorrow just as well. Philadelphia will still be there and so will our house and family."

"Ulys, I . . ."

"Julia, it's the president's request . . . and besides, Laura Keene is your favorite actress and *Our American Cousin* one of your favorite plays . . ."

"I've seen it before, and we can see it some other time . . ."

"I think we ought to go, being invited by Mr. Lincoln himself."

"But Mrs. Lincoln *herself* doesn't favor me and I don't mind returning the favor."

"Julia, that's not like you . . ."

"No, but it's like her. Ulys, please send our regrets."

Ulysses Simpson Grant thought for a moment.

"Would you mind if I went alone?"

"I would."

He thought for a moment more.

Somewhere in a dimly lit room nine conspirators—one woman and eight men—were meeting and going over their assignments in the plan to assassinate the most important leaders of the United States of America.

When it was his turn, the young man with a classic profile held up a six-inch twin-barreled brass derringer and spoke in a theatrically trained voice.

"Two shots. One for Lincoln. One for Grant."

Fate, Destiny, Providence, Chance, all played a card that would determine the course of two men—and in many ways, the course of a nation.

CHAPTER 34

April 17, 1865

> *It has been almost a week since Appomattox.*
> *This night I made camp alone. A strange thing*
> *happened . . .*

Those words were written in Yuma's journal after the "event"—the "event" still unknown to Johnny Yuma, who had been alone in the countryside for the last forty-eight hours—alone, within himself—and within his memories—memories from Mason City to Appomattox.

Johnny Yuma had been mustered out. For a short time he had drifted aimlessly, not far from what had been battlefields, and before that, villages and farms. He wanted to be away from everyone and everything.

He was tired. For the first time in a long while he realized just how tired he was. Of taking orders. Of being on the alert for an enemy who might have broken through the lines. But now there were no lines. And there was no enemy. He told himself he could relax. He had not prevailed, but he had survived, unlike so many who fought on either side, more than a half a million casualties.

It seemed that there was not enough land to bury them all, but buried they were.

There was land enough for all the dead and for all who lived. But those who lived had a choice. The dead would stay forever in their little plot of land.

The night was cool and becoming cooler. Johnny Yuma built a small fire even before unsaddling his horse. For a long time he had been carrying five twenty-dollar gold coins. Double Eagles. He no longer carried them. Four of the Double Eagles went for the horse and saddle, most of the fifth for supplies, food that would have to last until . . . until something happened.

It did. Yuma had relaxed too much. In trying to wipe away too many memories too soon, too hard, while looking into the yellow flames of the little fire, he was unaware until the man on horseback was too close.

Another time, another place, if the man on horseback had worn a blue uniform, Johnny Yuma might already have been dead.

But the man on horseback wore no uniform. He was dressed in civilian clothes, fine, expensive clothes but now dirty from what had to have been a long, hard ride. The horse, a buckskin, was lathered and seemed barely able to stand.

Against the firelight, the man looked ghostly. His garments and face were spattered with mud and dirt, but a face still handsome and finely chiseled, though thoroughly exhausted from the ride. The eyes like living jewels, but black and weary. Hatless, his long, dark hair curled down and across his formidable forehead.

Reflexively, Johnny Yuma's hand went toward his sidearm but stopped short as the man spoke. His voice was deep and cultured.

"Good evening, Reb."

"Evening." Yuma still wore his uniform and Confederate cap.

"Alone?" The man looked around.

"Not anymore."

The man smiled, a warm, charming smile.

"That animal looks beat." Yuma pointed to the buckskin.

"It is."

"So do you."

"I'm not," the man replied. "No, I am not." He said the words slowly, emphatically.

"Well, would you like to step down off that horse and have something to eat?"

"I would," the man said, and began to dismount. But it wasn't easy. It took great effort. He strained and grimaced. Yuma started to move toward him as if to help, but the man smiled and waved him away.

"I would," the man repeated. "I would like to stay

and enjoy your generous Southern hospitality, but I'm afraid it was not meant to be."

"Why not?"

"Because of this." The man removed a six-inch brass derringer from the pocket of his coat and pointed it at Yuma. "And because I need a fresh horse and need it now."

"You don't look like a horse thief."

"I'm not."

"I paid eighty dollars in gold for that animal as it stands. Four Double Eagles."

The man's left hand dug into another pocket. He held the contents in his fist for a moment, then let them fall to the ground. They glinted by the firelight.

"Five Double Eagles, and the buckskin in the bargain." He pointed toward his horse. "He'll be fit to ride by morning."

The man limped as he moved toward Yuma's horse, but kept the derringer aimed at the Rebel.

"And now I have an appointment to keep."

"I don't think you'll make it. But I won't try to stop you."

"I'll make it."

Yuma watched as the man struggled, but finally boarded Yuma's horse.

"I'm sure," the man said, "that you were a good soldier."

"Most of the good soldiers are dead."

"But not all, and believe me, I am sympathetic to your cause."

"Sympathetic enough to've fought in the war?"

"We all have different roles to play. Godspeed, Reb."

The man wheeled Johnny Yuma's horse and rode into the night—south.

CHAPTER 35

The "event," of which Johnny Yuma and most of the country didn't know at the time, took place the evening of April 14, 1865, at Ford's Theatre during the performance of *Our American Cousin* as President Lincoln, his wife, and their guests sat in the Presidential Box of the theater. Ford's Theatre had seating for an audience of 1,700 people and every seat was filled, since it had been announced that President Lincoln and his guests would be in attendance.

An hour earlier John Wilkes Booth had left the National Hotel. At nine p.m. he arrived at Ford's Theatre, where he himself had previously performed. The actor made his way along a back corridor, with which he was familiar, to the unguarded Presidential Box. Within, Lincoln, drained of most of his energy, sat in a rocking chair, nearly asleep, as the others in the box were enjoying the stageplay.

During the laughter and applause, Booth silently

opened the door and stood for a moment behind the occupants. He was surprised at what he saw, rather at whom he didn't see; Grant and Mrs. Grant were not in the box; instead, the president and his wife were accompanied by another officer and his fiancée, but Booth quickly took dead aim with the derringer at the back of Lincoln's head and fired. The officer sprang at Booth, but the assassin managed to free himself and leap from the box down onto the stage, breaking his leg as he landed.

Amid the confusion and shock of all the spectators, Booth turned to the audience and proclaimed:

"*Sic semper tyrannis!*" and then declared in English, "The South is avenged!"

Most in the theater were still not completely aware of exactly what had happened, and Booth ran, limping through the wings to a horse he had stationed in the alley.

The other conspirators, would-be assassins, were unsuccessful in their attempts to kill Secretary of State Seward and the other human targets.

But the dreadfully wounded president was carried across the street to a private residence, where several doctors did all that was humanly possible to save Lincoln's life.

Their efforts were in vain.

At 7:22 the next morning Lincoln's secretary of war, Edwin Stanton, spoke the words, "Now he belongs to the ages."

President Abraham Lincoln was dead.

CHAPTER 36

That day following the encounter with the limping man, Johnny Yuma sat at a table in the Willows Tavern in Narrows, Virginia. He had ordered, paid for, and consumed most of the soup, bread, and tankard of beer that remained on the table where he was writing in his journal.

Outside, the buckskin was hitched to a post. The animal still suffered somewhat from the effects of the stranger's reckless ride. It had been Yuma's intention to have the animal cared for at the local livery, but there was none. It had been closed due to the war, and had yet to open again for business, due to the death of August Gork, former proprietor and former infantryman.

Yuma finished the entry in his journal describing the stranger on horseback and what had happened. He then finished the last swallow of beer from the tankard and the last spoonful of soup from the bowl.

Gunshots!

Gunshots outside the Willows Tavern—and voices, footsteps, and attendant excitement. There were half a dozen customers in the tavern, all Southerners, most of them veterans, some still in uniform as was Johnny Yuma. The owner-bartender had a peg leg and had introduced himself as Mac when he served Yuma the soup and suds.

Ten or twelve men poured through the tavern door, led by a tall, middle-age, overweight man waving a newspaper and a younger man who had the same girth, features, and color hair as the man with the paper, red.

"Mac, listen!" Everybody, listen to this! He's dead! Been shot dead! That no-good Yankee son-of-a-bitch's been killed!"

"What no-good Yankee son-of-a-bitch you talkin' about, Kinkaid?" Mac took a peg step toward the man with the paper.

"Lincoln!" Kinkaid exclaimed.

"What?! Are you sure?!"

"Sure, I'm sure! Randy here just rode back with the paper from Charlottesville!" Randy, still standing next to his father, beamed with delight. "Yessir-ee-bob," Kinkaid went on, "deader than a can of corned beef!"

"Who did it? How'd it happen?"

"Well, according to this"—Kinkaid held up the newspaper—"a fellow named Booth, some actor, split the ol' Railsplitter's head with a derringer at a place called Ford's Theatre . . ."

At the mention of "derringer," Johnny Yuma stiffened. He thought of the stranger with the derringer pointed at him last night.

"Did they catch him doing it?" Mac asked.

"Hell, no! This fella jumped right on to the stage, said somethin' in Latin, then yelled, 'The South is avenged!' Got away clean even though he broke his leg or ankle in the jump. Hot damn! 'The South is avenged,' he said, and he was right! I'd admire to buy him a drink! Matter of fact, I'm buying everybody a drink! Mac, set 'em up on Tom Kinkaid and son! Yes-sir-ee-bob, we're all gonna drink to . . . lemmee see"—Kinkaid referred to the newspaper again—"Booth. John Wilkes Booth! The man who laid Abe Lincoln in his grave and avenged the South! And, by God, if he hadn't done it, I mighta done it myself!"

Mac started to draw beers. The reaction of the others in the room was not as exuberant. In fact some were subdued, even stunned.

But none as subdued or stunned as Johnny Yuma. He was certain that the man last night was Booth. John Wilkes Booth. He certainly had the carriage and voice of an actor. And the limp. And the derringer.

And now he had Johnny Yuma's horse, and was being hunted like no man had ever been hunted before. His fate was sealed, along with the fate of anyone else who could be implicated in helping him escape. Booth would be found and hanged, or shot. There could be no doubt about that.

Booth had Yuma's horse and Johnny Yuma still had the Double Eagles. It was unlikely that the Double Eagles could be traced to Booth. But could the horse be traced to Johnny Yuma? How far could Booth ride on that horse? Would he ride it into the ground and get another? If Booth were captured alive . . . What then? Would anyone believe that he, a Rebel, did not know about the assassination? He who had come so close to assassinating Grant?

Yuma's only chance was to get away, as far away from Washington and Virginia as he could. And as soon as he could.

All this flashed across his mind as he sat at the table in Willows Tavern. How long he sat there, stunned, he did not know. But he did know that now a lot of the others were drinking and thinking about what had happened.

The ones who were celebrating the most were the Kinkaids, drinking down beer after beer with relish and laughter.

Yuma looked at the journal still on the table. If anyone ever read the content of what he had just written, they would know about his encounter with Booth. But would they believe that that was how it happened?

He had to get out of the tavern, out of the town, and take the journal with him. Destroy those pages that mentioned the incident last night. He had to get out of there unnoticed.

But it was too late. He already had been noticed . . . by the Kinkaids. Tom Kinkaid was approaching with an extra tankard of beer in hand, accompanied by his son.

"Here you are, Johnny Reb." He set the beer on the table just as Yuma rose. "Looks like everybody's had a drink except you."

Johnny Yuma just stood there for a moment.

"Looks like you did some fightin'." Kinkaid grinned.

Yuma was silent.

"I said, looks like you did some fightin'."

"Some."

"Where?"

"What difference does it make?"

Kinkaid paused and looked around as the room fell silent.

"I just wanted to know. You *did* do some fightin', didn't you?"

"Did you?" Yuma regretted the words even before he finished speaking them. That hot Texas temper had erupted again. Even as he spoke, he knew he should have restrained himself. He should have been respectful to Mr. Kinkaid, answered the question politely, drunk the beer, thanked Mr. Kinkaid, taken his journal, and left quietly.

But there was something about the man that grated on Yuma. No, not something. Everything. His attitude. The smirking smugness. The vilification.

The bravado and boasting. Yuma had learned to read men, friends and foes, soldiers and civilians. And he did not like what he read in Kinkaid. There was deceit and weakness in the man's eyes, despite his size and bluster.

"What did you mean by that remark?" Kinkaid was not going to let it pass. Not in a room full of people he knew and lived among. Not from a stranger. And not after too many drinks.

"Nothing." Yuma said it, but without much conviction.

"Nothin'?! You musta meant somethin' . . ."

"No." Yuma made one more attempt at conciliation. "I'm sure that you," he glanced at Kinkaid's towering son who stood nearby, "and your son did more than your share of fighting. But it's over, so I'd just admire to get out of here and go about my business, Mr. Kinkaid."

Yuma did not know it, but he had said the wrong thing. Neither Kinkaid, nor his son, had served the Southern cause. At least not in the military, and everybody in the room knew it.

"And I'd admire to let you go about your business, whatever it is . . . just as soon as you"—Kinkaid pointed to the tankard—"pick that up and have a drink on me, to John Wilkes Booth, the man who avenged the South."

Johnny Yuma stood motionless. He knew the wise thing to do was what Kinkaid said. His good sense told him to do it. His common sense told him to do it.

But there was something uncommon about Johnny Yuma, and something unacceptable about the way Kinkaid put it. It sounded too much like an order, a command. And something in Johnny Yuma rebelled when it came to taking a command from someone like Kinkaid.

Still, he had decided he would. But it took too long for him to decide, or so thought Tom Kinkaid.

"What's the matter with you, boy? Where do you stand? What are you, some sort of Yankee lickin' turncoat?"

Yuma said nothing. Did nothing.

"Pick that up and drink to Booth!"

Nothing.

"All right, then . . . I'll pick it up."

Kinkaid reached down, picked up the tankard, held it for a moment, looked around the room, then flung the contents into Johnny Yuma's face.

Yuma's left fist smashed into Kinkaid's jaw, knocking him over a chair onto the floor. Randy Kinkaid leaped at Yuma, swinging a looping right. Yuma caught it on his left forearm and threw a straight right that sent the younger Kinkaid crashing against the table, then down.

Tom Kinkaid rushed in again, but met a backhand by Yuma that whirled the man into a wall. From the floor, Randy Kinkaid drew his gun and thumbed the hammer, but Yuma's gun fired first.

The slug hit bone in Randy Kinkaid's right shoulder and he dropped the pistol.

Another shot went off and hit the ceiling. It had

been fired by a man standing at the door. A man with one arm, holding the gun now aimed at Yuma. The man wore a badge.

"All right, that's enough."

"You saw it, Pete!" Tom Kinkaid rose from the floor. "This Yankee-licker shot Randy."

"Yeah, I saw it."

"He tried to kill my boy."

"I said I saw it."

"I want him arrested."

"You do, huh?"

"That's right, attempted murder . . . I . . ."

"You better get your boy over to Doc Reeves."

"But . . ."

"Never mind the buts, I'll handle this. Now get moving, Mr. Kinkaid." The sheriff looked toward Yuma. "You. Place that weapon on the table. Slow and gentle."

Yuma did. Kinkaid escorted his son toward the door and growled at the sheriff.

"You do your duty, Pete."

"I intend to." The sheriff walked to the table where Yuma stood. He holstered his gun, lifted Yuma's revolver, and motioned toward the entrance. "Let's go."

Johnny Yuma picked up the journal from the table and walked toward the door as the sheriff followed.

"All right," the sheriff said to the patrons, "go back to your drinkin'."

It was noon bright as Johnny Yuma and the sheriff, still holding Yuma's gun, walked outside.

"Stop right here," said the sheriff. "Is that your animal?"

Yuma nodded.

"Sheriff, all I did in there was . . ."

"I said I saw what happened, most of it."

"Then why am I being arrested? I just . . ."

"Who said you're arrested?"

"Well, Kinkaid . . ."

"Kinkaid is a blowhard bastard, never fought a lick . . . him and his fat-ass son stayed home and profited from the likes of you and me. Feed and grain . . . for gold, not Confederate currency. What was your outfit?"

"Third Texas . . . Rock Island, then with Jubal Early."

"Gettysburg." Using Yuma's gun, the sheriff pointed toward his empty sleeve. "What's that?" He nodded toward the journal Yuma had in his hand.

"Just some things I wrote down . . . Nothing important."

"Going back to Texas?"

"I don't know. Maybe . . . someday."

"Well, that's up to you, I guess, but I'm going to give you some advice, not as a lawman. Soldier to soldier."

"Yes, sir."

"Don't sir me, Corporal. I was no officer, just a Johnny Reb like you. What's your name?"

"Johnny, Johnny Yuma, Sh . . . Sheriff."

"Well, Johnny Yuma, get on that buckskin and ride out . . . to Texas, or someplace . . . and don't ever pass this way again. Will you do that?"

"I will."

The sheriff handed the gun to Yuma. He took it and slipped it into the holster.

"Thank you . . . Sheriff."

"Good luck, Johnny."

And, so far, Yuma's luck had held. Through the fighting with the 3rd Texas, at Rock Island, with Early, and at Appomattox. Then with Booth and at Narrows, thanks to a sheriff who had lost an arm at Gettysburg.

But how long would Johnny Yuma's luck hold? Booth was still at large and his trail might lead back to Yuma, who would have a lot of explaining to do, to people who might not be as sympathetic as the sheriff in Narrows.

He would make tracks—trying not to leave any— out of Virginia. He would read the newspapers and listen, wherever and whenever possible, for the fate of John Wilkes Booth and maybe of himself.

CHAPTER 37

After hearing the news of the assassination, Grant decided to leave Philadelphia immediately and return to Washington to do whatever he could to maintain order and continuity in the country.

"I'm going with you," Julia said.

Grant shook his head as he exhaled the smoke from his cigar.

"It still might not be safe. We still don't know who else might be involved in what happened . . . and what could happen. Julia, I . . ."

"I'm going."

"There's nothing you can do . . ."

"Yes, there is. I want to see Mrs. Lincoln and do whatever I can to comfort her. She must be frenzied with grief."

Julia moved closer to her husband.

"You know, Ulys, if we had gone to the theater that night, both she and I might now be widows."

"Or maybe I might have been able to stop Booth."

"Or be killed in the attempt. They say that you were also a target. No, my dear, you mustn't torture yourself like that. You and the country have suffered enough. My place, at this time, is with you—and Mrs. Lincoln. I'm going."

And she did.

Years later, in her "personal memoirs," Julia Dent Grant wrote:

> *His bereaved widow—still lingered at the Executive Mansion, alone with her little son, Tad. With my heart full of sorrow, I went many times to call on dear, heart-broken Mrs. Lincoln, but she could not see me.*

CHAPTER 38

Johnny Yuma had destroyed the pages in his journal referring to the stranger on horseback, but first he memorized them, in case he ever wanted to write about the incident again.

Near South Fulton, Tennessee, Yuma traded the buckskin for a sorrel, gave the farmer twenty dollars to boot, and continued to move west. The sorrel was a good-mouthed horse and responded to the slightest pressure on the bit.

As he rode west Johnny Yuma saw hundreds of them. On trees, barns, poles . . . on the sides of buildings, on boards at public squares—the posters:

WAR DEPARTMENT, WASHINGTON
APRIL 20, 1865

$100,000 REWARD!

THE MURDERER
Of our late beloved President,

ABRAHAM LINCOLN

STILL AT LARGE.

All good citizens exhorted to
aid public justice on this occasion.

EDWIN M. STANTON, *Secretary of War*

On April 26, twelve days after having killed the president, the end came for John Wilkes Booth in a tobacco shed in Port Royal, Virginia.

More than a hundred miles to the west, Johnny Yuma read the accounts in newspapers.

After a frantic two-week search by the army and Secret Service forces, and during which time he had received medical aid from a Dr. Mudd, Booth had been discovered hiding in a barn owned by a man named Garrett. The barn was set afire, and Booth was either shot by his pursuers or shot himself rather than surrender.

That ended it as far as Johnny Yuma was concerned. There was no mention of any assistance by, or encounter with, anyone except Dr. Mudd.

There were thousands like him in the South, tens of thousands, who had served and survived and lost. Johnny Rebs. But like snowflakes and cinders, no two were exactly alike.

They had buried and left their brethren behind, in fields, on hillsides, near streams and forests, north and south of the Mason-Dixon line. Eternally asleep by one another. Countrymen again and forever.

They had come from the streets of the cities, from the fields of farms, rich and poor, from plantations and backwoods shacks, across the flowing waters of the Mississippi, the Missouri, the Red, and the Shenandoah to heed the call of the Confederacy— at first to the trumpets of victory, and finally, the dirge of defeat.

For those who returned, the journey was bittersweet. The men could never be the same and neither could the places from where they came, and now returned. Most were anxious to get back. Some traveled day and night. Home, no matter how much it had changed, had to be better than where they had been.

And some of the survivors, by choice, would never go home. They were the ones who had fallen in love with other places and other people, who had been looking for a way to escape and found it—in a lost war.

Johnny Yuma fell into neither category. He knew that he would go home someday, and he was heading in that general direction, west. But for the first time since he left Mason City, which wasn't a city, not really much more than a village, he was not being ordered, told in which direction to go— where and when.

And there were things and people in Mason City that he was in no hurry to face. His father. Mr. Dodson. Rosemary.

Even as a young boy, Johnny Yuma had run away from home more than once. And always his father had come after him and, like the lawman that Ned Yuma was, tracked him down and brought him back. This time Johnny Yuma would go back when he was ready. When he was somebody, or something. Money would make a big difference, at least in people's eyes, and Johnny Yuma at this time didn't have much. He'd see to it that he had more, a lot more, before he went home.

Then there was Rosemary, Rosemary Cutler. Red hair aflame, eyes green as jade, the prettiest girl in town, who grew into the most beautiful lady anywhere.

And Elmer Dodson, owner, publisher, editor, and staff of the *Mason City Bulletin*, except when Johnny Yuma worked there. It was what Dodson wrote and the way he wrote it that started Johnny reading and wondering about a lot of things.

When he had left Mason City he was in a hurry to get to the war. Like so many others who had left in a hurry from so many other places, he didn't want to miss out on it. Everyone said the fighting would be over in six months or less. They all wanted to come back with tales of glory and victory.

But the six months or less had turned into three years and more. And the garlands of glory and victory had turned into the bitter taste of ashes and defeat. There would be no brass bands and celebrations for the returning Rebels.

They knew that they had done the best they could.

Better than the best. But better was not good enough. Not good enough to beat, or even withstand, the overwhelming war machine of the North. A machine that produced an unending supply of men and materiel; a naval wall that blocked the harbors and ports of the agrarian South, the South that produced cotton and tobacco, sugar and grain, not guns and ammunition.

Still they had reaped more than a measure of glory, even in defeat. But glory in victory rang loud and strong. Glory in defeat was silent and subdued.

Yes, Johnny Yuma would go back, but in his own time and on his own terms.

CHAPTER 39

There were Southerners, such as some of those at Willows Tavern, who had rejoiced, even celebrated, at the news of Lincoln's death.

But most of the land mourned, filled with lamentation, as the beloved and martyred president lay in state at the Capitol and later was carried in great sorrow to his final resting place in Springfield, Illinois.

Among those mourners was George Armstrong Custer, who was still in Washington. Like thousands of others, he had watched the funeral procession and prayed in church.

But unlike the others, Custer had decided on a silent farewell to the fallen leader by paying a solitary tribute at the scene of Lincoln's assassination.

So it was that he was now in the upper corridor of Ford's Theatre listening to a voice through the partially open door, listening to words being spoken

by a voice rich and deep—a voice he had heard in
the distant past.

> *"If it were done when 'tis done, then 'twere well*
> *It were done quickly: if th' assassination*
> *Could trammel up the consequence, and catch*
> *With his surcease success; that but this blow*
> *Might be the be-all and the end-all—here,*
> *But here, upon this bank and shoal of time,*
> *We'd jump the life to come. But in these cases*
> *We still have judgment here, that we but teach*
> *Bloody instructions, which, being taught, return*
> *To plague the inventor. This even-handed justice*
> *Commends the ingredients of our poison'd chalice*
> *To our own lips."*

Unnoticed by the man speaking the words,
Custer had gently nudged the door and stepped in.

"A grand and moving performance, as usual, Mr.
Booth."

"You know me?"

"Years ago I saw Edwin Booth performing as
Hamlet while touring in Monroe, Michigan."

"But this was not a performance, General
Custer . . ."

General Custer couldn't disguise his surprise as
Booth mentioned his name.

"I've seen your picture in the newspapers and
read of your exploits. As to what you just heard,

that was not a performance, but a prelude to . . . penance."

Edwin Booth raised his right hand holding a derringer, and with his left hand pointed to his temple.

"Since you know who I am, you know who my brother was . . . and what he has done . . ."

Edwin Booth paused, looked to the dark, empty stage for a moment, then down and across to the vacant seats where the audience had watched; from there, to the place where Lincoln had sat.

". . . and now the whole world knows."

Booth faced Custer directly.

"The once famous name of Booth is now an anathema, forever consigned to infamy."

"You're right," Custer said without hesitating.

Booth arched an eyebrow, then nodded, but Custer proceeded.

"You're right about the name of John Wilkes Booth, but not *Edwin Booth* . . . unless you end it with a gun."

"What else is there for me to do?"

"Fight back."

"With what?"

"Talent."

"What?"

"Your talent. It's the best weapon you have—not that." Custer pointed to the derringer still in Booth's hand.

There was a moment of silence.

"When is your next performance?" Custer asked.

"What do you mean?"

"I mean when is your next performance on stage? And where?"

"Oh, that." Booth shook his head. "I'm scheduled to do *Hamlet*, just down the street . . . but, of course, I'm canceling it . . ."

"Why? Are you afraid the audience won't come?"

"No," Booth said with an ironic half smile. "I'm afraid they *will* come. They'll want to skin me alive. In this case, not for the sins of the father . . . but for the sin of a brother."

"Your brother's paid for his sin—at least on this earth. He may pay forever—wherever he is. But no man can pay for another man's crime, not even his brother's . . ."

Once again Custer pointed to the gun.

". . . Not by turning that on himself. Besides, that's the coward's way out."

"And who says I'm not a coward? It's easy to be brave on stage. You know how the play will turn out . . ."

"Not in this case, you don't. I've seen brave men . . . and cowards."

"Yes, General, I imagine you have."

"I've seen men in battle tremble, turn, and start to run away, not knowing how it would come out, but somehow, something from within made them turn back and even lead other men into the thick of it. I say you're that kind of man, not a coward. Prove it, Mr. Booth, by going on that stage, not knowing how it will turn out, and doing what you do best . . . to vindicate the name of Booth . . . *Edwin Thomas Booth.*"

Booth's eyes narrowed ever so slightly.

"I . . . I . . . don't think I could go on."

"Go on?! Mr. Booth, I'll be there to see it . . . and you'll give the performance of your life!"

CHAPTER 40

It was more like going to a funeral service.

In the history of the theater there had never been anything to compare to the thick, diffident atmosphere that prevailed that night.

Not in the ancient, open-air amphitheaters cradled between the slopping shoulders of Grecian hills where audiences first viewed the works of Euripides, Sophocles, and Aristophanes.

Nor in the Elizabethan structures of The Swan, The Globe, and Whitehall Theatre, which housed the dramas and comedies of Shakespeare, Marlowe, and Jonson.

Nor the palatial nineteenth-century American playhouses such as the Winter Garden, the Astor, the Adelphi—not at the Western saloons with squalid stages, the makeshift platforms of sordid mining camps, or the raucous minstrel stages of the South.

At all these places and events there was always

chatter, laughter, all manner of ceaseless small talk and gossip that preceded the rise of the curtain.

Not tonight. Not at this theater, the Grand Palace.

The theater where Edwin Booth and Company would perform *Hamlet.*

A shroud of silence prevailed as battalions of men and woman streamed forth, seemingly in stocking feet, and with throats hushed as death—looking straight ahead, without a word to each other, making their way to their respective seats, then gazing straight ahead to the curtained stage.

Among those who had entered were George and Libbie Custer. General Custer had put aside his uniform and donned evening clothes in the same manner that many of the other spectators were dressed. The Custers were seated in second-row aisle seats.

"George, I still don't know why you insisted on not wearing your uniform."

"Because, Libbie, I did not want in any way, to draw attention from Mr. Booth. This is his night."

"Maybe in more ways than one." Libbie's sweeping gaze took in the faces of the audience. "I don't like the look of some of these people . . ."

"Shush, dear, the curtain's going up."

It did.

To no reaction. No cheers. No applause—as was customary.

Only ominous silence.

And a mumbled curse from the burly man seated behind Custer.

The audience began to stir, and a few voices, not from the stage, but from various sections of the theater, became increasingly audible, unfriendly voices, with disparaging remarks attached to the name of Booth—and from some sections, the perceptible stomping of shoes.

By then the actors were obviously aware of the growing untoward reaction but went on, speaking slightly louder.

KING CLAUDIUS continued: *"But now, my cousin, Hamlet, and my son,—"*

HAMLET: *"A little more than kin, and less than kind."*

As Edwin Booth spoke his first line the burly man behind Custer cupped his hands and this time shouted. *"What about your kin, Booth! The sonofabitch who killed Lincoln!"*

Custer turned and looked at the man, but said nothing as the players continued.

KING CLAUDIUS: *"How is it that the clouds still hang on you?"*

At the word "hang" the burly man behind Custer rose to his feet and shouted, "Hang that bastard Booth—all Booths are alike! Traitors! Scum! Assassins! Don't listen to the bloody bastard!"

Others in the audience took up the cry, stomped their feet, booed, and there were those who began to fling tomatoes and eggs toward the stage.

The burly man behind Custer continued his tirade as Custer stood, turned to him, and spoke.

"Suppose you shut up, mister."

"Suppose *you* shut up, Curly Locks; I paid to come in, and Booth, the bastard, should pay . . ."

So fast that it was seen by not more than a few of the spectators, Custer's right fist struck out into the burly man's chin and he sank back into his chair unconscious, as Custer addressed the audience.

"That man on stage had nothing to do with his brother's crime. Edwin Booth is an actor, a great actor. For God's sake, and for your own, allow him to act!"

By this time, some in the audience had recognized George Armstrong Custer and his name raced through the throng—first whispered, then louder.

Custer stood defiantly.

"I'm here to watch the greatest Hamlet who ever lived! If any of you have any other idea—GET OUT NOW!"

No one moved.

Edwin Booth drew himself to his full height and with a strong unwavering voice went on through the play as if invigorated, impelled by a renewed motivation.

"*. . . but I have that within which passeth show;*
These but the trappings and the suits of woe."
Applause.
"*He was a man, take him for all in all,*
I shall not look upon his like again."
More applause.

"*. . . this goodly frame, the earth, seems to me a sterile promontory . . .*"

"*. . . in action how like an angel! in apprehension how like a god!*"

Cheers and applause.

Through the acts even the other actors caught fire.

"*To be, or not to be: that is the question:*
Whether 'tis nobler in the mind to suffer
The slings and arrows of outrageous fortune,
Or to take arms against a sea of troubles,
And by opposing end them . . ."

Louder cheers through the last act.

"*. . . And in this harsh world draw they breath*
    in pain,
To tell my story . . ."
"*Good night sweet prince:*
And flights of angels sing thee to thy rest."

By then there was a continuous standing ovation that included the burly man behind Custer, who had regained consciousness.

Edwin Booth had given the greatest perform-ance of his life.

On the way home, Libbie smiled at her husband. "Had you ever met Booth before?"

"Just once," Custer acknowledged.

"You did see that Edwin Booth took a bow and smiled directly at you."

"I didn't notice." He shrugged.

"The hell you didn't, Custer Boy."

CHAPTER 41

Halleluiah! The war is over,
Reconstruction has begun!
Lincoln's gone to heaven
to get a bit of rest.
Carpetbaggers are a comin',
Me, I'm movin' west.

Johnny Yuma saw the lines scrawled on what was left of a barn near Clarksdale, Missouri. The farmhouse had been burned down, maybe by Yankees, maybe by the owner himself, who had decided to follow the sun. Other owners who had also abandoned property knew that they could not prevent those who would take over from benefiting off lost land, but the carpetbaggers and bankers would have to build their own houses to live in, or sell.

The former owners usually did not scorch the land, but many of them scorched everything on it.

Yuma decided to sleep in the ruins of the barn. He wrote a few lines in his journal, wondering about who had lived there and where the family was now, if they were still a family.

While there was light enough, Johnny Yuma read an article from a newspaper he had found earlier that day on a street in Clarksdale. The article was about the new president, Andrew Johnson. Yuma knew very little about Johnson. Always eager to read, Yuma learned more about Lincoln's successor before dark.

Born in a shack in Raleigh, North Carolina, Johnson was three when his father died. After a desolate childhood, Johnson, at age fourteen, became apprentice to a tailor. At eighteen he moved to a poor mountain village in Tennessee, where he married Eliza McCardle, who encouraged him to pursue his studies as well as the tailoring trade. In 1843, he was elected as a Democrat to the United States House of Representatives.

On that floor, Jefferson Davis had done his best to insult Johnson with reference to "the common tailor from Tennessee." Johnson did not reply directly but in his next speech on the same floor he referred to the "son of a common carpenter from Nazareth."

When Tennessee seceded, Johnson stuck with the Union and after Grant invaded and reclaimed the state, Lincoln appointed Johnson military governor. Even though Johnson was a Democrat, Lincoln chose him as his running mate in 1864.

But since the day of Abraham Lincoln's inauguration on March 4, 1865, Vice President Andrew Johnson's tenure in high office had met with criticism and vituperation, seemingly from everyone in office, except Lincoln himself.

The inauguration day had been cold, interspersed with drizzles and even driving rain. Vice President–elect Johnson spoke, actually mumbled and maundered incoherently as more than 30,000 soaked and shocked spectators tried to make sense of what the obviously inebriated Johnson was saying. In truth, Johnson had been drinking, but in a vain attempt to assuage the effects of the typhoid fever he had just suffered.

But the result was devastating.

The two most impressive images in the minds and memories of those present, and in the later newspaper reports, were the brilliant and passionate speech delivered by Abraham Lincoln and the stumbling, whiskey-soaked performance of Andrew "Tennessee" Johnson.

In the newspaper that Johnny Yuma read there was also a photograph of the inauguration in which one of the spectators was later identified as an actor named John Wilkes Booth.

After Johnson became president he also became the object of swelling tides of resentment—and even revolution.

CHAPTER 42

The meeting was being held in the office of the President of the United States.

Only two men were present—President Andrew Johnson and General Ulysses Simpson Grant.

"General Grant, it was most kind of you to be here today."

"Sir, I am a general, but you are the commander in chief."

"But for how long?"

"At least another three years."

"Maybe . . . we'll see about that, and please be assured, General, that this was not an order—a request."

"In that case, Mr. President, do you mind if I light up a cigar?"

"General, I don't think I'd recognize you without one—and neither would anybody else. Please, go ahead and light up."

Grant did, as Johnson pushed an ashtray closer to the general.

"Sir,"—President Johnson grew serious—"there has been talk, more than just talk."

"About what?"

"About me, as president—and you as president."

"Sir, I don't . . ."

"I happen to know, from reliable sources, there have been meetings, secret meetings, with politicians from both parties, high office holders, and, yes, army officers, generals—they'll be coming to you. All they need is a word—even a nod—from you."

"What word? What nod?"

"That you would accept the presidency—no, not three years from now, but *now*, and there would be an immediate upheaval—a revolution."

"Never, but may I ask you one question?"

"Please do."

"There have been many rumors, conflicting rumors. Mr. President, where do you stand in regard to the treatment of the South?"

"The radicals, even now, are demanding that Jefferson Davis, my old congressional adversary, be taken out of prison, tried, and hanged for treason . . ."

Grant inhaled from his cigar and waited for Johnson to continue—not for long.

"To sum it all up, sir, I have always stood, and will always stand, with President Abraham Lincoln—reconciliation—'To bind up the nation's wounds'—one nation, North and South—the United States of America."

Grant nodded and again drew from his cigar as Johnson went on.

"But . . . they say I'm incompetent—and a drunk . . ."

"That description sounds familiar. It was often directed at me."

"It's true, I was drunk at the inauguration, but General, I swear I haven't had a drink since."

"Mr. President, by the time I was forty-one I was deemed a flat-out failure, drummed out of the army as a drunkard, and after that, a stranger to success in business. And you, sir, attained your education the hard way, had already served in Congress, chose loyalty to the United States when Tennessee seceded from the Union, served as military governor over the state of Tennessee by appointment of the president, and President Lincoln chose you as his vice president before he chose me to be chief general of the Army."

"Yours was a heavy burden in the military pursuit of the war."

"Not as heavy as your burden now in pursuit of peace."

"I need your help . . ."

"President Lincoln's faith in you is good enough for me. Mr. President, if any group of politicians, generals, or insurrectionists asks me where I stand, or even if they don't ask, I intend to make it known that if anyone, any radical group, tries to storm the

White House, in any way, shape, or form, I'll stand at the door with a gun in one hand and a sword in the other. That is my pledge to you and to my country."

At Grant's response, much of the great burden was obviously lifted from President Johnson as he relaxed and smiled.

Grant also smiled.

"Mr. President, would you care to join me in . . . smoking a cigar?"

"No, thanks, General, but there is one more thing . . ."

"Name it."

"There's a photographer named Brady in another room. Would you mind having your picture taken with me?"

"Mr. Brady has taken my picture with a lot of people, including President Lincoln. It would be my pleasure to have him take one with President Andrew Johnson."

CHAPTER 43

Late in the afternoon, Johnny Yuma, astride the sorrel, was crossing a shallow stream. He had already spotted the wagon in distress that had not quite made it to the other side.

He continued the crossing, moving closer to the wagon and to the people who had occupied it. The woman and a young boy, about eight, stood on the bank at the edge of the stream. The man was in the water, up to his thighs, working where a wheel had broken off.

They were a family. A black family.

During the early days of Reconstruction, surging waves of carpetbaggers were flowing south and many of the freed slaves were moving north—but not all of the former slaves who left were moving north.

"Howdy," Yuma said, as he reined the horse to a stop in the stream a few feet away from the wagon.

The man looked up at the horseman, still in the uniform of the Confederacy.

The man's clothes were wet. He was huge, even in the water, with a dark-brown handsome but unsmiling face, power-laden shoulders and arms, narrow waist, coal-black eyes glistening.

Silence.

Yuma's look went to the woman and little boy. She was a comely woman in her late twenties and the boy next to her appeared to be a miniature replica of his father.

"Ma'am." Yuma smiled. "Hi, young fella."

Silence still. The woman nodded slightly, but the boy just stood, looking at his father.

"Name's Yuma, Johnny Yuma." He headed the sorrel a little closer to the man. "Looks like you could use a hand."

The man went back to work.

"I'd be glad to be of some help."

The man kept at his work. Johnny did not move.

"Ben," the woman said, but the man did not look up.

"Quite a load on that wagon." Yuma rose in the saddle and pointed, "That looks like an anvil."

"It is," the woman said. "Ben's a blacksmith."

"That so?"

"Listen, mister . . ." The man spoke with a deep, strong voice, but didn't look up. "Are we botherin' you?"

"No." Yuma smiled.

"Then why don't you leave us be?"

"All right, I will."

But Yuma did not move.

"Well?" the man finally said.

"Well, what?"

"Why don't you move on?"

"I will, but first I need some help."

"You?"

"Yeah, me."

"What kind of help?"

"Horse's got a loose shoe. Must've knocked it on a rock some ways back."

"That so?"

"Yep. Hate to keep on riding him like this. Might get crippled. He's a good horse. Don't you think?"

The man looked at the sorrel and nodded.

"Say, Ben . . . that your name . . . Ben? I got an idea . . ." Yuma glanced at the woman, then back to the man. "Maybe we could help each other out . . . me with the wagon, you with the shoe. I'm sure this horse would be mighty grateful. What do you say?"

"Ben," the woman repeated.

The man looked at the woman, then the boy. He rubbed the massive palm of his wet hand across his face.

"All right."

"Good," Yuma said. "We'd better go to it before it gets dark."

They worked until after dark, but the wagon was repaired. Not many words passed between them, only words needed in the repairing. Yuma didn't press for conversation. He knew that the sight of his uniform was not a pleasant reminder to the man and his family. But the wagon now stood near the campfire ready to roll in the morning.

The woman had asked Yuma to stay and eat what she had prepared while they worked. There was little conversation while they ate. Later, Yuma spread his bedroll some distance from the others and was about to lie down and get some sleep. Fixing the wagon had been hard work, but Ben had gone about it almost without conversation or effort.

"Mister Yuma." The woman stepped out of the darkness and spoke softly. "My name's Louise."

"Well, I'm pleased to know you. My name's Johnny."

"I just wanted to . . . well . . ."

"What is it, Louise?"

"To thank you for helping . . ."

"Nothing to thank me for. Like I told Ben, my horse . . ."

"Yes, I know. About Ben . . ."

"What about him?"

"Well, I know he appears to be kind of . . . starchy."

"Starchy? I wouldn't blame him for being down-right resentful. I don't expect that gray is his favorite color."

"And I wouldn't blame you for . . ."

"For what?"

"Well, you know that we were slaves, and you fought for . . ."

"Louise, I wasn't fighting for slavery, I was fighting for Texas, or I thought I was. There weren't any slaves where I come from, out west."

"There weren't?"

"No, ma'am."

"That's where we're going you know, west."

"That's a good idea. I'm going back myself, someday. Where'd you come from?"

"Georgia."

"Georgia, huh?!"

"Ever been there?"

"One step ahead of Sherman." Yuma smiled.

"Ben's awful good with his hands, can do most anything, and he's got a gentle touch for such a powerful man."

"He's powerful, all right. You're a lucky woman."

"I know that."

"And so's the boy . . . what's his name?"

"Benjie."

"Lucky to have such a father . . . and mother."

"Thank you for saying that, and for what you did this afternoon. Now I'd better get back."

"Good night."

"Good night."

"And Louise . . . all of us . . . we've got to get used to all colors . . . including gray, white, and black."

The next morning, Ben was examining a hoof on the sorrel as Yuma approached.

"Morning, Ben."

Ben only nodded.

"Did you get a good night's sleep?" Johnny Yuma inquired.

"I did, but there's something I want to talk to you about."

"Sure."

Before Ben could say anything else, both of them noticed the three riders splashing through the stream toward the camp.

Ben let go of the sorrel's leg.

The three men were big and dirty. Yuma saw that the biggest man wore an army hat. Union army. Neither Johnny Yuma nor Ben said anything as the men reined up.

"Well, what we got here?" said the man with the Union hat. He looked at Yuma and Ben, then at Louise and Benjie, who now were standing nearby. "Joe, Charlie, what do you make of this?"

"I don't know, Sam. What do *you* think?"

"I think we ought to get down and find out."

All three dismounted with hands never too far from their weapons.

"What's your name, boy?" Sam was looking at Ben.

Ben didn't answer.

"I said, what's your name?"

Ben said nothing.

"Well, it don't matter. What else we got here?" He took a step away from Yuma and Ben toward

Louise and her son. "Oh, yeah, a fine-lookin' Negro woman and her child. That is your child, isn't it?"

She didn't answer.

"Hell, fellas, looks like we come across a band of dummies. Nobody here can talk." He turned to Yuma. "What about you, Reb? Can you talk?"

Johnny Yuma didn't answer.

Sam's fist slammed into Yuma's midsection. Joe pulled out his gun and all three laughed.

"We all know you can't fight," Sam said. "We found that out all right. Didn't we, boys?"

The men laughed harder.

"Say, I think I know what's goin' on," Sam said after he quit laughing.

"You do, Sam?" Joe's gun was pointed at Yuma.

"Sure I do. You want to hear?"

"Tell us." Charlie nodded.

"All right. This here Reb, why, he's trying to run away with his slaves. That's what's goin' on."

"Could be," Joe agreed

"Could be, hell! That's what it is! Plain as a piggin' string. We got to do something about that."

There were tears in Benjie's eyes.

"Don't you cry, little boy. We're here to help you people." Sam turned toward Ben. "What's the matter with you? Ain't you heard you're free? You don't have to tend to his kind any more. We done whipped their ass clear across the South, didn't we, Reb? I said didn't we, Reb?" His fist rammed into Yuma's stomach again.

"Stop, please!" Louise cried out.

"I'll stop when I please . . . *ma'am.*"

"You want to fight?" Yuma said. "Put away those guns. I'll fight, all of you."

"All of us?" Sam grinned.

"All of you."

"Three to one? Tall chance. Them's unfavorable odds, Reb."

"We're used to it."

"You hear that, fellas? He's used to it. Well, you're gonna get used to something else, and I don't need no odds against the likes of you. Watch this, boys!"

Sam swung at Yuma's jaw. This time, Yuma blocked the punch and landed a hard left, followed by blows to Sam's face and body. Sam fought back as the other two watched and cursed and urged Sam on. He was bigger than Yuma and maybe stronger, but Yuma was faster, and knew how to use his speed.

Sam managed to grab Johnny and wrestle him to the ground. But Yuma broke free and clubbed Sam with both fists.

"Joe!" Sam yelled as he dropped.

Joe leveled his gun at Yuma, but Ben slapped it away and smashed a boulder fist into his face, then backhanded Charlie before he could draw.

Yuma sprang up, panther quick. The two of them, Ben and Yuma, back-to-back, with exploding blows. Still on the ground, Sam went for his gun, but Yuma kicked it out of his hand, lifted him to his feet, and dropped him with a right as Ben collected the artillery and set it in a pile on the ground.

"Three to *two*." Ben grinned.

"Thanks," said Johnny Yuma.

"You're welcome." Ben nodded.

"All right, get up!" Yuma motioned to the fallen men. "Get up, get on your animals, and get out."

All three staggered to their feet. There was blood on their faces, and broken cartilage, but they managed to climb on their mounts.

"We'll keep these"—Yuma pointed to the ground—"as mementos. This is one fight you Yanks didn't win, but I got to admit our side had some help." He smiled at Ben.

The three rode away without looking back.

Louise ran to Ben and kissed him. Benjie was not crying anymore.

"Are you all right, Johnny?" she asked.

"Like I said, Benjie's lucky to have a mother and father like you two."

"Johnny." Ben stopped smiling. "I said there was something I wanted to talk to you about."

"Sure, Ben, what is it?"

"About your horse . . . there's nothing wrong with those shoes."

"There isn't?"

"No, there isn't." Ben smiled again.

"Well, I'm sure glad to hear that. I must've been mistaken. Oh, one more thing, Ben . . ."

"What's that?"

"Those guns." He pointed at the guns the three men left behind.

"What about them?"

"You might as well keep them. You being a black-smith, maybe you can make something useful out of 'em."

CHAPTER 44

The Custers had gone back to Monroe amid cheers, parades, and assorted celebrations—all of which lasted longer than their stay in the old hometown.

Not a day, almost an hour, went by that someone, some company, or some delegation didn't offer the "hero of heroes" an opportunity to shed the restrictions and limited monetary potential of army life for some business or political venture with unlimited societal and financial prospects.

One afternoon they managed to get away from everything and everyone and ride horseback along the Raisin River.

"Libbie, I don't know how much more of this I can bear."

"What do you mean by 'this'?" she asked, even though she knew.

"This morning a delegation showed up saying

they wanted to back me if I'd run for governor of Michigan. A few hours later it was a group of portly politicians who came to urge me to run for governor of Ohio. Then a committee from the Monroe Chamber of Commerce wanted me to make a speech in front of the courthouse so they could raise money to build a statue of me on horseback near city hall."

"That would be nice." Libbie smiled.

"The horse I'd want to be on would be alive, leading a charge into battle."

"That will happen, but you've got to be patient."

"For how long? Until I get my third set of teeth and need a stepladder to mount a horse?"

"George, the last time I looked at a calendar, which was this morning, you were twenty-six years old."

Libbie, in her heart, knew that she had married a soldier who was a soldier no more, and never could be as long as he stayed in Monroe and waited for something to happen.

Something did happen—but not what Libbie had hoped for.

A few days later, Custer waved the paper in front of her.

"Libbie, what do you think? An offer from Benito Juárez down in Mexico. A commission as major general of the Mexican revolutionary forces. Sixteen thousand a year, sixteen thousand, to organize and lead a cavalry command against Maximilian. All paid for by Juárez."

"George, that cavalry command would be American mercenaries, wouldn't they? And so would George Armstrong Custer—wouldn't he? That's what I think of it."

"Libbie, it would be for a cause—to free Mexico. Give me a thousand Wolverines and I'll chase Maximilian back across the Atlantic Ocean." Custer grinned.

"Our savior was content to merely walk on water and you're going to do it on horseback?"

"I didn't mean that literally."

"You didn't?" she bantered.

"No, I just got carried away, I was talking—well, figuratively."

"George, I was always happy to follow you before you went into battle, but that was in our own country, *for* our own country—but would you expect me to go there with you?"

"I don't know. I haven't thought about that yet—besides, I'd have to get a leave from the army for at least a year."

"What you really want is a command out west, isn't it?"

"I've been trying, but it seems that nothing will happen while we sit around here and wait."

"Then"—Libbie smiled—"let's go back to Washington, Custer Boy."

* * *

They did. And weeks later, it was more of the same.

The Custers were ensconced in a suite at the Grand Palace Hotel. Libbie was in another room while three men, Jason Andrews, Benjamin Blake, and Samuel Curtis, talked to her husband.

". . . and the corporation would be called Custer and Company Development." Andrews smiled.

"And what would the 'company' develop?" Custer asked, not smiling.

"Oh"—Blake shrugged—"various enterprises. Land, lumber. We'd sell stock and keep our eyes open for business opportunities. We have $50,000 seed money, half of which would go to you immediately as president, and . . ."

"And what would you *gentlemen* be?"

"Oh, uh, the board of directors," Blake said.

"In other words you'd use my name to sell stock and then you'd make all the decisions."

"Well, General," Curtis said, beaming, "we do have the experience in business . . ."

"Yes, indeed, monkey business." Custer rose and took a step nearer the door. "The name of Custer is not for rent, or sale . . ."

"General, you'll never have a better offer," Andrews said.

"I already have, one from Mexico, and I'm waiting for one from the U.S. Army. This meeting is over."

Custer opened the door. To his and the others' surprise, another general stood there, about to knock.

Ulysses Simpson Grant.

"Good day, 'gentlemen,'" Custer said, "and maybe you'd like to make that offer to this officer."

"They already have," Grant said as he drew from his cigar.

The three men scurried out without further comment.

Grant stepped in as Custer closed the door.

"How much did they offer you, General?" Custer asked.

"Forty thousand."

"Rank does have its privileges." Custer smiled. "They offered me twenty-five."

Libbie opened the door and came in from the other room.

"Yes,"—she smiled—"I've been listening. How do you do, General Grant?"

"Very well, Mrs. Custer."

"Sir, do you have news?" Custer asked.

"Yes."

"Good, or bad?" There was anxiety in Custer's voice.

"Your request for leave to join Juárez . . ."—Grant drew again from his cigar—". . . has been refused. The president doesn't want any army officer to get involved in a foreign conflict, especially you."

"But the Monroe Doctrine . . ."

"The Monroe Doctrine can wait."

"Sir, I can't . . ."

"Yes, you can. George, you have my word, and that of President Johnson, and General Sherman and Sheridan, that you'll receive an assignment worthy of you talent out west right after . . ."

"Right after what?"

"You accompany the president and me on an eighteen-day tour to be called 'Around the Circle.'"

"To do what?"

"Help us convince the public to follow Lincoln's last command—a policy of reconciliation with the South, 'and bind up the nation's wounds.'"

Custer looked as sheepish as he was able.

"Sir, would I have to make any speeches?"

"No, George. President Johnson will do the speechifying. You'll just stand there next to me and, also . . ." Grant took another, even deeper draw.

"Also, what?"

"Be his bodyguard. I've got a feeling he's going to need one."

There was a sigh of relief and satisfaction on Libbie's face as she looked at her Custer Boy.

CHAPTER 45

July 4, 1866

Today I won a rifle shooting contest in St. Louis. It cost 20 dollars to enter. That's about a month's wages for just about any job. Trouble is, for just about any job, there are about 20 job seekers.

I was down to my last thirty, so I risked two thirds of my fortune and won by a dog hair—finally. The prize was worth well over a hundred. A new model Henry rifle—.44 caliber—15 shot—weight 9 1/2 lbs.—with breech made of shiny golden brass . . .

The entries Johnny Yuma had written into his journal through, and shortly after, the war had always been grim. Times were grim and his entries reflected those times. Things were still grim, but the grimness was not as stark. There no longer was death and danger in every living minute of every day and night.

And while Johnny Yuma still was a serious young man, more serious than most, a touch of humor had begun to seep into his aspect and into at least some of the notations he made in his journal.

That night of July 4th, the celebration was still going on on the streets of St. Louis and in the saloons. Johnny Yuma was in one of the saloons, the Lady Luck, and his luck was running good.

The Henry leaned against one arm of the Douglas chair he sat in, and near the rim of the table in front of him were three stacks of chips worth ten dollars a stack. He felt flush, what with a brand-new, shiny-golden, brass-breech Henry at his side, thirty dollars in front of him, and a red flush in his hand. Yuma pushed one of the stacks toward the center of the table.

"I'll raise," he said, looking at the well-dressed gentleman opposite him.

The three other players in the game had dropped out of the hand. The well-dressed gentleman had only one stack of chips in front of him. He studied Yuma, then the lone stack. His eyes went back to Yuma.

"Too bad. I got you beat, son. But I only got enough to call . . . so I call . . . with a straight to the nine."

"All red." Yuma turned up the cards.

"Damn!" said the gentleman. "Well, son, this is your lucky day, first the rifle and now the biggest pot of the night. Well, I'm busted. Good night, gentlemen!" He rose and moved away from the table, broke, but still with dignity.

Johnny Yuma liked to play cards. He played with Danny Reese and other prisoners at Rock Island. But here in St. Louis, it was a far different game. With whiskey drinks, candled chandeliers, loud music, and a new deck of cards. And if a player lost, he could get up and go out the door.

At Rock Island, they were lucky if there was enough water to drink. It was always too dark. The only music came from a harmonica played by a near-blind young prisoner named Ralph. The cards in their only deck were bent and dirty and soggy from the sweat of the prisoners. And, win or lose, nobody could leave the compound.

Yuma gathered the chips from the center of the table.

"You boys mind if I sit in?"

Yuma looked up. It was the man who had come in second in the rifle contest, barely. Nobody minded. The man removed his hat and sat.

"They call me Red," he said as he settled.

"How come?" one of the players inquired. "You ain't got no red hair."

"Red for danger." The man smiled. "And I've just got a feeling that your lucky streak has come to a finish, Mr. . . . sorry." He looked at Yuma. "Didn't catch your name earlier today."

"Yuma. Johnny Yuma."

"I guess it's your deal, Mr. Yuma." Red called for chips. He was in his late twenties, a tall, handsome man, not as handsome as he would have been without the telltale effects of a long-ago bout with smallpox.

Johnny knew that Red was a good shot. The truth was that Yuma wasn't all that anxious to find out how good a poker player Red was. He would have been content to leave the game with his winnings and his rifle, but he dealt the cards.

Half an hour later, Yuma hadn't won or lost much, but the rest of the players had. They had lost to Red, who sat with close to two hundred dollars' worth of chips in front of him. He won the next hand, too. Three of the other players said they'd had enough.

"How about you, Mr. Yuma? How about one more hand? Just you and me, five card draw, to make the night worthwhile?"

"Thanks, I don't think so."

But the spectators urged Johnny on. One of the saloon ladies, the prettiest of the lot, leaned down and kissed Yuma on the cheek.

"That's for luck," she said. "Go ahead and play, Johnny."

Everybody laughed and clapped, and Johnny Yuma didn't have much choice. All he really stood to lose was the ten dollars he started with. The rest he had won. And there was always the chance that he could win some more.

Yuma nodded at Red. Everybody clapped again.

"Cut for the deal," Red said.

Yuma drew a jack. Red turned up a queen, then dealt.

Johnny looked at a pair of kings, a pair of deuces, and a six.

He opened for ten dollars.

Red saw the ten and raised twenty.

Yuma saw the raise. That left him with twenty. Yuma discarded the six and took one card.

Yuma didn't know it, but Red held three aces, a six, and a seven. He discarded the two numbers and drew two cards.

Neither player looked at his new cards.

Johnny bet the twenty.

There was a pause. A long pause.

"See it," Red said. "And raise a hundred and fifty."

There was an audible reaction from the spectators, then silence, dead silence.

"Table stakes," Johnny reminded the man across from him.

"I know that," Red smiled. "As far as I'm concerned that rifle's on the table and it covers the difference. You drew one card, I took two. Haven't looked at my hand and won't. Two hundred dollars against the pot and the Henry. What do you say, Johnny?"

There was a murmur from the watchers, but this time nobody laughed or clapped.

"Well?" Red goaded.

The same saloon girl leaned down again and

kissed Johnny Yuma again, this time full on the mouth, sweet as syrup.

"I'll call," Yuma said. He turned up the first four cards, two kings, two deuces. Then he turned over the fifth card. He had caught another deuce. Full house.

Red did not change expression. He showed the three aces. Then one at a time, the two other cards. First, a nine. He looked across at Yuma and turned the final card. A king.

Now everybody did laugh and clap and cheer. Everybody except Red, who rose, put on his hat, and left without a word.

Yuma cashed in. He had never had so much money in his life. He had never even seen as much. He was rich. Over $250 in legal tender and a brand-new Henry rifle to boot. He thought it best to get away from the Lady Luck before somebody else suggested a game.

Somebody did. A different kind of game.

"My name's Cherry," the pretty saloon girl said. "Don't you think I deserve a drink?"

"Uh, yes, ma'am."

"Don't call me ma'am. I'm not as old as you. Jake!" She called to the bartender. "Johnny Reb here is buying me a drink, aren't you, Johnny?"

"Yes, uh . . . yes."

It didn't take long for Jake to pour the drink.

"What about you?" Cherry looked at Yuma. "Don't you want a drink?"

"No, thanks."

"Is there anything else you do want?"

Johnny Yuma hadn't much experience with saloons or saloon girls, and Cherry was attractive. More than attractive. Her face was beautiful, and didn't need all the paint and powder she laid on it. And her body was enough to stop a stampede.

But Johnny Yuma was not about to expose himself to the likely consequences of what Miss Cherry had suggested.

He had heard stories from some of the older soldiers about big-city saloons, and some saloons in not such big cities. Especially stories about big winners in card games. The upstairs rooms, the painted ladies, the drinks called Mickey Finns—and waking up in some alley with a turbulent head and empty pockets.

Not for him, not for Johnny Yuma.

"I said, is there anything else you want?"

"Uh, look, ma'am . . . uh, Miss Cherry, please don't take offense . . ."

"Oh, oh, I think I know what's coming." She smiled.

"No, what I mean is . . . I appreciate your rooting for me, and bringing me luck, and . . ."

"And?"

"And all . . . but . . ."

"But what?"

"Well . . ."

"Is it because you've never been with a woman?"

"No, ma'am."

"What does that mean? You have? You haven't? Because the time comes . . ."

"Cherry, listen . . ."

"No, Johnny, you don't have to explain. That's not what I'm here for, to listen to explanations . . . but you listen to me. I like you. I really do. And I'm sorry we met like this. So, thanks for the drink. You take care of that poke you won, and the rifle. See you sometime. I got to get back to work."

She turned and walked away.

Johnny Yuma felt embarrassed and ashamed. Ashamed of the way he had treated her. He thought of going after her. But what would he say? "Excuse me, but I've changed my mind. Let's have a drink and go upstairs. Let's . . ."

No, he would do the smart thing and get out of the Lady Luck, and out of St. Louis, while the getting was good and while he was still lucky.

The sorrel was tied out back of the saloon. He'd take it over to the livery, get a room for the night, and sleep with his money under his pillow and the Henry by his side. In the morning he would buy some clothes and supplies and head for other parts. That's what he would do, and he would start now.

Yuma walked down the dark alley alongside the Lady Luck toward the hitching posts in the rear. He held the Henry in his right hand and thought about Cherry at work upstairs.

She said she was younger than he was. She didn't look it. But it was hard to tell with all that rouge and talcum on her face. He wondered what her face looked like without all that war paint. He would never find out.

He loosed the sorrel's reins from the hitching post. First, he heard the hammer click back. Then the voice of the man who stepped out from around the corner behind him. The man tried to change his voice, but still it was familiar.

"Drop the rifle and put your hands out front."

Yuma did both.

He could hear the man's footsteps come closer.

"Take the money out of your pocket and drop it next to the rifle. Don't turn around."

Yuma thought about going for his sidearm. But he knew he had no chance.

"The money," the man said. "On the ground. Now!"

"Okay." Yuma slowly started to remove the roll of bills as he mapped out his strategy. He would make sure the bills scattered out as they fell so they would spread all over the ground. He might have a chance to make his play as the man went to pick up the scattered currency, if the man didn't knock him out or shoot him first.

But the man seemed to have read Yuma's mind.

"Hold it!" he said. "Don't drop it. Just hold it out back of you."

"Okay," Yuma repeated. Slowly, he moved his hand close behind him with the money in it.

"Out further."

"Right."

He could hear the man take another step forward. Then Yuma heard something else.

A hard, dull thud.

Johnny Yuma whirled with the gun in his hand as the man fell forward on the ground and lay unconscious where he dropped.

She stood over the man with a bunghammer gripped in both hands.

"I said I'd see you sometime." She smiled.

She was the loveliest sight he could remember seeing in a long, long time. War paint and all.

The unconscious man on the ground wore a bandanna across his face. Even so, his identity was apparent. Yuma reached down and pulled the kerchief from Red's pockmarked map.

"I had a feeling," Cherry said. "He's a poor loser."

Yuma put the money back in his pocket, then picked up Red's gun as Red groaned and began to stir.

"All right," Yuma said. "Up."

Red struggled to his feet, wiping his left hand over the lump behind his ear.

"I . . . I'm sorry. I . . . I just wanted that rifle . . ."

"And my money," Yuma added.

"Yeah . . . I guess so."

"Well, you're gonna get neither."

"I know . . . all right, let's go see the sheriff."

"Red, you want to make a deal?"

"What're you talking about?"

"I was lucky today. At the contest and at cards. You weren't. Let's let it go at that."

"You mean it?"

"I do, but if I ever see you again, or she does . . ."

"You won't, neither of you."

"Here's your gun. Good-bye and good luck."

"Thanks, Reb."

"You're welcome, 'Red for danger.'"

Red disappeared in a hurry around the corner of the Lucky Lady.

Johnny Yuma picked up the Henry and brushed the dirt from the shiny, golden brass. He looked at Cherry.

"Say, you're pretty handy with that bunghammer."

"A girl in my business has to be. Well, so long Johnny." She started to turn.

"Cherry."

"Yes." She looked back.

"Could I . . . buy you a drink?"

"Are you sure you want to?"

"I'm sure."

CHAPTER 46

The Grand Tour turned out to be not so grand.

It had been President Johnson's idea to "swing around the circle" as he called it, on an eighteen-day trip, speaking in twenty-two cities in nine states: Maryland, Pennsylvania, New York, Ohio, Michigan, Illinois, Missouri, Indiana, and Kentucky.

Johnson's administration faced serious opposition in Congress on at least a half-dozen postwar issues, including the pardoning of Confederate office holders and army officers, the status of newly freed slaves, and the empowerment of the ex-Confederate states.

Congress had taken a strong stance against "reconciliation" and for further punishment of the South as a defeated enemy.

Johnson's ego was not wide and deep enough to think his appearance and orations alone would draw crowds to listen to his views.

He knew he needed marquee names to attract attention and audiences.

Johnson had managed to assemble a compelling cast, including General Ulysses Simpson Grant, General George Armstrong Custer, Admiral David Farragut, Secretary of State William Seward, and Navy Secretary Gideon Welles.

All had agreed to appear on the condition that none of them would have to speak.

Andrew Johnson's ego was more than wide and deep enough to agree to their nonvocal condition.

That was a big mistake on the part of all participants.

The so-called Grand Tour consisted of an imperfect geographical "circle" and a downright political blunder.

The "swing" started off satisfactorily enough in the friendly eastern states but gained momentum in the wrong direction as the "swing" swung into the midwestern Radical Republican strongholds where opposition became vocal from attendees— more than vocal.

Grant, Custer, and the rest were always greeted with cheers and applause as they appeared, smiled, and waved, but once Johnson began to speak, not just speak, but harangue and insult the gatherings, while deviating from prepared remarks, he was bombarded with return fire.

As the tour progressed, actually regressed, it was obvious that Tennessee Johnson had reverted to his old habit of fueling up with liquid fire in the belly, which also inflamed his brain.

Hecklers and plants of Republican Radicals rattled the already intemperate president, who spat back curses and accusations.

Crowds cheered and clapped at the appearance of Grant and Custer and called for them to speak, but neither acquiesced, and Johnson grew even more hostile and vituperative toward the crowds.

In Cleveland even fate seemed against him as a temporary grandstand creaked, swayed, then gave way as more than two thousand spectators hurtled earthward from seats to their doom, death, and gaping bloody wounds.

Grant, Custer, and Farragut had seen death and broken bodies on the battlefields and at sea, but this was too much in time of peace.

All three were overcome with tears at the sight of women and children with broken and bloodied bodies crisscrossed among the wreckage.

At the next stop in Ohio a half-dozen men made their way to the front of the platform waving hangman's ropes and shouting, "Hang Johnson"—"Hang the sonofabitch"—Custer leaped from the platform and faced the would-be rioters.

"You'll have to hang me first, you bastards! I was born two miles from here, but I'm ashamed of you bastards and what you stand for. This isn't why we fought, and I'll fight any and all of you who take another step!"

The crowd cheered Custer as the men with ropes

backed away, and many in the crowd even saluted General George Armstrong Custer.

That night in the hotel, Libbie, who was the only wife to accompany her husband on the tour, lay awake in bed while her husband slept with two loaded revolvers on the bed stand next to him.

Suddenly, his eyes opened wide, and still in his bedclothes, he rose quickly and grabbed both guns.

Libbie leaned forward.

"What is it, George? What's the matter? Did you dream . . ."

"Shussh, Libbie. Just stay here!"

Custer moved toward the door.

In the hallway there were three men, one of whom had inserted a key into the lock of President Johnson's door and was trying unsuccessfully to twist it.

"Damn thing!" the man with the key slurred. "Sonofabitch! I'll get it open! Stand back!" He pulled out a revolver and aimed at the lock.

"Hold it!" Custer commanded, both guns pointed at the intruders.

All three men trembled and tried to speak at the sight of the pointed guns.

"What the hell do you think you're going to do?" Custer barked and noticed all three had cranberry eyes and swayed visibly.

"Take . . . take it easy, mister . . . we . . . we're just trying to . . . get into our . . . room . . . but it won't . . . work . . . key . . . it . . ."

"Hand me that key!"

"Yess . . . sir." The man's hand was unsteady as he handed Custer the key.

"We're . . . we're . . ."

"You're drunk."

"Had . . . had a few," one of the other men managed.

"What's your room number?" Custer asked.

"Two . . . two thirteen."

"This is the third floor," Custer said and pointed to the door with a gun. "And that's *three* thirteen."

The door opened and President Johnson in his nightclothes stood next to a lieutenant with a grim face, who held a gun.

"What the hell is going . . . going on . . . here?" Johnson said.

It was obvious that President Johnson had also "had a few."

"Jesus Christ!" another of the men gulped.

"It's all right, Mr. President," Custer said. "Just an honest mistake. Go back to sleep." Then he turned to the three men. "The stairs are over there, boys."

The boys weaved toward the staircase.

"General Custer," Johnson said.

"Yes, sir."

"You care to have a . . . nightcap with me?"

"No, thanks, Mr. President," Custer smiled, with both guns still in his hands. "Think I'll call it a night."

* * *

"What was it, George?" Libbie asked when he came back into the room.

"Nothing to worry about, Libbie, just a few drunks out in the hallway . . ." then added, "and in the next room."

"General," Custer said to Grant when there was no one else in the room, "I remember a quotation—think it was from Shakespeare—'Some are born great, some achieve greatness, and some have greatness thrust upon them.' Andrew Johnson missed the mark on all three counts."

By the end of the tour Johnson had managed to turn formerly friendly newspapers against him, as well as the previously supportive Congress, and more and more every day, the majority of those who would vote in future elections.

Thomas Nast, the most famous and influential cartoonist in the country, lampooned Johnson in a series of biting illustrations labeled "Andy's Trip."

Articles proclaimed him a "vulgar, drunken, demagogue, disgracing the presidency."

Ulysses Simpson Grant puffed on his cigar as Custer continued.

"General, that man's a real blister. The more he talks, the more he blathers. He's talking his way out of the White House and into the doghouse—and he's taking President Lincoln's policy of reconciliation with him."

"Yes." Grant nodded. "That's the worst part."

"Not only could he not get reelected, he couldn't even get nominated. He's damn lucky if he doesn't get impeached . . ."

"For what?"

"They'll think of something. And, General, you'd better think things over."

"For instance?"

"There's a groundswell building for you. The presidency is yours for the taking in the next election, and if you give the word that you're interested, they might even let Johnson stay in office knowing that you'll run."

"George, that's a big decision . . ."

"It's the right decision, and you know it, but . . ."

"But what?"

"Crafty Johnson's got to get you out of the picture, out of sight, away from the public eye. You saw the reception you got, and so did he. Everyday you're around here, whether it's Washington, Philadelphia, or New York, and the papers write about you, you grow bigger and Andy Johnson shrinks away."

"I've talked things over with Julia, and I don't intend to go anywhere without her and our family."

"Good enough, but that might conflict with what Johnson's got in mind. He's still the president, and I've found out it's not as easy to protect your flanks in Washington as it is in war."

"All right, George, enough about me. What do you intend to do?"

"Since I can't go to Mexico, I'll go back to Monroe." Custer grinned. "And wait for the Three Musketeers—Grant, Sherman, and Sheridan—to get me that assignment out West. That's the only war I've got left right now."

CHAPTER 47

Johnny Yuma sat at a corner table at a flyspeck saloon in a flyspeck Southern town drinking a glass of beer and reading a newspaper.

There were a half-dozen other tables, half of them empty, opposite the bar being tended by a man he had heard called Baldy by a couple of the customers.

A short man sat on a piano stool doing his best to play "Dixie" on an out-of-tune upright piano.

Three men came in through the batwings, all three wearing remnants of Confederate uniforms, including black leather belts with oval Confederate buckles and sidearms. The biggest man, who was in the lead, also wore sergeant's stripes on his sleeves.

The sergeant paused, looked around, then proceeded toward Yuma's table.

"Evenin'," he said when he got there.

"Evening."

"You play poker?"

"Sometimes."

"Care to join us in a hand or two?"

"No, thanks."

"Why not?"

"Just going to finish my beer . . . and the news-paper."

"Then you're finished."

"How's that?"

"This is our poker table."

Johnny Yuma looked round the room.

"There're some other tables, some of them empty."

"Yeah, but this 'uns ours." He waved toward the bartender. "Ain't it, Baldy?"

The short man at the piano stopped playing

Baldy hesitated, then shrugged.

"Ain't it, Baldy!?"

Baldy nodded.

"So beat it, Corporal, besides"—he pointed to the stripes on his sleeve—"I outrank you."

"Not anymore. The war's over."

"Yeah? Did a squirt like you do any fightin'?"

"Some."

"Where?"

"Different places."

"Not around here."

"No."

"Well, we did." The sergeant grabbed the news-paper.

"What're you readin'? Look here, boys. Paper says that Grant is visitin' veterans' hospitals up north. That hog-face sonofabitch, I'd like to put *him* in a hospital, better yet a casket."

"Can I have my paper back?"

"Why? You want to read about that craven Grant sonofabitch?"

"I just want my paper back."

"When we get this table." The sergeant turned to the other two southerners. "Right, boys?"

"If you say so, Sergeant," one of the men replied.

Yuma pointed to the newspaper still in the sergeant's hand.

"The paper."

"In all that fightin' you done—you ever come across that Grant sonofabitch?"

Johnny Yuma thought back to the shack at Vicksburg and the McLean house at Appomattox, but said nothing.

"You can have the paper . . . if you can take it away from me—and even keep the table, squirt."

With that the sergeant slapped Yuma across the face, then tore the paper, holding one half in each hand.

Yuma's left fist smashed into the sergeant's nose, splattering blood; then he crashed a right into his rib cage—and another left and right into body and jaw.

The sergeant buckled and went down.

Yuma had already drawn his gun. With the other hand he reached to the floor and picked up both pieces of the paper.

For a second it looked as if the other two might make a move.

"Hold it, boys!" the sergeant commanded and wiped the blood from his face. "I told him he could have it if he took it away . . . and that he did."

The sergeant made it to his feet.

"Reb . . ." the sergeant managed to smile, "I'm glad you were on our side."

"Thank you, Sergeant. The table is all yours."

CHAPTER 48

George Armstrong Custer was right about two more things: (1) It's not as easy to protect your flanks in Washington as it is in war. (2) Crafty Johnson had to get Grant out of sight, away from the public eye as the general was becoming more popular every day, and Andy Johnson was shrinking away.

Unfortunately for Crafty Johnson's plan to get rid of Grant, it included a major role for William Tecumseh Sherman. Johnson summoned Sherman and offered him Grant's position as chief of generals, if and when Ulysses Simpson Grant accepted a diplomatic mission to Mexico, a prestigious position, but where little would be heard or read about him in the coming United States congressional and gubernatorial elections.

Sherman never intended to play that role in Johnson's scheme; what he intended to do—and did—was to go straight to Grant and warn him of what to expect.

Grant's reaction was brief and to the point.

"Thanks, Bill."

"General," Sherman replied, "you stood by me when a lot of people thought I was crazy and wanted me dismissed from command—and maybe I was a touch crazy temporarily—we both know that war'll do that—but you set me straight—and I'll be hanged before I let that Tennessee Judas rope me into any scheme against you."

"I want to thank you, too, General Sherman," Julia, who had been listening at the open parlor door, said.

"What's the matter, Julia?" Grant smiled. "Don't you want to spend a quiet vacation at a luxurious villa in Mexico?"

"I'd rather spend a not-so-quiet time at the White House in Washington when you're elected president in '68, where you can do more for your country than that 'Tennessee Judas.'"

"Well, Bill"—Grant grinned at Sherman—"I guess that seals it."

Grant had been asked to attend a cabinet meeting where President Johnson asked Secretary Seward whether General Grant's appointment for the Mexican mission was in order.

Seward nodded and began to read. Before he

completed the first sentence Grant was on his feet and interrupted Seward in a firm voice.

"I will not accept that order. I will not go."

"What?!" Johnson's face was red, his body visibly shaken.

"I will not go."

"You would defy a direct order of the commander in chief?!"

"Not a military order, but this has nothing to do with the military; this is a so-called diplomatic mission and I'm not a diplomat. I will resign first and let the public know why. Good day, Mr. President, and gentlemen."

General Ulysses Simpson Grant made straight for the door without looking back.

"How did it go, Ulys?" Julia asked her husband.

"I hope you didn't waste any time packing for Mexico."

"I certainly did not. But . . ."

"But, what?"

"Won't President Johnson do something . . ."

"To me?"

"Yes."

"President Johnson can't afford an open break with me. As Billy Sherman said when I told him what happened: 'Crafty Johnson would rather have you be a part of his administration—better to keep you in the tent blowing cigar smoke out, than out of the tent blowing smoke in.'"

"I see." Julia nodded.

What Grant didn't tell his quite proper wife, Julia, was that he had paraphrased Sherman's remark, which had been: "Better to have you, General, inside the tent pissing out, than outside, pissing in."

CHAPTER 49

For a dozen nights, sky had been his ceiling, saddle his pillow, and rabbit his menu.

When Johnny Yuma rode into Baton Rouge he decided to treat himself to an unaccustomed luxury at the Grand Palace Hotel, which was neither grand, nor palatial; however, it had survived the siege of Union commander Thomas W. Cahill almost four years ago.

The luxury, or luxuries, included a single room with hot tub bath, a tolerable steak, and a small pitcher of beer.

Adjacent to the dining room there was an area designated for smoking, reading, and letter writing.

Yuma had just finished writing on a page of the journal he kept and set the sheet aside on the table.

There was no one else in the room until a gentleman wearing a rumpled suit, carrying a newspaper, and smoking a freshly lit cigar entered.

The man sat not far from Yuma, opened the

newspaper, started to read, then glanced at the nearby journal page on the table.

It became more than a glance as he read aloud.

"'The dark clouds drifted east, and the search-light of the sun broke through and by high noon scorched the no-path terrain.'"

"You turn a handsome phrase. Writing a story?"

"Sort of . . ." Yuma took the page and placed it on his other side, "a diary, journal, since I left home and joined up."

The man noted Yuma's Confederate cap on the table.

"With the South?"

"Third Texas. Rock Island. Appomattox. Going home the long way."

"That's a good story . . . so far."

"That's as far as I've got . . . so far."

"Well, you're young yet."

"A lot of my army buddies aren't going to get any older . . . and that's pretty grim, might even say solemn . . . and that's the truth."

"Okay. But you know there's humor in truth, too. You got any humor in them there words?"

"A dollop or two."

The man took a deep draw from his cigar.

"What percent?"

"What percent of what?"

"What percent of the words have to do with humor?"

"Like I said. Third Texas. Rock Island. Appomattox. Not much humor has happened to me, when I think about it."

"Well, maybe it's the *way* you think about it."

"What do you mean?"

"I'd say a solemn background is the best contrast for humorous effect. When it comes to writing, some say humor is as good as gold."

"The way I heard it, gold is where you find it, and not many people do . . . find gold, that is."

"True again. But it's also true that there's different kinds of gold . . . when it comes to thinking and writing."

"Different kinds of gold?"

"In writing, and thinking."

"For instance?"

"Well, there's the gold in a sunrise. The gold in a young lady's hair. Even some specks of gold in the skin of a frog."

"A frog?"

"A frog, or a fall. Somebody trips on a banana peel and falls. It's not funny to him, but maybe it's funny to them who see him fall, maybe even to the banana peel, if he's not hurt. Depends on your point of view . . . and that's up to the writer . . ."

"Meaning me?"

"Meaning you . . . or me."

"Are you a writer?"

"Well . . . would you care for a cheap cigar?"

"No, thanks."

"I don't have any expensive ones."

"No, I mean I don't smoke cigars. Hard on the lungs."

"Well, that depends on your point of view, too . . .

and lungs. Some find 'em salubrious. Now, U.S. Grant and I have a different point of view . . . and lungs. We think smoking cigars serves to steady nerves."

"I see your point . . . and U.S. Grant's, but what's a cigar go to do with humor?"

Another deep draw.

"If you gagged on a cigar that'ud be funny to me and Grant, but not to you."

"What if you go to heaven and they don't allow cigars up there?"

"Then I won't go."

"Would that be humorous?"

"Depends on your point of view . . . and mine."

"What are you, mister? A philosopher? A teacher? A writer, or what?"

"Might say a ventriloquist, who puts words in other people's mouth. Just a southern fella like you who does a little scribbling once in a while."

"Well, so do I, do a little scribbling, but I didn't have the benefit of a higher education."

"Neither did I"

The man held up the newspaper.

"All I know is what I *don't* read in the newspapers. Education, like gold and humor, is where you find it. In places and people. In plush times and hard-scrabble. In life. Anyhow, I think I'll have a drink or two. Care to join me?"

"No, thanks."

"Don't tell me you don't drink either."

"Oh, I take a drink . . . or two, at times. But this time I reckon I'll just sit here a while and think."

"Can't hurt. But neither can a drink or two. Well, good luck . . . say, what's your name anyhow?"

"Yuma. Johnny Yuma."

"*Yuma*? Sounds too . . . geographical for a writer. Why don't you change it?"

"To what for instance?"

"Oh, I don't know." Another deep draw. "Something like Herman Melville, Bret Harte . . . or maybe with three names like James Fenimore Cooper, or even four . . . Walter Van Tilburg Clark. Something that sings."

"Yuma doesn't sing?"

"Not to me, it doesn't."

"I'll think about it." Johnny Yuma smiled. "And, by the way, what's your name?"

"Sam."

"Sam what?"

"Doesn't matter." Sam rose. "I'm thinking of changing it."

"To what?"

Sam shrugged.

"I'm still thinking about that, too. And by the way, which way are you heading?"

"West."

"Taking Horace Greeley's advice, huh."

"Who's Horace Greeley?"

"Oh, just a newspaperman in New York who's thinking of running for president."

* * *

Johnny Yuma didn't know it at the time, but Greeley had written "Go West, young man."

A lot of young men and women and families were taking his advice.

As far as the Indian tribes were concerned *too many.*

It was becoming a multi-forked invasion, from the Oregon Trail in the north to the Santa Fe Trail in the south—all aiming west. Covered wagons, riders on horseback, and, as the Indians called it, "the Iron Horse"—the railroad, cutting through the plains and peaks, which, for centuries, had been Indian domain.

But not anymore.

Not for the Sioux, Blackfoot, Mandan, Arika, Shoshoni, Nez Perce of the north.

Or the Cheyenne, Osage, Arapaho, Paiute, Ponca of the plains.

Or the Kiowa, Apache, Comanche, Cherokee of the southwest.

The tribes had a saying: "Where the sun rises, white man's land. Where the sun sets, Indian land."

But the white man had a different saying: "Manifest Destiny."

Nothing much was said about the destiny of the Indians. But more and more, the Indians would have something to say about it—and something to do.

From the Mississippi on the east, to the Columbia

on the west, from the Missouri on the north to the Rio Grande on the south, the land would be littered with paint, feathers, and blood.

And the United States would have infinite need of men of war like Grant, Sherman, Sheridan, and Custer—and even men like Johnny Yuma.

CHAPTER 50

Part of the letter Libbie Custer had written to General Philip Sheridan, War Department, Washington, D.C., read:

> He's like the main spring of a pocket watch that's wound up tight, much too tight—and I fear that spring might snap and render the watch broken.
>
> George is doing his soldier best to remain calm and useful, but, at heart he is, and always will be, a soldier, who now feels thrown on an ash heap instead of being on the firing line, on horseback leading a charge.
>
> He's almost given up running to the mailbox everyday hoping for a letter from the "War Department Three Musketeers," as he put it, with an assignment to active duty—with an accent on _active_.
>
> As yet he hasn't slipped off "the wagon"—as they say—we only have one drink together, but

*he's spending more time at the pub, and everyone
keeps proposing toasts to him. He responds by
sipping sarsaparilla—so far.*

*I don't want him to know about this letter, but
after all the two of you have been through together,
I urge, no, General, I beg you to do what's best for
him, for the army, and for the country.*

Libbie's letter had been written over two weeks
ago and still no response, but everyday she has-
tened to the mailbox, and everyday provided another disappointment.

On a Thursday afternoon Custer had taken
Libbie's favorite mare, Bluebelle, for a three-mile
exercise and was making his way back to Monroe
along a narrow bridle path meant for one horse at
a time.

"Gangway! Gangway, mate!!" a deep-throated
voice from behind bellowed as fast-paced hoofbeats
thundered closer and louder. "Gangway!"

Custer was not about to give up what little space
he could have.

"Go to hell!!" Custer looked back and shouted at
the rapidly approaching horseman.

"Been there and back!" an accent-tinged voice
retorted. "Gangway!"

Custer prodded Bluebelle, and the mare charged
ahead.

But in a moment the horseman, a bulky man
with bushy sideburns, in lieutenant's uniform and
beetled eyebrows that almost met at the deep

crease in the middle of his forehead, was alongside Custer, pressing him and Bluebelle hard against the thorny brush of the bridle path. The horses, neck and neck, flank to flank—the riders, elbow to elbow and boot to boot, galloped at breakneck speed without either rider giving an inch, both riders lashed by the whip-like thorns and branches that rimmed the trail.

"Let me by, mate—I'm thirsty!"

"Get off that horse and you'll go to hell thirsty!"

"Some other time, mate!"

There was no doubt about the lieutenant's horsemanship—nor Custer's, as the two riders bolted ahead. In truth, Custer was enjoying the challenge—until Bluebelle suddenly shuddered, favoring her right front hoof, and Custer reined her to a stop as the lieutenant raced ahead grinning and waving back.

Custer dismounted and examined Bluebelle's hoof and the shoe that had been knocked loose and askew.

Not much later, Adam Dawson, formerly Captain Dawson, was at the piano in the White Horse Tavern playing and singing some of his favorite songs when a bulky lieutenant came in, ordered a bottle, took it to a table, and began to pour and drink.

This went on until the lieutenant's bottle was almost half empty and George Armstrong Custer walked in and Dawson rose, greeted his boyhood friend and Wolverine commander, and walked with him to an empty table.

Custer watched as the lieutenant took up his bottle and glass, made his way to the piano, and began to play and sing.

"Autie, you're late, been expecting you."

"Bluebelle threw a shoe, took her over to the blacksmith."

The bartender brought over a sarsaparilla and set it in front of Custer.

The lieutenant continued pounding on the piano, and between drinks, singing:

> *"Let Bacchus' sons be not dismayed,*
> *But join with me each jovial blade,*
> *Come booze and sing and lend your aid,*
> *To help me with the chorus:*
> *Instead of spa we'll drink down ale*
> *And pay the reckoning on the nail,*
> *For debt no man shall go to jail;*
> *From Garryowen in glory."*

With each verse the lieutenant's voice grew louder.

So did Adam Dawson's.

"Autie, have you . . . damn it, I can't hear myself talk with that loudmouth lieutenant bellowing . . ."

Dawson started to rise.

"Let him sing, Adam, I like that tune—never heard it before."

"I'll be right back," Dawson said and moved toward that singing lieutenant.

"Hey, fella, do you mind putting a mute on that bellowing so my friend, General Custer, and I can carry on a conversation?"

"I do mind, and you and your friend, General Custer, can go outside and talk. I'm mustered out of the army, mate, and intend to celebrate."

"Celebrate softer."

"Like hell, mate."

"No, like this . . ."

Dawson grabbed the lieutenant and pulled him to his feet.

But Custer was there.

"Hold on, Adam."

"Oh, no." The lieutenant grinned. "So this is General Custer, that half-ass horseman . . ."

Dawson pulled back his fist.

"You can't talk like that to . . ."

But Custer slugged his friend, Dawson, square on the jaw, then turned to the lieutenant.

"You said 'some other time.'" Custer's fist flew again, and the lieutenant fell against the piano, but grabbed the bottle before it toppled.

"Shall we continue?" Custer smiled at the lieutenant.

"No, mate, I guess that evens things." The lieutenant grinned. "I'm Willie Cooke, glad to meet you, General."

"Then sing that song again—it's got a beat to it, like a cavalry charge."

"Sure, it's sung by the Queen's Own regiments—the Irish from Limerick—goes like this." He sat back at the piano as Dawson rubbed his jaw and whispered to Custer.

"Autie, what'd you hit me for?"

"When you want to confuse the enemy—hit a friend." Then to the lieutenant, "Go ahead, Queen's Own, sing."

And sing Queen's Own did—even louder than before.

> *"We'll beat the bailiff out of fun,*
> *We'll make the mayor and sheriffs run,*
> *We are the boys no man dare dun,*
> *If he regards a whole skin."*

Lieutenant Cooke took a swig directly from the bottle.

"Sing along, mates, just follow me."

First Custer, then the others did.

> *"Our hearts so stout have got us fame,*
> *For soon 'tis known from whence we came,*
> *Where're we go they dread the name,*
> *Of Garryowen in glory."*

Just before they finished, Libbie Custer rushed into the room, with one hand behind her back.

Custer was not surprised. He was astounded—and moved close to her, speaking just above a whisper.

"Libbie, what the devil are you doing here! What's wrong?"

"Wrong! *You're* wrong, General Custer. I'm not Libbie! I'm a mail carrier." She brought a letter from her back and thrust it toward her husband. "It's from the War Department, and I took the liberty of opening it. Read it, Autie. Read it out loud!"

Custer took the envelope and letter, cleared his throat, and began.

> *"We three, General Grant, General Sherman, and I, Philip Sheridan, and nearly all the officers of your regiment, have asked for you. Can you report at once? Eleven companies of your regiment, the 7th Cavalry, will move soon against the hostile Indians.*
>
> *"Grant, Sherman, Sheridan, The Three Musketeers"*

"Can I report?" Can I report!? Well, Libbie, my sweet, can *we* report?!"

"You bet your boots we can!" She smiled. "You bet your boots we will!" and kissed him. "We're practically packed."

"What about you, Adam?"

"I thought you'd never ask,"—Dawson grinned.

"Hold on, mates." Lieutenant William Cooke

held up the nearly empty bottle. "I suddenly feel like reenlisting, if you'll have me."

"Have you?! Why, Queen's Own, you're the best horseman I've met since the war . . ." Custer looked at Dawson. "Well, one of the best. We'll need you and that song. It's our good-luck tune, 'Garryowen,' let's give it another go, right now, all of us."

They sang.

> "Let Bacchus' sons be not dismayed,
> But join with me each jovial blade,
> Come booze and sing and lend your aid,
> To help me with the chorus:
> Instead of spa we'll drink down ale
> And pay the reckoning on the nail,
> For debt no man shall go to jail;
> From Garryowen in glory."

Once again George Armstrong Custer was in pursuit of glory.

CHAPTER 51

From Johnny Yuma's journal:

I'll never forget what happened when I decided it was time to quit drifting for a while; it was time to go and see Danny Reese's mother and sister— maybe be of some comfort to them.

Someday I'll write the entire episode in detail just as it happened, but for now, while I'm still on the move, I've jotted down a few bare-bone notes to suffice until I'm at least somewhat settled with a table, or even a desk, instead of a saddle, and maybe even a fireplace instead of a campfire.

I reached for the brass knocker on the door of the colonnaded house a few miles from Natchez; the house, like most places and people of Natchez, was in disrepair and had suffered from the war.

Miss Morrison, a crusty retired schoolteacher, with an oval face and downward slanting grey eyes magnified by spectacles, opened the door.

My name meant nothing to her, but when she repeated it in a loud voice, another lady's voice came eagerly from within: "Please tell Johnny to come in."

In the parlor, now converted to a bedroom, I was first greeted by a venerable Dr. Pickard, then Mrs. Amanda Reese, Danny's mother, propped up in bed—arms extended, face suddenly moist with tears.

Amanda Reese told me how, for months, and even sometimes now, she looks out the parlor window and hopes for a miracle. And then the inevitable question of how did her son, Danny, die—was it heroic?

In the telling, I made it even more heroic.

After a while I asked about Danny's sister, Cynthia.

"Who?"

"Your daughter."

"I have no daughter."

"Cynthia isn't your daughter?"

"No," said Amanda Reese—"she's a whore."

I recalled with what love, devotion, adoration, Danny always spoke of his sister Cynthia. Gentle and strong. Wise and genial. Beautiful without vanity.

How she tended and nursed him back to health—rallying, challenging, demanding— willing him to live, when at the age of eight he

*nearly expired from an epidemic of deadly fever
that hit Natchez.*

*Later, Dr. Pickard told me how Cynthia was
the first to volunteer as a battlefield nurse for
the South—hundreds of operations—a bomb
exploding too close—how she continued in the
makeshift operating room with shrapnel torn into
her back, until collapsing—herself being operated
on—and then given something to relieve pain—
something called morphine.*

*Then more morphine—until the solution became
worse than the affliction—until she began to inject
herself—and had to be sent home—while her
fiancé, Captain Hurd Renfield, was away fighting,
and by the time he came home it was too late.*

*Cynthia was an addict, who met a man named
Will Cameron, owner of the Emporium, who
provided her with what had become a necessity—
while, at first, she provided him—and now
customers—with herself—just one of the upstairs
whores.*

*Thousands of soldiers had become addicts—
wounded victims of the needle.*

*But this was Danny Reese's beloved sister—
and I had to do something about it.*

I had to start at the Emporium.

*I made the necessary financial arrangement
and went upstairs—after meeting Will Cameron's
"Enforcer"—Al Rattigan.*

Cynthia was pale, a little too thin, but still beautiful.

"My name is . . ." I began.

"It doesn't matter."

"Maybe it does . . . Johnny Yuma."

"Johnny . . . Johnny . . ." she sobbed, "Danny wrote . . ."

Minutes later, after we talked, and after I found the needle and smashed it—the first step—"They won't let me go—Cameron and Rattigan."

"Yes, they will. I'll be back tomorrow—I'll get you out—we'll help you through it. Dr. Pickard and Hurd Renfield and me—we'll be with you all the way—and so will Danny."

On the way out I met Will Cameron, a handsome, imposing man, and told him I'd be back tomorrow to take Cynthia with me.

"They're free to go." Cameron smiled. "Including Cynthia. All they have to do is walk past Mr. Rattigan."

"Fine," I said. "We'll do just that."

Dr. Picard took me to see Captain Hurd Renfield, tall, with a saber scar on his cheek and in need of a cane from a war wound. At first I talked—then:

"It's no use . . . I tried . . ." he said.

"*Try again. I'll help you. So will Dr. Picard. She's willing to try. It'll help if she sees you there.*"

It did.

But as the three of us came down the stairs, Rattigan was there waiting, and Cameron was watching.

"We're your friends," Rattigan said to Cynthia. "We take care of you. You need something right now. Go back upstairs."

"Yeah," I said, "and what's the next step? The cribs out back? And then a wooden box!"

"Reb, you still have to get past me." Rattigan smirked and went for his gun. But my Colt was already leveled at him, and Renfield whipped his cane across Rattigan's hand, and the gun fell to the floor. I leathered the Colt and smashed Rattigan's face with a left cross. He put up a good fight, but not good enough. Rattigan dropped to the floor, but reached for his fallen gun. I drew and hip-fired. His gun sparked and shattered inches away from his outstretched hand.

As we moved toward the batwings, Will Cameron smiled.

"Mr. Yuma, she'll be back."

"Never," I said, not smiling.

"War is hell," General Sherman said, and he was right. But there are other kinds of hell.

Torment, terrifying and unspeakable. Torture of
the body and mind, a living hell, called . . .
withdrawal.

    We were there to help, sometimes taking turns,
Renfield, Dr. Picard, and me. A room at Renfield's
place had been stripped bare of everything but the
brass bed and the straps that held her down when
she turned wild and furious—hurtling her
distorted mind and aching body deep into a
fathomless pit with billowing pain, beating a
tattoo of torment into her fevered brain for more
than a week—time, twisted and stretched, snaked
and spiraled—time—but a clock with no hands.

    The chemise she wore clung to her writhing
body—her breasts and thighs—pulling against
the straps that held her legs and arms.

    "Johnny, I want to die."

    "No! Live!"

    "Give me a knife . . . a gun . . . anything . . ."

    "Think of Danny."

    "Danny?"

    "You saved him . . . and he got us out of Rock
Island . . . He saved us . . . like you saved him . . .
that's why I'm here . . . and so is Danny . . . Now
you're going to fight and save yourself."

    And fight she did.

    But Amanda Reese had suffered a stroke.
Dr. Picard was with her and sent word with
Miss Morrison that Cynthia's mother had asked
to see me.

I left Cynthia with her fiancé and rode to be at Mrs. Reese's bedside.

Mrs. Reese's words were slow and slurred.

"Now that Danny's gone . . . you're my family . . . I wanted you to be with me . . . when . . ."

"Mrs. Reese, you're going to get well, and I'm going to bring someone to see you . . . someone who is your family . . . your flesh and blood."

"No."

"Yes. She's been sick, too, but she's going to get well . . ."

"No."

"Listen to me, Mrs. Reese. Your daughter was a soldier of the South, as much as Danny . . . and on a lot of battlefields with cannons and blood and death all around her. We had guns and bayonets. She had nothing but faith in God . . . and courage. Cynthia was wounded in action . . . a terrible wound. She kept fighting and she's fighting now. For her life and your love. If Danny came home wounded, would you have turned your back on him? You said you still look out the window, well, what about your other soldier, sick and wounded? She can come back. Mrs. Reese, I'm going to bring your other soldier home. So keep looking out that window."

Amanda Reese smiled and nodded.

* * *

Later, I found out what had happened while I was away, what happened to Cynthia and Renfield.

"Hurd," Cynthia said, "I'm going to make it."

"We're going to make it. Together. First thing I'm going to do is untie those straps."

There was a knock on the door, then again. Renfield went to answer it. When he opened the door the butt of a pistol sledged across his forehead knocking him back into the room.

Al Rattigan stepped inside and viciously kicked Renfield in the back, walked to the inner doorway, and saw Cynthia Reese strapped to the bed.

"Well, ain't that handy. All tied up and ready for pluckin'."

She screamed.

"Go ahead and yell. There's nobody to hear but me and them chickens outside."

Rattigan ripped a cord off the drapes, tied Renfield's hands behind his back, and dragged him through the doorway, a few feet from the bed.

"He's comin' to, Cyn, and he's gonna watch and see you in action like at the Emporium. But first, I'm gonna give you somethin' to settle your nerves and take you back like I promised Mr. Cameron."

He removed a black leather case from the inside pocket of his coat, snapped it open, and took out the syringe with the long shiny needle.

She screamed as Hurd Renfield struggled against the cord that bound him. Rattigan held the syringe in one hand while the other moved down against the surface of her body, across her breasts, and finally came to rest on her left arm.

I leaped across the room and sprang at Rattigan. We slammed against the wall. The syringe flew into the bed near Cynthia's arm.

I held Rattigan by the throat with one hand, while the other fist crashed again and again into his face until he dropped.

I went to Hurd Renfield, pulled a knife from my pocket, and cut the cord.

"Johnny . . ." he muttered.

"It's all right. I saw the open door, heard her scream . . ."

And as Cynthia screamed again I spun, drew, and fired.

Rattigan fell, this time dead, with the gun still in his hand.

"That's just what I wanted him to do," I said, then walked to the bed, cut the straps, and helped Cynthia Reese to her feet.

She reached toward the bed, picked up the syringe, and hurled it against the wall. It broke. The pieces fell where Rattigan lay.

I stayed in Natchez until Mrs. Reese recovered enough to attend her daughter's wedding, where I *served as best man, and Miss Morrison beamed as septuagenarian bridesmaid.*

As I rode out of town, I saw Will Cameron on the boardwalk escorting a young lady who appeared to be fresh from the farmland.

And as is usual, the "Enforcer" took the fall and the "Headman" is still in business.

CHAPTER 52

"You can't outguess fate."

"Inevitable."

"Just as sure as the turning of the earth."

"The will of the people."

"New savior of the nation."

"Your destiny."

There were countless other encouragements, entreaties, pleas, promptings, assertions, affirmations—along with supplications and sweet logic. As the postwar weeks and months went on, the groundswell for Grant's ascendency to the presidency of the United States of America gained even more momentum.

Andrew Johnson had imploded. Shattered by his stubborn clash with Congress; his intransigent position that the president prevail on every issue; his hot temper and cold conduct; his bombast and unbridled stance that he would legislate as well as execute the laws of the land—until, led by Representative Thaddeus Stevens, one word resounded and unceasingly echoed in the House chamber . . . IMPEACH! IMPEACH! IMPEACH!

George Armstrong Custer's prediction to General Ulysses Simpson Grant was coming true; Custer had said about Johnson: "He's talking his way out of the White House and into the doghouse. Not only could he not get reelected, he couldn't even get nominated. He's lucky if he doesn't get impeached . . ."

When Grant asked, "For what?" Custer replied, "They'll think of something."

Congress was coming closer and closer to that "something."

And even if Congress failed in its impeachment trial to throw Johnson out of the presidency, he would have no chance for reelection.

As for any other potential nominees, the *New York Times* summed it all up:

"General Grant's heavy guns have almost completely silenced the small artillery of his traducers."

But as the election of 1868 was drawing nearer—there were some warning signs, one in particular from General Sherman to Julia Grant:

"You must soon be prepared to have your husband's character thoroughly sifted."

"Why General," Julia exclaimed, "Ulys is my Admirable Crichton. He does all things well. He is brave; he is kind; he is just; he is true."

"My dear lady," Sherman replied, "it is not what he has done, but what *they will say* he has done, and they will prove, too, that General Grant is a very bad man indeed. The fact is, you will be astonished to find what a bad man you married."

In a way General Sherman was teasing Julia Grant, but in another way, he was preparing her for what he thought was to come—before and after the election—if Grant made the run.

Ulysses Simpson Grant was an indisputable war hero.

But—

While the vast majority of citizens believed that Grant would make as great a president as he had been a general—the man to lead the nation to prosperity and progress, as he had led the Union to victory and glory—there were those few—politicians and speculators—who saw in Grant, if he were elected, a simple, unsophisticated midwesterner, honest, naive, a man inexperienced in the sophistry of politics—a man who could be mislead and manipulated to the advantage of those few.

Grant had said that in war it was easy to tell who was the enemy, because of their uniforms, but in civilian strife there were no discernible uniforms—

and as Shakespeare noted, "There is no art to find the mind's construction in the face."

Julia Dent Grant and their three children were in favor of his declaring that he would run.

As yet, Ulysses Simpson Grant had not said yes.

But he didn't say no.

CHAPTER 53

Lt. Colonel George Armstrong Custer had not announced the date of his arrival at Fort Abraham Lincoln.

And as it turned out, he was glad that he hadn't.

The parade grounds were crowded with officers, troopers, civilians, and even some "friendlies"— Indians who toed the white man's mark.

But they were not assembled to greet the fort's new commander.

Custer, Dawson, the Queen's Own, and a cavalry escort were on horseback. There were two covered wagons conveying the Custers' personal belongings, and Libbie, in traveling regalia, rode on the bench of one of the wagons.

"Attention!" one of the parade ground officers commanded at the sight of Custer's uniform and rank.

"What the hell is going on here?" Custer barked at what he saw.

What he saw was an Indian, stripped to the waist, tied to a post, being lashed by a moose of a sergeant, who ceased lashing and stood at attention as Custer dismounted and strode toward the whipped Indian—tall, well-muscled, maybe twenty years of age.

"What's this all about?" Custer addressed the sergeant.

"Orders, sir," the sergeant replied.

"Whose orders?"

The sergeant looked toward the approaching major, a stiff-back marionette of a man.

"Mine," the major saluted as he answered Custer's question.

"Who are you?"

"Major Thomas Benton in command of the fort, sir."

"Not anymore. I presume you received orders that you were relieved upon the arrival of Colonel Custer."

"Yes, sir."

"Well, you're relieved, and why is this man being lashed?"

"By this 'man' I presume you mean this Indian."

"Answer the question."

"Here? Now?"

"Here. Now."

"This Indian struck a white officer of the United States Army."

"Which officer?"

"Major Thomas Benton, sir."

"Why?"

"Because . . . because he's a recalcitrant . . . savage . . . sir. And I'd prefer to continue this conversation in private, sir."

"I wouldn't, so we'll continue here and now."

By then, both Dawson and Queen's Own had dismounted and approached. Libbie watched and listened from the wagon.

There was an apprehensive silence from all the parade ground spectators as Custer turned toward the stolid red man with black-bullet eyes and twin-knife-blade mouth.

"You speak American?"

"I speak English," the Indian replied without turning to look at Custer.

"Cut him loose," Custer said to the sergeant, looking at the red man's bleeding back.

The sergeant obeyed and the Indian turned and faced Custer in silence.

"You're welcome." Custer smiled as he studied the grim red face. "Suppose I continue the conversation with you? Why did you strike the officer?"

"Because he struck me."

"All right." It was obvious that Custer appreciated the succinct answer. "Why did he strike you?"

"Because I held up to his nose a stinking piece of meat he had rationed to my tribe."

"What tribe?"

"Lakota, Sioux."

"Anything more?"

"Much."

"Go ahead."

"We are given meat that only buzzards would eat. Indian agents use our warriors and children to dig coal for their own comfort and profit. Your soldiers and scouts sneak on our land and take away our women. White men hide in ridges and shoot our people for target practice. Many other wrongs . . ."

"That's enough wrongs for now. And I give you my word that from now on these wrongs will stop if the Lakota will live in peace. Do you believe the word of Custer?"

"I believe what happens . . . when it happens."

"Fair enough, now . . ." Custer turned toward Major Thomas Benton.

Before Custer could continue, the Indian raced toward a cavalry horse, leaped on it, and galloped through the men and mounts on the parade grounds as soldiers and civilians scattered away from the pounding hooves. Rider and horse flew over a water trough and raced toward the open gate.

Several soldiers drew their sidearms and aimed, but Custer's command stopped their action.

"Hold it! Let him go! Who the hell is that fellow?" Custer asked nobody in particular.

A short man with whiskered face crisscrossed with creases, a mouth with more teeth absent than present, dressed in faded buckskin, stained with tobacco juice and dried whiskey, stepped forward and spat a stream of chaw.

"Crazy Horse," the short man said.

Custer looked at Dawson, Queen's Own, and then Major Thomas Benton.

"He's the best cavalryman I've seen since we left Monroe."

"Crazy Horse," Benton sneered, "is also an unregenerate miscreant, a barbarian, and liar; he's attacked . . ."

"That'll do for now, Major. You're dismissed and so are the rest of these troopers on the parade ground."

"Are you going to believe that red bastard or an officer of . . ."

"I said 'dismissed,' Major."

"Yes, sir." Benton spun, repeated Custer's order to a lieutenant, and marched away.

The soldiers, and most of the spectators on the parade ground, scattered, but not Dawson, Queen's Own, and the bewhiskered man in buckskin.

"General Custer, heard a heap about you, and I'm proud to know you."

"I am now a lieutenant colonel, and who are you?"

"They call me California Joe."

"Born there?"

"Nope, but hope to die there—not too soon."

"What do you do around here, California?"

"Scout some. You want to hear another opinion about this here situation?"

"Whose?"

"Mine."

"Go ahead."

"It happened like the Horse said. He ain't no saint, no more'n the rest of us—but it happened the way he laid it out about Benton—and the rest of what he said had more truth than tilt, though he bent it some. Them injuns ain't all as straight as the arrows they shoot, but they got grievances all right. There's right and wrong on both sides. That's my opinion, General."

"Duly noted, and I hope you stick around and do some more scouting."

"Like I said, I ain't in no hurry." California Joe started to turn away, but stopped and looked back. "By the way, that horse that Crazy Horse stole belonged to Major Benton."

"That so?" Custer smiled, "I once stole a horse belonging to General Sheridan to get back to my regiment."

"I ain't surprised." California Joe nodded and moved off.

"Well, gentlemen"—Custer stepped toward Adam Dawson and Queen's Own—"what do you think?"

"I think we're in for a lot of surprises," Dawson said.

"Right-o," Queen's Own added, "things do need a lot of attending to."

"That's just the beginning, chums." Custer looked around. "We didn't come out here to do any picnicking."

* * *

Custer dismissed Major Thomas Benton not only from the parade grounds of Fort Abraham Lincoln but from his command, which took in a string of other forts from the Yellowstone to the Dakota Black Hills, with an assortment of tribes: Sioux, Blackfoot, Mandan, Arika, Shoshoni, Nez Perce, and Cheyenne.

It was difficult to determine the friendlies from the hostiles because those same tribes were sometimes friendly and sometimes hostile—too hostile—when it suited them. When snows painted the peaks above the timberline and winter came—when there was no food to feed the women and children—their leaders would take them back to the reservations.

And then, in spring, with full bellies they would bolt the reservations on stolen horses, carrying stolen guns and ammunition to hunt not just buffalo, but whatever resources they could forage from the white settlers, wagon trains, and travelers west.

"Libbie," Custer one night posed the question, "was it a mistake?"

"Was what a mistake?"

"To bring you out here and to all this?"

"Custer Boy, how could you ask such a question when 'all this' includes our being together?"

"We've always wanted a son and daughter—and out here . . ."

"*Out here* people have sons and daughters all the time—or haven't you noticed?" She smiled.

"I'll have to be away a lot of the time . . ."

"Then we'll have to make up for it while you're here . . . and there's no better time to start than right now, Custer Boy."

Things at Fort Lincoln and the other forts Custer was in charge of did need attending—and then some.

They needed overhauling and Custer set about doing that—and then some. The officers, troopers, and scouts were to become the most efficient fighting machine the West had ever seen.

California Joe warned Custer: "Just when you think Indians will go in one direction, they'll go 'tuther."

Custer met with all the officers, scouts, and Indian fighters in his command and became quickly oriented in the strategy, tactics, and machinations the Indian tribes utilized in their resourceful sort of warfare.

Custer was a fast learner and so were his troopers as they drilled and drilled and drilled. It wasn't long before the 7th Cavalry was ready.

Custer's intent and orders included:

"We're going to force ride and force march on short rations, and show up where the hostiles least expect us."

"We're going to feint in one direction and strike in another two or three directions."

"Those Indians who want to settle down and live in peace will be fed and comforted—and no more unfit meat and spoiled food will be rationed. They'll be fed what the troopers are fed, and any agent caught cheating will be punished severely, and the tribal chiefs will know about it."

"But if those chiefs want to fight, we'll show them what it means to fight the U.S. Cavalry."

"We'll outthink, outflank, and outfight them until they're dizzy and defeated."

"What's been treatied as their land will remain their land. But they will not stop the westward movement, nor will they savage what has been agreed upon as ours."

"And there will be no winter respite in warfare. We'll strike in cold and frost, in rain and sleet and snow."

"If they attack a wagon train or ranch, railroad camp, or travelers and kill, they'll be attacked tenfold and suffer scores killed and captured."

"They'll find that warfare doesn't just mean war paint and warrior yells. They'll find out that some warriors wear blue uniforms, ride hard, and shoot straight, and all to the tune of 'Garryowen'—and Glory."

* * *

Custer's orders were carried out, resulting in victory after victory, and he gained the respect of his troops—and even of the Indian tribes, who found that Custer never broke his word.

But Custer was not in charge of government policy and of those politicians, speculators, and expansionists whose word was not sacrosanct.

Before long, land that was ceded to the Indian was receded to the white man.

The Indians had signed treaties that they didn't understand, but the white signers fully understood and took advantage of those treaties and the Indian signers.

The railroads and settlers encroached on hunting grounds and sacred burial grounds. Rumors of gold and silver brought more invaders, and more tribes were consigned to reservations against their will and their ways.

All this was exacerbated by the buffalo hunters who killed thousands and thousands of buffalo— buffalo for the men who built the railroad, buffalo for foreign hunting parties, including royalty, buffalo for robes, and buffalo tongues, smoked and sent back East, considered culinary delicacies— while heaps of meat lay rotting.

General William Tecumseh Sherman, the complete warrior, welcomed these buffalo hunters.

"Take away their commissary and you take away their way of life—and their will to fight. No more buffalo, no more Indian war. Just a weak, defeated enemy."

But the Indians had other ideas. They struck back in the only way they knew how: arrows, bullets, fire, and fury. Retaliation that the whites never conceived—capture, torture, gouged eyes and arms, legs amputated, bodies disemboweled, burned, and skinned alive.

Invaders who wanted Indian land would pay for it—body and mind—in ways they would never forget—those who survived and those who lost fathers, mothers, brothers, sisters, sons, and daughters.

But Custer's tactics, using the bone-hard disciplined 7th Cavalry, soon took effect. With marathon marches, midnight maneuvers, and winter forays, it was Custer who surprised the Indians, not the Indians who surprised Custer.

When they logically expected attacks from one side, Custer would—as California Joe said, "hit 'em from 'tuther."

More often than not, Custer was at the head of the charges, red scarf flowing and drawn sword leading.

The Civil War was over and won, and Custer had reaped more than his share of glory. But the West was far from won, and George Armstrong Custer was determined to reap a second glory.

CHAPTER 54

Through the months that followed, the pages of Johnny Yuma's journal were filled with myriad experiences—recalling events and people encountered—pages that he sent back to Elmer Dodson in Mason City: his stint in Longview, where he served as deputy sheriff while also working on the *Longview Chronicle*—and where he utilized his tracking skills, taught him by his boyhood friend, a Kiowa named Pony that Flies, in rescuing a young bride kidnapped by outlaw brothers; a tranquil visit to Reverend Doug Baines, his wife, Cora, and their expanded family; how he met the eminent Kiowa chief, Satanta, known as the "Great Orator of the Plains," saved his life, was made the chief's blood brother, given an eagle claw to wear around his neck signifying Satanta's gratitude and friendship; how he met a newly formed brigade of the 3rd Texas, led by a colonel who intended to form a new Confederacy in Mexico. Yuma refused the colonel's invitation to rejoin the Ghost Brigade—all this and much more—an abundance of adventures, some that answered questions he was seeking, and others that left questions unanswered—because he decided there were some answers that could only be found at a place he had called home.

Johnny Yuma realized it was time to return to Mason City—his father, Sheriff Ned Yuma, Elmer Dodson, his aunt Emmy, and most compelling, the one he loved more than anyone, beautiful Rosemary Cutler.

Two of the most unpredictable times, Johnny Yuma thought to himself, were when you left home and when you went back, and as he now rode that last mile to Mason City he glanced up at a cave, a cave with Indian markings that brought back a vinculum of memories:

On that Sunday years ago, a sudden summer storm. Johnny Yuma and Rosemary Cutler had intended to picnic near a stream, when thunder bellowed, a north wind with rain slapped into their faces and clothes, eyes blinded by the downpour, but they made it into the cave.

He had kissed her many times before, at picnics near a stream, on the porch before she went inside, even on horseback, but never before like this, and both of them knew without saying a word, at first through the wetness of their clothes and later against the wetness of their naked young bodies . . . They always had torn themselves apart, but not this time.

Later that same Sunday, when Johnny Yuma got back, his father, Sheriff Ned Yuma, was waiting with pent-up fury ready to explode.

Events had preceded Johnny's meeting on that Sunday morning: His father and Deputy Jess Evans went after a wanted outlaw, leaving Johnny with Goober Brown, drunk and asleep on the bunk of a cell, drunk and disorderly since his wife died over two weeks ago. Sheriff Yuma had locked him up that morning as much for Goober's protection as anything else and left him with Johnny.

Then Rosemary Cutler came in with a picnic basket. Johnny had promised to take her on a Sunday picnic and he didn't intend to break that promise, not on account of his father or some drunken fool, who was snoring away in jail.

It was the worst decision Johnny Yuma ever made.

In Johnny's absence, Goober Brown had hanged himself with his own belt.

"I'm . . . I'm sorry." Johnny managed, "I just . . ."

"Don't say anything. I don't want to hear the sound of your voice. Just turn around and get the hell out of my sight."

Still wet in the moonlight, he knocked on Rosemary's door.

"I'm leaving, Rosemary. I've got to."

"Because of us?"

"No, but you'll hear about it."

"Johnny, I thought you loved me."

"I do."

"Then I'll wait."

"No. I've got a feeling I'm not coming back. I'm joining the 3rd Texas."

"Your father . . ."

"The hell with my father and Mason City."

"And with me?"

"No, Rosemary, never with you. I love you and I always will. I'm sorry for what happened. I'm sorry for a lot of things; I love you, but don't wait for me. I . . ." He touched her hair, her cheek, turned without finishing, mounted his horse, and rode east.

And now four years later, he was riding west, less than a mile from Mason City. Johnny Yuma hoped for a lot of things, among them that he would walk into the sheriff's office and just stand there and that his father would put his arms around his son and hold him close, even for a moment. Something that Ned Yuma had never done.

But his sorrel nickered, pulled up to a stop, and pawed the ground. Yuma climbed down, inspected the hoof. Loose shoe, couple of nails missing. Yuma tore off the shoe.

"Well, horse, looks like we walk the rest of the way. Not far. Just a good stretch of the legs—the two of mine and the four of yours."

Mason City raddled in an uneven pattern of tired buildings, wood and adobe, baking under the sun.

Yuma led the sorrel down the main street past the sign in front of the large store:

TOMPKINS SUPPLIES
GENERAL STORE—MINING EQUIPMENT

Farther down the quiet street, other signs, other establishments on both sides. A large circular wooden watering trough squatted in the middle of the street. An uneasy quiet prevailed as Johnny Yuma and the sorrel moved toward the tank. Two wagons loaded with families and possessions were leaving town. Several citizens on the boardwalk waved them a silent good-bye.

A half-dozen men who didn't look or act like the other citizens stood in front of Zecker's Saloon and Hotel, guns slung lower, faces dirtier, except for the obvious leader, bigger, cleaner, smoking a stogie as if surveying his own domain, Dow Pierce.

"Hey, Dow!"

The flat-faced man with flat black eyes, flat nose, wearing a flat-crowned hat with twin gun belts crossed over his waist, each with a pearl-handled Colt, looked up at Yuma, "Lookie there, some stray Reb come here to roost."

Yuma allowed the sorrel to drink its fill, took off his Rebel cap, and set it on the horn of the saddle, then plunged his head into the tank, once, twice.

"Hey, Dow,"—flat face grinned—"see that?"

"Yeah," Dow Pierce smiled and said, "that boy looks like he really needed that."

A small man walked out of the saloon batwings toward the big man.

"Mr. Pierce"—his voice and attitude overly solicitous—"my wife'll have some food for you all in a few minutes. She's . . ."

"Dow," flat face interrupted, "I think I need to have some fun with that Reb . . . Mind if I rawhide him some?"

"Sure, Bart, you go ahead, have some fun."

"Johnny!" the small man stared at the Rebel.

"You know him?"

"I do . . . Mr. Pierce, he's . . ."

"Later, Zecker. I want to watch Bart make his acquaintance."

Yuma dunked his head into the tank again as Bart hummed "Dixie" and approached leading his horse.

A stiff finger poked twice into the Rebel's ribs.

"Hey you, Reb . . . this here water's for horses, it ain't for no jackass." Bart laughed hard at his humor and turned toward the men in front of Zecker's saloon. They, too, were laughing, all but Zecker.

"I said I need to water my horse, Reb."

"Then you do that."

"Not with your face in it. I don't want him contaminated."

"Don't push."

"Push! Why, Reb, you ought to be used to being pushed." He shoved at Yuma's shoulder. "Why we pushed you clear from Gettysburg through Georgia . . . You been pushed real good."

"Yeah." Yuma did not flinch. "The war's over."

"So it is . . . but I'm not. I enjoy pushin' the likes of you." He shoved Yuma again. "I'm gonna push you . . ."

Yuma's left exploded into Bart's nose. A right smashed into his gut. Bart staggered, regained his balance, then charged toward Yuma, who spun him around and somersaulted him into the tank, drew his gun with the barrel an inch from Bart's dripping nose.

"Now, you don't push me no more . . . I'll blow your eyeballs out . . . both of 'em." Yuma holstered the Colt, picked up his cap, and led his limping horse away as townspeople murmured approval.

Bart managed to climb out of the tank and stagger toward the saloon.

"You had enough fun for one day?" Dow Pierce grinned.

"I tried to tell you, Mr. Pierce." Zecker was breathless—"That's Ned Yuma's boy."

"That a fact, Zecker? Why, that makes him your kin, don't it?"

"Not exactly, Mr. Pierce. He's my wife's nephew, not mine."

"Ned Yuma's boy, huh?" Pierce took a puff from his stogie. "Maybe the fun's just starting . . . all over again."

As Yuma approached the sheriff's office, a young boy, six or seven, ran up to him.

"I'm Clem Bevin's boy, Clay." He pointed to a large red barn, Bevins Stable and Livery—Blacksmith. "Pa sent me over to pick up your horse. Said he'd fix that shoe . . . you'd be needing that horse soon enough . . ." Clay took the reins and hurriedly led the sorrel toward the barn.

"Hey, wait . . ."

But the boy didn't.

Johnny Yuma opened the door of the sheriff's office—the place was sloppy, dirty; empty and broken whiskey bottles were strewn in pattern-less disarray—an unconscious figure wearing a deputy's badge was sprawled on a bunk. Yuma walked toward him.

"Hey . . ." The man stirred as Yuma prodded his shoulder. "Hey, come on . . . get up . . ."

"Lemme be . . . I ain't hurtin' nothin' . . . go on . . . Johnny!?! Uh, no!!"

"Jess . . . my pa out of town? He comes back and finds you like this you're gonna be in deep trouble . . . We got to get some coffee in you and . . ."

"Johnny . . . you shoulda come back sooner . . . you . . ."

"Say, what's the matter with you . . . What's hap-pened to this town . . . I never saw you drunk before." Yuma looked around; his eyes rested on a hanger on the wall with a hat, gun, and gun belt . . . a sheriff's badge pinned on it.

Yuma grabbed the deputy, who was nearly crying, a broken, humiliated relic.

"Now you're gonna tell me . . . Jess, where's my pa?!

The inscription on the tombstone in the church-yard read:

NED YUMA
1820–1867

Johnny Yuma wiped at the moisture in his eyes, turned toward the stooped figure of Deputy Jess Evans, and waited.

"A couple weeks ago, Johnny . . . they rode in . . . took over the mine . . . forced the owners to sell out cheap . . . Everybody just backed down . . . lot of family people moved away after they killed him." He pointed to the grave.

"Did they shoot him in the back?"

"They didn't have to . . . there was enough of 'em in front of him."

"Was he alone?"

Jess Evans took a breath and nodded.

"Why was he alone? Where was the rest of the town . . . all his friends . . . where were you . . . *Deputy?*"

"Where were *you*, Johnny? The war's been over more'n . . ."

"Has it? There's different kinds of wars . . . There's wars that go on inside." Yuma turned and started to walk away. "Well, I'm here now."

"Johnny, don't do anything crazy. You didn't come back all this way just to die."

Johnny Yuma stopped when he saw her standing by the church where they might have been married. Rosemary, her beautiful face a portrait of sadness. Beside her a young boy, a towhead with blue eyes, held her hand.

"Hello, Johnny." She did her best to smile.

He managed to nod, but not to speak. Not yet.

"Johnny, this is my boy, Jed . . . Jed Tompkins. Jed, this is Johnny Yuma, an old friend of your mother's. Say hello to Mr. Yuma."

"Hello, Mr. Yuma."

"Jed, you're a fine-looking young man. I'm sure your mom . . . and dad are proud of you."

"Thank you, sir."

"Now, Jed, you go over there with your uncle Jess while I talk to Johnny for just a little while."

Jess Evans came closer and led the boy away.

"Johnny, I waited for a letter."

"Not very long . . ."

"As long as I could . . . and Gary . . ."

"That jellyback . . . I did tell you not to wait, but . . ."

"I *couldn't* wait, Johnny, not after what happened in the cave. Our baby had to have a father. I was beginning to show . . ."

"Rosemary, I didn't know. If I'd have known . . ."

"What could you have done? Leave the 3rd . . . the war? Come home to be a husband and father? Could you? Gary knew. I told him, still he asked me to marry him. He's a good man . . . he's grown up since you left. His father's crippled and Gary's taken responsibility . . ."

"I wrote to Mr. Dodson. He's written back. Why didn't he tell me about you being married and . . ."

"I asked him not to. If you had written me I would have told you . . . and when the war was over, if you were still . . ."

"Still alive?"

"Yes, I knew that someday you'd come back . . . and see your son . . . and me."

"Well, I'm back and now there's something else I've got to do. Those men . . . my father . . . There's a lot of us going to die in this town. I'm going to try to be the last."

"Johnny, if you have any feeling left for me . . ."

"I'll say this just once, Rosemary. I love you, now and from this world into the next, but somebody once wrote, 'I could not love thee, dear, so much, loved I not honor more.' Now take the boy and go back to your husband."

"Don't you want to say good-bye to your son?"

"I already did."

"But not to me . . . not yet."

She put her arms around him and kissed him and he kissed her. At first soft and tender . . . and then it was the same kiss as in the cave. But this time they tore themselves apart.

Rosemary reached out and touched Johnny Yuma's cheek, then walked past him toward the deputy and her son . . . Johnny Yuma's son.

* * *

In Zecker's Saloon Dow Pierce and three of his men—Steve Miller, and the twin brothers, Tim and Tom—nobody knew their last name or cared—were playing poker. Slim, a lunger, who smiled and coughed a lot, was acting as bartender, and Bart, whose clothes hung from a makeshift line to dry, while in his underwear, was fanning the hammer of his unloaded gun.

"If the sun hadn't been in my eyes," Bart said, "he never woulda got that first one across. I'm gonna put six slugs right through his breastbone . . ."

"Is that before he gets your eyeballs?" Slim smiled.

"What?"

"Sure you will, Bart." Slim poured a couple shots of whiskey.

"I'm gonna kill him."

"Bart"—Pierce looked up from his hand—"you better wait till your britches dry."

"Yeah . . . well, I killed me plenty of them Rebs."

"From a distance," Pierce said. "But this one's up close."

"Yeah . . . well, I'm gettin' tired of waitin' for a lot of things"

"Is there anything you'd like to do about them other things?" Pierce looked back at his cards.

"Yeah . . . well, when are Lathe and Chet gettin' back with them Mexicans?"

"They'll be here. Then all we have to do is sit

back and stack all that gold they take out of that mine, but if you can't wait, maybe you'd like to start digging in that hole yourself."

"Yeah . . . Well . . ."

"Bart, you say 'yeah' like that one more time and I'm gonna crack your skull, now shut up . . . Raise five dollars."

Zecker minced out of the back room, followed by his wife, Emily.

"Beg pardon, Mr. Pierce . . . but we're about out of provisions . . ."

"So, get some more."

"Well, Mr. Pierce . . . it's the money. I'm all out. You promised me money, that you'd pay for all this. Well, I've spent all the cash I had . . . if you'd just . . ."

"I just raise again . . . You're credit's good at the store, put it on your bill."

"But you promised . . ."

"That's all, Zecker. Say, Mrs. Emily, you never even went to your brother's funeral. Now Bart here says he's gonna kill your nephew. I'm not of a mind to let him, but just in case he does, you gonna miss that funeral, too?"

Pierce's men all laughed as she walked away followed by Zecker.

Slim, who had walked to the batwings, whiskey glass in hand, glanced back at Pierce.

"Dow, it looks like ol' Dodson's taking your advice. He's over there loading his buckboard."

Elmer Dodson carried a stack of books and was

walking toward the buckboard on the street in front of the *Mason City Bulletin*. Dodson, a rope-thin man in his sixties, with stringy white hair spiked down across his narrow face, paused as Johnny Yuma approached from the direction of the church.

"Mr. Dodson . . ."

"Hello, John."

"You turning out like the rest of them?"

"I'm just a small businessman going out of business."

Dodson's attempt at an impersonal relationship didn't quite come off.

"You closing down the *Bulletin* on account of them?"

"That's correct. Oh, yes, I saw what you did to one . . . and as soon as they want to, my innocent lamb, they'll devour you like the ravishing jackals they are."

"If you leave, everybody else will."

"That's up to them. There's just the quick and the dead . . . and Dow Pierce in between. The jackals'll inherit the earth, at least this part of it . . . and they're welcome to it."

"How'd they do it, Mr. Dodson? Why haven't you sent for government troops?"

"We did. And we're still waiting. I guess they're too busy tending to the defeated Confederacy and the undefeated Indians . . . so the town's died and so did your father."

"You and Pa, Mr. Dodson, you were the two people I . . ."

"John, I loved your father like my own brother, but I'm not anxious to join him. I'm sorry, that sounds cruel and cowardly. I don't mean to be the former . . . I guess I can't deny being the latter."

"The things you wrote about, Mr. Dodson . . . that's mostly what set me off to reading and writing."

"Stay ignorant, John. Ignorance is the greatest comforter of all."

"I remember something you printed in your paper. 'For everybody there's a time to decide, and that's when the brave man chooses and the coward steps aside.'"

"That was a reprint, like most of my stuff. I finally realized that those kind of words were a shield to protect me from the fact that I've mostly led a meaningless, unproductive life, which ironically enough, I am now trying to save."

"It's funny. I thought of asking you for a job."

"John, I read those pages you wrote, the ones you sent. They were beautifully crude and expressive. You *could* be a writer."

"I wanted to say things the way you do, Mr. Dodson."

"I suppose after all my brave words I should be ashamed. But they've smashed my press and promised to smash my head. I don't want my head smashed, so I'm not staying. I looked at death and trembled. John, I'm sorry if those brave words confused you."

"Good-bye, Mr. Dodson." Yuma walked off.

Slim, from the batwings, was still watching.

"Hey, Bart. There's your Rebel friend now. I think he just come back from visitin' his daddy."

"I'm gonna get his nose." Bart bolted for the batwings.

"Bart!" Pierce commanded, "When I tell you and not before."

Bart stopped, disappointed.

"But . . ." Pierce smiled. "You can rile him up some in the meantime."

As Yuma walked, Bart's voice called out from the batwings.

"Hey, you, Yuma. You have a nice talk with your daddy?!"

Yuma's pace slowed. There was something about that voice coming from a distance.

"How'd he look to you, Reb? A little pale!? It's me, Bart Vogan! I'm gonna get you like I got those yellow-belly Confederates. Like I got your yellow-belly daddy!"

Hate. A wild, chaotic hate, for a man whose face he had never seen, the man who had killed Danny Reese during the war. The man who killed his father.

"Hey! You little cottontail . . . you better scat while you can . . ."

Yuma hesitated, then turned, and continued

walking as Bart Vogan's voice continued taunting, singing to the tune of "Dixie."

"Look at that cottontail get . . . Oh, I'm glad I'm not in the land of cotton, they lost the war and their bones are rottin'. Look away, look away, Johnny Reb."

From an upstairs window, Aunt Emmy and Ainsley Zecker were watching.

Ainsley Zecker had been pleading with the man in the wheelchair, Ben Tompkins, while Ben's son, Gary, Rosemary, and young Jed stood by.

". . . Ben, you've go to let me have them provisions . . . They've promised me a share of the mine . . . I'll have lots of money . . . I . . . we'll all make out . . . just till they give me the money . . ."

"Go to the bank."

"The bank's closed; you know that."

"Then talk to Gary. I signed the store over to him."

"Gary . . ."

"Save your breath, Mr. Zecker." Gary Tompkins was tall, thin, and pale. Not an imposing man for his height. "You picked your side from the start. We had a chance at the beginning if we'd backed the sheriff, but we didn't."

"Including you!"

"That's right, including me."

"Gary, you've got to do this . . . everything I've got left's at stake . . ."

"Zecker," Gary Tompkins said, "Just what have you got left?"

"You're a damn fool. You'll regret this."

Ainsley Zecker turned in a fury, stormed out, slamming the door.

"He's right, son," Brad Tompkins said. "You'll regret it. Maybe we all will."

"Maybe so. But I'm not helping Zecker. You all stay here. Rosemary, lock the door. I'm going out back."

"Where are you going?" Rosemary asked.

"I'm going to do my best to stop some killing."

"Please, Gary, be careful."

"I've always been careful."

Young Clay Bevins had delivered a note from his father to Johnny Yuma, who was in the sheriff's office with Jess Evans.

Johnny, your horse is shoed, rested, and fit to ride, tied up out back of the sheriff's office. For everybody's sake, including your own, get out of town before bullets start flying and more people die—including you. Sorry about your dad. He was a good man.

Good Luck,
Clem

There was a knock on the office door. Jess Evans opened it and Gary Tompkins stepped in and faced Johnny Yuma.

"Can I talk to you, Johnny?"

"Sure."

"I'll be back," Jess Evans said. "There's . . . there's something I got to do." He left.

"Aren't you taking a risk coming over here?"

"Not nearly as big a risk as you. Johnny, I know that Rosemary talked to you at the cemetery. She and the boy . . . She told me all about it."

"*All?*"

"All I need to know."

"All right. So I'm back now, and what are you going to do about it?"

"Ask you to leave."

"That figures."

"Not for the reason you think."

"Then suppose you go ahead and explain it."

"If you go up against them, they'll kill you."

"Then your troubles'll be over."

"Not if she watches you die. Then I'll have to live with your ghost for the rest of our lives . . ."

"There's not much I can do about that."

"Yes, you can. Leave now. Sooner or later, Pierce and his gang will take what they came for and go away. Then if you want to come back . . . we'll tell the boy about you and decide what happens next." Gary Tompkins looked away from Yuma and toward the floor.

"You know something, Gary? You're a hell of a man after all. But you forgot one thing. You forgot that those bastards killed my father . . . and some other people."

"Well, what are you going to do about it, and how are you going to do it?"

"I'm not sure yet. But there's a general named Custer who always says 'ride to the sound of the guns.'"

"Johnny . . ."

"Look, you tried. No matter what happens, I'll remember that and know you'll take care of Rosemary and the boy. Now go back to them. They need you."

It wasn't long after Gary Tompkins left and Jess Evans returned that Johnny Yuma had another visitor, his aunt Emily, whose attitude was kindly, almost motherly.

"Johnny! Johnny!" She went to him and kissed him as he stood rigid, tolerating it. "You've gotten to be a strapping young man. Why haven't you come by to see your aunt Emmy?"

"I thought my aunt Emmy was too busy catering to her brother's killers."

"Johnny, that's not fair. We're just tryin' to keep things goin' . . . tryin' to keep the town together. Somebody around here has to show some common sense."

"You trying to make sense with the ones who killed your own brother?"

Her attitude became less kindly.

"Just 'cause your father was a fool don't mean the rest of us don't have to go on livin'. He let himself be goaded into bein' shot dead. He was a fool, Johnny. What did he ever do for you?"

"Don't you talk that way about my father!"

Jess Evans spoke for the first time.

"And what about the other ones they killed, and what . . ."

Emily Zecker paid no attention to the deputy.

"Your father thought more about 'law' and 'duty' and 'honor' than he did about his own family . . ."

"And you never thought about anything but your own skins . . ."

"Why'd you run away a dozen times before you was fifteen? Why'd you go to war? To fight for a cause? You didn't know anythin' about any cause. It was just another kind of runnin' away. Well, why don't you *keep* on runnin'? All you can do around here is cause trouble for the rest of the town."

". . . You don't care about the rest of the town."

"I came here to help you . . ."

"You just care about you and your boot-licking husband."

"Oh . . . all you Yumas"—she moved toward the door—"you Yumas hold your nose when Zecker walks by, 'cause you can't stand the scent of good sense. Well, Zecker knows what he wants . . . He wants to take care of what's hisin'. He's smart. He's what a husband should be."

She slammed the door.

Zecker's face was roundly slapped by Dow Pierce. Ainsley Zecker could not stop trembling.

"You had no cause to do that, Mr. Pierce; it's that damn Tompkins kid. Like I told you, he's stubborn . . ."

"So am I. The sight of you makes me puke."

"Why do you talk like that, Mr. Pierce? I've been the only one to help you." Zecker reached into his backpocket. "I've got bills here . . ."

Dow Pierce's fist smashed into Zecker's face. Zecker fell into Bart Vogan's arms. Vogan spun him around, and laughing, exploded his fist into Zecker's rib cage, then pushed him again toward Pierce, who grabbed him.

"If them provisions ain't here in an hour, I'm coming after them and you." Pierce crashed his fist into Zecker's jaw, sending him careening through the batwings onto the boardwalk.

Johnny Yuma and Jess Evans watched from the sheriff's window, as Zecker landed on the street. Emmy ran toward him. A couple other onlookers came to assist. They steered him toward Tompkins' store.

* * *

"That's the way it is, Johnny," Deputy Jess Evans said. "You can't fight 'em and you can't do business with 'em."

"Well, I've got no notion of doing business with them."

"We're all of us changed, Johnny . . . mostly me. They shamed me. They called me down and I ran . . . right for a bottle. I got no right wearin' this badge. It's just got too heavy for me since they killed your pa."

Yuma had already started to take off the gun belt he had been wearing as he walked up to the belt, badge, and gun that hung on the wall peg. He placed his own gun and holster on the desk and strapped on his father's rig. His manner had changed from uncertain to calm determination. He unpinned the star that was on the belt, looked at it for a second, then put it on the desk.

"Jess, I'm getting awful sick of you whimpering and bellyaching." He walked toward the door. "And another thing, quit following me around like some puppy dog. You're supposed to be a man."

"John." It was the voice of Elmer Dodson. He stood just inside the open door of the *Bulletin*. He held an ancient pistol in his hand, hidden from the view of the street. "John," he repeated.

"What is it, Mr. Dodson? What're you doing with that gun?"

"I've been reading over my old editorials. It

may be that a man who listens to himself is twice a fool . . . but I'm staying . . . Maybe long enough to write my own obituary. But I can still pull a trigger, and I think I can fix that press."

"That's fine, Mr. Dodson, but there's more around here needs fixing than that press."

"What can we do, John?"

"You already did. Now please, just stay inside someplace, Mr. Dodson."

Johnny Yuma walked on and heard Bart Vogan's voice, who stood looking out of the saloon batwings.

"Hey, boys, lookee . . . here comes the soldier boy again . . . and he's got his daddy's gun on. He wants to die the way his daddy did."

There was no reaction from Yuma as he kept on walking and Vogan kept on taunting.

"You gonna be by your daddy's side, sonny. I'm gonna put you there, me, Bart Vogan. Remember that, Reb!"

Johnny Yuma walked past the sign—

TOMPKINS SUPPLIES
General Store—Mining Equipment

—and into the store.

Rosemary was cleaning Zecker's battered face while his wife held his hand. Brad Tompkins sat in his wheelchair while Gary stood behind the counter; Jed watched from a distance. The people who had brought Zecker in from the street waited in silence as Johnny Yuma approached Gary Tompkins.

"Gary, I'm going to ask you to do something. I need your help."

"You want me to get my rifle?"

Rosemary took a step forward before Yuma answered.

"No. I want you to give me the key to the room back there."

"Gary," his father cautioned, "you better wait and think this . . ."

"Dad, we've done too much waiting. This is my store, and for once in my life . . ." He reached out near the cash register for the key on a large brass ring, picked it up, and handed it to Yuma.

Johnny Yuma took it and walked toward the door. He unlocked it, went in, and closed the door behind him.

"What's he gonna do in there?" Emily Zecker asked.

Nobody answered. Nobody knew. But they all looked at the sign on the door of the room.

DANGER
DO NOT ENTER

Inside Zecker's saloon, Pierce, Vogan, Slim, Miller and the twins, Tim and Tom, were playing poker. Bart Vogan was seated next to Pierce.

"Dow, what you think that Reb's doin' in that store?"

"Don't know. Don't care. How much of that hour's left?"

"'Bout twenty minutes." Slim smiled.

"Then let's keep playing poker."

"Dow . . ." Vogan scratched his head. "What're you doin' . . . besides playing poker? I mean with that Reb?"

"Ever see a cat play with a mouse? Sometimes the mouse goes plumb crazy without the cat's ever really hurt'n him. You had your fun with him, now I'm having mine, just to pass the time 'til that work gang gets here. We're playing draw—jacks or better to open, deuces wild."

They all stared in fascination, fear, and awe as Johnny Yuma stepped through the doorway of the back room . . . his aunt Emmy, Zecker, Brad and Gary Tompkins, and everybody else in the room. Rosemary, with her hand on the young boy's shoulder, cried out.

"Johnny!"

But Yuma kept moving through the store and out the door into the street. He turned and walked toward the saloon. His right hand hovered near his father's gun. The Rebel's left hand held a home-made bomb with a lighted wick that hissed and steadily burned down toward the payload.

With each advancing step there was less of the wick left . . . less . . . and less.

The Rebel stopped in the middle of the street directly in front of the saloon. He looked down at the bomb with the flickering wick, switched the bomb into his right hand and screamed the Rebel yell as he hurled the missile over the batwings and onto the floor of the building.

The explosion rocked the building, blasted off the batwings, splintered the doorway, and shattered the windows into countless shards of jagged glass scattering onto the street.

Black smoke billowed; white and yellow flames flared up the wrecked structure as the charred men coughed and staggered out. Miller led the way, followed by Tim, then Pierce and Bart Vogan. Tom and Slim were dead, their bodies burned inside the ruins.

Miller managed to pull his gun out of its holster.

In a smooth hook and draw, Yuma's father's gun was leveled and the Rebel started to cock the hammer and he squeezed the trigger.

But the hammer stuck. He tried to fan it with his left palm. Still stuck.

As Miller fired, so did someone else. Deputy Jess Evans from beside a wagon on the street. Miller dropped, and his shot went wild.

"Johnny!" Evans hollered.

Yuma spun as Jess Evans stepped out and tossed him a sawed-off shotgun.

"Scattergun, Johnny!" Deputy Evans fired again.

Yuma dropped the Colt and caught the shotgun. He rolled onto the ground, cocking the hammers of the double-barreled scattergun.

Tim fired at Yuma but missed; Jess Evans didn't. Tim took the shot in his heart and dropped.

Dow Pierce shambled through the smoke and aimed, but Yuma squeezed off a blast that tore into Pierce and pitched him back through the broken window.

"Vogan! Bart Vogan!" Yuma yelled.

Vogan's answer from out of the smoke was two fast shots that winged past the Rebel.

At the sound of the gunfire, Yuma blasted off the other shotgun barrel through the smoke and haze.

Bart Vogan caught the load in his chest and face, lurched backward, and fell on the boardwalk twitching.

Yuma looked at Jess Evans and nodded. Still holding the scattergun, the Rebel moved closer to where Vogan lay.

He leaned down. Vogan was still breathing, barely.

"Vogan. Bart Vogan. Can you hear me?"

Vogan's eyes blinked.

"It's Yuma. Third Texas. Lee's Army of Northern Virginia. I was on that bridge near Appomattox. *Johnny Yuma. Remember it . . . in hell.*"

* * *

Through a Chinook wind, gentle and warm from the northwest, the morning sun caught the curvature of the thick, gleaming white tombstone between the two graves on the slanting green mantle of ground.

The inscription, recently carved, was chiseled deep—deep enough to be there through the end of the century and long beyond.

YUMA
෬

Elizabeth Yuma	Ned Yuma
1824–1850	1820–1868

Loving
Wife and Husband

Beloved
Mother and Father

Johnny Yuma knelt near the flowers he had placed at the base of the tombstone. A mother long dead, a mother he barely remembered. A father murdered just days ago, a father he should have known better. The sadness of a lone son kneeling near the graves of his mother and father.

A slender shadow appeared on the tombstone. The Rebel knew without looking.

"Johnny," Rosemary said. "Jed and I picked some wildflowers. Would it be all right if I put them next to yours?"

Yuma nodded.

She placed the flowers beside the ones already at the tombstone. Johnny rose.

In the distance, Gary Tompkins stood next to the boy near the church, close enough to watch but not to listen.

"Mr. Dodson said you were leaving this morning."

"In just a few minutes."

"Johnny, will you ever come back? Will you ever settle down?"

"Maybe I'll come back someday . . . and I suppose I'll settle down sometime, someplace . . . but not here. I couldn't do that, Rosemary . . . I couldn't look at you every day and not touch you or hold you . . . or him. I couldn't even try."

"I know."

"Do you, Rosemary? Do you?"

"I read in a poem, just a short time ago, 'of all sad words of tongue or pen, the saddest are these— it might have been.'"

"Not always. Things usually work out for the best. We've got to keep thinking that, both of us. Promise you will."

"I will, Johnny." She kissed him gently on the side of his face. "But I'll always remember."

"So will I, Rosemary."

They walked toward the church where Gary Tompkins and the boy waited.

"Jed." Rosemary tried hard to compose herself. "You say so long to . . . Mr. Yuma."

"So long, Mr. Yuma. Why do you have to go?"

"I just do, son." Yuma didn't mean to call him that, but it was too late.

"Why?" the boy repeated.

"Someday, you'll understand." He turned to Rosemary. "Mrs. Tompkins, you've got two good men here."

"Three," said Gary Tompkins and put out his hand.

Johnny Yuma and Gary Tompkins shook hands.

Johnny Yuma turned from Church Street onto Main Street, where Ainsley and Emily Zecker were waiting.

"Johnny . . ." Emily Zecker took a step toward him.

The way Yuma looked at both of them prevented her from finishing.

The Rebel moved toward the rail in front of the *Bulletin* where the sorrel was tied and where Elmer Dodson and Deputy Jess Evans waited. Evans held the scattergun in his left hand. Yuma loosened the reins from the post and turned to the two men and smiled.

"Johnny." The deputy held out the scattergun. "I know your pa would want you to have it."

Yuma nodded and took the gun.

"I thank you, Mr. Dodson, for everything."

"You sure you don't want to stay and . . ."

"No, sir. The things I got to find aren't here . . . not yet. This was just another stopping-off place."

"I know that. You can't just watch the parade, you've got to march in it. Keep writing, John."

"I intend to. And I'd like to send you what I put down from time to time. Maybe you can keep it and help me fix it up later."

"I'd like to do that, son. You've got a lot to see, and I think one day you'll have a lot to say. But you can't write about it unless you've lived it."

Johnny Yuma put his boot into the stirrup and swung onto the saddle.

"Where'll you go?" Evans asked.

"Here and there." Yuma looked down from the sorrel. "And Jess, I don't think that badge is a bit heavy for you."

As he started to ride out, Gary Tompkins, Jed, and Rosemary turned off Church Street. They waved when he went by. Rosemary took a step forward from the others.

Johnny Yuma didn't look back as he rode along the street—the street where he had ridden in just a short time ago—when he thought he had come home.

CHAPTER 55

The decade of the 1860s, a turbulent decade of secession and Civil War, of painful reconstruction, was fading. To the surprise of only a few, including Horatio Seymour, who ran against him, Ulysses Simpson Grant was overwhelmingly elected president of the United States in 1868 after the impeachment of Andrew Johnson.

The East and West were united by railroad at Promontory Point. Much of the land west of the hundredth meridian was surveyed and partially settled. States were added to the Union.

But as the decade of the 1870s flowed in, much, including the lives of U.S. Grant, George Custer, and Johnny Yuma, remained unsettled.

And as the pendulum of life's clock marked time, destiny's three brothers—Grant, Custer, Yuma—participated in or witnessed the century's most expansive era.

By sea and land the young nation underwent unprecedented flourish.

The whalers of Gloucester swarmed into the Atlantic and returned weighted with carcass cargo. Frigates flowed into what was once the Spanish Main and came back with the bounty of the Caribbean Islands. Schooners sailed south around the treacherous Horn loaded with settlers and goods destined for the California coast.

More and more Conestogas crossed the hundredth meridian fanning into the vast empire of the West, while being outpaced by the newly joined Union Pacific and Southern Pacific railroads.

And cattle drives—cattle drives—cattle drives. Out of a bankrupt Texas, hundreds of thousands of cows, bulls, and steers, worth a dollar a head south of the Red River, were being driven north by intrepid cattlemen blasting their way through border raiders, hostile Indian country, swollen streams, and then drought-drained terrain, into Missouri and Kansas, where eager buyers offered twenty dollars a head—on the hoof.

Outlaws: mostly ex-Confederates, who had ridden with the likes of Quantrill, Mosby, Stuart, and Nathan Bedford Forrest, Frank and Jesse James, the Daltons, the Youngers, and bands of others— turned brigands, bandits, and worse, hitting stage-coaches, banks, and even railroads—shooting, looting, and killing their way to ill-gotten gains, and—more often than not—violent death.

The Star Packers: Hickok, Henry Brown, Ben

Wheeler, Ben Thompson, Bat Masterson, the Texas and Arizona Rangers, who responded to bullets with more bullets that spat out Law and Order—but not all of the time.

And the red men: from the Apaches of the Southwest to the Horse Indians of the Plains and the Dakotas, who revolted against an unconquerable foe and inevitable defeat, but inflicted a terrible toll.

Through the early years of the dawning decade, Grant, Custer, and Yuma each played his part, each came closer to his destiny.

Grant, as president of the United States—the largest part of him—survived what might have been devastating crisis after crisis to a less honorable man—the Crédit Mobilier Scandal—the Salary Grab—the Whiskey Ring Frauds—the Dakota Land Grab. However, Grant withstood the intrigues of dozens of not-so-honorable men, men such as Fisk and Gould, who attempted to corner the nation's gold, control it, and capitalize on their scheme. But Grant beat them at their own game by flooding the country with gold stored up by the government.

He fought against the night-riding Ku Klux Klan, ordering troops in the South to break up bands of disguised night marauders. No one was a stronger advocate, or better friend, to the freed Negroes. Henry Ward Beecher proclaimed, "There has never been a president more sensitive to the wants of the people."

But there were those who opposed Grant's policies; among them was *New York Times* publisher

Horace Greeley, who ran against Grant in 1872 and lost in another landslide victory for U.S. Grant.

And while the indomitable Grant impassively suffered the slings and arrows of his attackers, there was one denigration he would not tolerate.

There were whispers not only denigrating President Grant, but even alluding to his beloved wife as "wall-eyed Julia." Grant overheard one of those whispers, leaped on the whisperer, inflicting on him the beating of his life, until a half-dozen Secret Service men managed to prevent Grant from doing further, maybe fatal, damage.

And Grant not only championed the plight of the black man, but also advocated fair treatment of the red man, in upholding the agreed-upon treaties with the Indians—unless the Indians turned hostile.

And that was part of the duty imposed upon George Armstrong Custer.

Unfortunately, too many of the Indians, lead by young, aggressive chiefs—Bloody Knife, Sitting Bull, Crazy Horse, Gall, Black Kettle, and others—did turn hostile—some with good reasons—some with reasons of their own.

And Custer, in his newfound glory, with the red-scarfed brigades under his command, soon became the most celebrated officer of the U.S. Army. Sensational, and sometimes exaggerated, accounts of his exploits were heralded in newspapers, magazines, and books across the country. And each time "the Custer Boy" would return to the welcoming arms of his Libbie at Fort Lincoln along the Missouri near Bismarck, North Dakota.

There were no two people more in love, with more fame, glory, harmony, and happiness than the Custers of the West, but they still lacked only what they coveted most—children.

The pendulum of life's clock was not as notable, nor as kind, to Johnny Yuma as it was to Ulysses Simpson Grant or George Armstrong Custer.

"Seek and ye shall find" the old adage pronounced. Johnny Yuma went on seeking, learning, and writing, but was still unfulfilled. He had sailed to the Sandwich Islands, unsuccessfully mined for gold in Virginia City where he met up again in a newspaper office with the fellow named Sam, who now wrote articles and short stories, currently working on a piece he called "The Celebrated Jumping Frog of Calaveras County" and had changed his name to Mark Twain. Twain read a dozen pages of Yuma's journal and encouraged him to "keep scribbling." One spring and summer Johnny Yuma scouted for General Crook, then blazed a trail from Texas to New Mexico with John Simpson Chisum's herd of longhorns, rode shotgun on Butterfield's stage, and served as railroad detective for Pinkerton. Adventures enough to fill hundreds of pages in his journal, which he sent back to Elmer Dodson, but not enough to fill the craving that dwelt within him. Yuma could not help remembering a lost love and a growing son—remembering with a heart flooded with emptiness.

And then fate, destiny, chance intervened.

He came across a cattle drive led by a man named Tom Riker—and that made an indelible difference.

CHAPTER 56

Johnny Yuma didn't know the destination of the drive when he met Tom Riker and it didn't make much difference at the time.

But it did.

Indian Territory. Johnny Yuma had crossed the Platte two days ago and for the two nights that followed he had made dry camp.

No sign of Indians, but to the trained eyes of a scout, signs of Indians. Pony That Flies had trained Johnny Yuma well. And Yuma had often thought of his Indian friend—as a young boy and into his early teens Johnny Yuma had spent countless hours with Pony That Flies, called that because he left no tracks, who had scouted for the Texas Rangers against the bloody Comanche when Ned Yuma wore a Ranger badge. How the two men became blood brothers, Johnny Yuma was never told, not by the Kiowa, not by his father. But a few days after

Johnny's mother died, Pony That Flies showed up, stayed until Ned's son was fourteen, then just disappeared again without a word of farewell—but not until he had taught Yuma how to track, how to scout. But the Indian had said that part of it was inborn in his pupil. Not everyone could be taught the rudiments of scouting. Not one in ten, or a hundred, or even a thousand. Not if the hunter's instinct was not there to begin with. That instinct seemed to be a part of Johnny Yuma's mind and body. His eyes were made for the unseen trail. But good eyes didn't necessarily make a good scout.

Pony That Flies had honed Johnny Yuma's natural abilities and perception. The Kiowa had taught his eager pupil to accumulate and evaluate what had happened, what was happening, and what to do about it with accuracy and alacrity.

The Rebel saw signs, some obvious—a cattle drive, not far ahead—some not as obvious, left by unshod ponies. A snapped branch. A feather, fallen from an Indian headband—more than enough to semaphore a signal to a scout schooled by Pony That Flies.

Yuma rode close to every rise, tree, and rock cluster that gave him cover. Still, he could make out the scattered tracks of at least a half-dozen beeves that had broken away from the herd—and tracks of shod ponies, two, maybe three drovers in the process of rounding them up.

Then the echoing reports of gunshots just over

the rise ahead and the faint reverberation of yells—not Rebel yells, but screams—red men on the attack.

Yuma spurred his horse and rode to the sounds of the gunfire and screams.

From the rise he saw six or seven beeves scurrying away from the melee, the sprawled body of a dead white man, another white man behind the skimpy shelter of a rock, and a handful of red riders firing at the white man, who fired back, but with little chance of survival.

Yuma charged ahead past the sprawled body on the ground with his gun spitting out three rapid shots. Two of the Indian attackers fell even before they and the three others saw him coming.

The three other attackers turned their ponies and their attention toward Yuma, who was swerving his mount from one direction to another.

From the rock came another shot, this one finding its target, the back of one of the attackers.

Yuma's next shot caught one of the two Indians in the throat, and the survivor, wearing a speckled green headband, looked back at the Rebel, raised his fist in defiance, and sped away.

It was over.

Yuma rode to the rock and dismounted as the drover rose, holstered his gun, smiled, and extended his hand.

"My name's Jim Carew. How do you do?!"

CHAPTER 57

". . . That's how it happened, Mr. Riker," Jim Carew summed it up. "If it weren't for this Reb"—Carew pointed at Yuma's cap—"I would've been a goner like Keeler, and we would've lost them beeves that strayed away last night."

"Much obliged, Mr. . . . . what'd you say your name was?"

"Yuma, Mr. Riker, Johnny Yuma."

Johnny Yuma looked around at the outfit. Drovers from the drive standing by, some drinking coffee from tin cups, others smoking cigarettes, pipes, and cigars, while finishing their noon meal. A freshly dug grave that held the body of Fred Keeler, which Yuma and Carew had brought back. And circling the makeshift camp—cattle—cattle—cattle.

Then the Rebel looked back at Tom Riker, a no-nonsense man in his early fifties, a creased face, square-built body, an air of authority.

"Where from, Yuma?"

"Here and there."

"Where mostly?"

"Texas."

"Me, too. I see you joined up,"—Riker pointed to the Rebel cap—"with the South."

"Yes, sir."

"Me, too . . . with the North."

"Uh, huh."

"You want to join up with us?"

A quizzical look came over Yuma's face.

"Mr. Riker, I . . ."

"We're mostly Texans and mostly broke. I gathered this herd, two thousand beeves not worth a plug nickel in Texas . . . Twenty dollars a head where we're heading. I've got a contract with the U.S. Army. Beef for troopers, for civilians, and for friendly Indians."

"Well, I . . ."

"Thirty dollars a month and found, a ten percent share split among the drovers . . . twenty of 'em . . . nineteen now . . . unless you join up."

"Where're you heading? If you make it?"

"We'll make it."

"There'll be more Indians along the way. It's called Indian Territory. This is their land."

"And this is my herd. We'll make it."

"To where?"

"North Dakota. Fort Abraham Lincoln."

"The 7th Cavalry?"

"The 7th Cavalry."

"Where do I sign?"

"You already have." Riker smiled.

Indian Territory, it was called.

Land set aside by the Federal government primarily for the so-called Five Civilized Tribes—Cherokee, Seminole, Creek, Choctaw, and Chickasaw. But during the Civil War the Five Civilized Tribes gambled on the side of the Confederacy, and since then the vast region had become a cauldron of chaos.

Tribes, justifiably not called civilized—Cheyenne, Arapaho, Comanche, Kiowa, and Apache—charged in and considered fair game everything they could kill, rob, rape, and exploit.

Much of the land was rich and fertile, suitable for farming. But these Indians were not farmers. Not like white people, who built houses and barns, raised cattle and crops.

These Indians were hunters who owned no land—who owned all the land and felt no compunction in taking from other tribes whatever they needed or wanted. They lived by precepts the whites did not grasp—nor did the Indians grasp the ways of the whites.

But one thing the Indians did grasp—that this territory belonged to them, by divine right and by treaty with the white government, and whoever crossed their territory could rightfully be considered invaders.

Besides the Indians there was another breed.

Comancheros, dirty men in a dirty business; called Comancheros because they did business with the Comanche and other tribes—providing guns, ammunition, whiskey, assorted provisions, and prisoners, often women—stolen and kidnapped— often from wagon trains moving west—or cattle drives moving north.

Comancheros. Scalawags, highbinders, back-shooters, outlaws from both sides of the Civil War.

Tom Riker's drive of more than 2,000 beeves, 2,222 by count when they started out, provided Johnny Yuma with ample material for his journal— vivid descriptions of the drovers, their hopes, and dreams, much of which depended on the success of this drive; descriptions of the land itself—some horizons flat and fertile; others, as the days and miles passed by, rugged, with towering snow-clad peaks where lone eagles flew, rivers gurgling with white water daring the cattle and wagons and drovers to cross, but cross they did—all but one drover who drowned in the crossing. All this and more.

And as the drive went on, Tom Riker realized that as good a drover as Johnny Yuma was, he was even more adept and valuable as a scout—reading tracks that spelled trouble ahead, where and when Johnny Yuma warned them of danger, and to take a longer, but safer, pathway.

But once, after a devastating storm that held

them back, Tom Riker made the mistake of not taking the Rebel's advice.

Or did he?

In his journal, the Rebel wrote a more modest version of what happened, but these were the events, places, and people.

"I just don't like the looks of it, Mr. Riker. I don't like the looks of it."

"You saw Indian signs?"

"Sort of . . . sort of sensed 'em. And mostly I don't like the geography."

"What?"

"If I were an Indian and wanted to hit a cattle drive, that's the place I'd do it."

"We've gone through narrower passes than that."

"This one starts out okay, but later on a couple miles, it funnels down into what could be a neat trap where just a few Indians on both ridges could . . . well . . ."

"What do you suggest, Yuma?"

"Go farther north. I could see the ridges start to decline. There must be another way through."

"Sure, and if there is one it could be a couple of weeks away, or more. We've already lost too much time with that last storm . . . and I haven't told the boys yet, but we get a fifty-cents-a-head bonus to split if we make it by the due date, and we've only got a slim chance as it is. I say we take 'em through."

"Whatever you say goes, Mr. Riker." Yuma turned

to Jim Carew. "You heard the boss, Jim. Let's start moving 'em through."

Just short of two miles in, at the narrowest point of the pass, Johnny Yuma slowed his horse.

"Mr. Riker . . ."

"I see 'em."

"There's more that you don't see."

"How many more?"

"Can't tell. Let me try something. Anybody got a white kerchief?"

"This one used to be white," Jim Carew said, and drew a kerchief from his back pocket.

Yuma took the kerchief, removed his scattergun from its boot, tied the kerchief to the tip of the barrel, then took off the eagle claw and thong from around his neck. He let the reins drop over the saddle horn, held out the white flagged shotgun in his right hand and the thong with the eagle claw out in the other, and began a slow advance into the narrow clearing ahead.

"He's got more guts than brains," Carew said.

"Let's hope not," Riker muttered.

"Well," Carew shrugged, "I could be wrong."

"You better be." Riker nodded.

Yuma stopped in the clearing, still holding out the scattergun and eagle claw, and waited what seemed like a long time—too long.

Finally, three mounted Indians appeared out of cover; the leader, in a multi-feathered headdress, carried the coup stick of a chief. A coup stick that was at least as old as the chief. All three, the chief and the other two, looked undernourished.

"Ya-ta-hey," Johnny Yuma said.

"I talk your language," the chief replied.

"Good. Then let's talk."

"We'll talk . . . at first." The chief, with his coup stick, pointed around at armed Indians on both sides of the ridges.

"My name's Johnny Yuma. Yours, Chief?"

"Red Bear, chief Blue Snake Lodge."

"Chief, I see you have two of your council with you. Can I bring two of our party? One is our chief."

Red Bear paused. He studied Yuma, the eagle claw in one of his hands, the Rebel cap on his head, the Confederate buckle on his belt.

"Why not? Better targets."

Yuma ignored the second part of what Red Bear said, and waved for Riker and Jim Carew to come ahead.

They did.

"Chief Red Bear, this is our chief, Mr. Riker."

Both men nodded. Then Yuma spoke.

"You are Cheyenne."

"Blue Snake Lodge . . . Cheyenne." Red Bear nodded again.

"You fought against the blue coats during the war."

Another nod.

"So did we." Yuma pointed to his Rebel cap.

"For different reasons."

"Maybe not so different. If we fight here many will die on both sides . . . for what?"

"For honor." Red Bear pointed to the herd of cattle. "And for food. Our lodge is hungry."

"There's food at the agency."

"Agency many days away. Lodge hungry now. Honor here now."

"Right. About honor first. Will Red Bear, Cheyenne, not honor the thong with the eagle claw?"

"Claw of the eagle," Red Bear said. "I saw."

"Given by Satanta, great chief of the Kiowa, blood brother of the Cheyenne . . . and my blood brother. And as for food . . ." Yuma looked at Tom Riker.

"Keep talking, Johnny."

"We will give Red Bear's lodge food for many days to get to the agency, nobody fights. Nobody dies. Mr. Riker, I'll give my share of the money coming from the cows we leave behind."

"Throw in my share," Jim Carew volunteered. "Weren't for Yuma I wouldn't be breathin'."

"That's not necessary, Jim . . . or Johnny. How many cows, Chief?"

Red Bear paused, looked at the two bone-lean Indians with him, then back at Riker.

"Twenty."

"No," Riker said, then added, "Thirty. Nobody fights. Nobody dies."

Red Bear held up the coup stick and nodded.

But a mounted brave sped out from a boulder,

rode up to the group, pointed to Johnny Yuma, and spoke to the chief in the language of the Cheyenne.

The brave wore a speckled green headband and his black eyes were burning with hate.

"He says you killed his brother." Red Bear looked at Yuma.

"He and his brother were trying to kill us."

"Moondog claims the Blood Rite," Red Bear said. "It is Cheyenne law, a fight to the death."

"I'll fight him." Yuma nodded.

"No, you won't." Riker shook his head.

"We've got no choice," Yuma said.

"*We*?"

"I've got no choice, Mr. Riker."

The narrow passageway became an arena. Moondog now looked considerably bigger than he had at a distance on horseback.

Yuma and Moondog were tied left wrist to left wrist by a leather thong six feet long. Red Bear threw a razor-sharp knife onto the ground twenty feet away. The two started a no-holds-barred run to get the knife and plunge it into the other's body.

The Rebel and Moondog ran toward the knife, Moondog a couple paces ahead, until Yuma braced himself and jerked back with all his strength against the thong and Moondog, who came to a stop abruptly.

Pony That Flies not only had taught Yuma the

ways of Indian tracking, but also the way of Indian fighting, including the Blood Rite. But Moondog was also well schooled. He looped the thong. It circled Yuma's neck. They both spilled to the ground, twisted over each other's body. Yuma's elbow exploded into the Indian's face, stunning him. The Rebel freed his neck from the encircling thong.

But the red man's right hand secured the knife and he lunged—Yuma sidestepped and hammered a fist into Moondog's jaw.

Yuma crashed into him. Both fell to the ground. The Rebel grabbed the knife hand with his left and smashed the Indian with the other. Still Moondog raised the knife and plunged it down.

Yuma moved just in time, and the knife was buried almost to the hilt in the ground near Yuma's ear. In the same instant, Yuma's right fist burst into Moondog's face, splattering bone and gristle, with blood spurting from his nose and mouth.

Yuma made a tight loop around Moondog's neck and pulled hard—his other hand gripped the knife handle and pulled it away from the earthen sheath, then brought the blade close to the Indian's throat—slowly the deadly blade came ever closer. The red man's eyes flashed with fear and frenzy. The veins in his neck swelled into thick, throbbing cords, as he struggled in vain to hold back Yuma's hand. The blade of the knife barely nicked Moondog's neck, drawing a dollop of blood. But suddenly Johnny Yuma's hand holding the knife moved in another direction, with one swift stroke, slashing the thong that bound his own wrist, freeing himself, and relieving the pressure from around Moondog's throat.

Yuma rose to his feet—knife still in hand—turned the handle toward Red Bear and extended it.

"Red Bear," he said, "we're still on the same side. You'll have food to feed your lodge."

Red Bear took the knife and nodded. "We go now."

The drive moved north, luckily avoiding an attack from Comancheros, who were otherwise occupied in pillaging and plundering other prey in other places.

Fair weather prevailed as the herd crossed into the South Dakota Territory, skirting the Black Hills near Rapid City and near the Aberdeen Reservation. Then into North Dakota Territory, across the Missouri, past Bismarck to within sight of Fort Abraham Lincoln.

That chapter in Johnny Yuma's journal was finished.

CHAPTER 58

"Johnny Yuma, you son of the Southern sod, I never expected to see you this far north!"

"Well, I expected to see you, General." Yuma smiled.

"Colonel." Custer thumbed toward a shoulder epaulet.

"Not for long, I'll wager."

The two men unashamedly hugged each other in front of the group.

"You knew I was here?"

"Everybody does. Everybody who reads about the exploits of the most-talked-about frontier . . ."

"That's enough of the malarkey. How you been, Johnny, m'chum?"

"Well," Tom Riker noted in surprise, "it's obvious you two know each other."

"Since Vicksburg, Appomattox . . . and other places," Custer said.

"But"—Riker pointed to the Rebel's cap—"on different sides."

"Sometimes." Custer smiled.

"I don't understand." Riker shrugged.

"We do. Don't we, Johnny?"

"Well, I'll tell you this," Riker added, "if it weren't for this young fellow, I don't know if you would've gotten those beeves. He signed on as a drover, but he's the best damn scout I ever saw . . . Reads tracks and thinks like an Indian . . . Why, he . . ."

"That's enough of that malarkey," Yuma interrupted with a smile. "We made it, and that's what counts."

"Right." Custer grinned and looked at Yuma. "And we've got another friend who's done even better, over in Washington, huh, Johnny?"

"Have you heard from him?" Yuma asked.

"He's mostly the reason why I'm here . . . and now, so are you . . . and we've got to talk about a lot of things."

They did have a lot to talk about—and as usual, Custer would do most of the talking. He was the first, and so far, the only commander of Fort Lincoln.

"But first, Johnny, I want you to meet some people and then show you around."

Yuma met Captain Adam Dawson, Lieutenant William W. Cooke—better known as Queen's Own—California Joe, who had lately suffered an arrow wound just above his left knee, and, of course, Libbie, who was her usual gracious self. And when Johnny Yuma met her, he couldn't help thinking of another girl, a girl named Rosemary, and "what might have been."

"And now, Johnny, I want to take you on a little bit of a tour of my 'home away from home,' at least for the foreseeable future. But before that, I want you to watch something on the parade grounds."

Johnny Yuma could already hear the martial strains of the fort band, trumpets blaring, drums beating, not just a song but a challenge as voices, first a chorus, then a company, a regiment, sang out to the accompaniment, not only of music but to the tempo of hoofbeats, voices, deep and triumphant.

> *"Let Bacchus' sons be not dismayed,*
> *But join with me each jovial blade,*
> *Come booze and sing and lend your aid,*
> *To help me with the chorus:*
> *Instead of spa we'll drink down ale*
> *And pay the reckoning on the nail,*
> *For debt no man shall go to jail;*
> *From Garryowen in glory."*

And then, framed by the morning sun, he saw them, the flower of Custer's 7th Cavalry, lead by Captain Adam Dawson and Queen's Own.

Line after line, under regimental guidons and the United States flag, horses and riders in perfect formation and harmony. Red scarves fluttering, sunlight glancing off brass buttons and yellow stripes, faces precise and powerful, disciplined and determined, veterans of Sheridan's Yankee brigades and JEB Stuart's Confederate Invincibles, now under the same flag in the same fighting force.

And as they began to pass by Colonel George Armstrong Custer and Johnny Yuma, Captain Adam Dawson gave the command; Custer took their salute and returned the compliment with pride in his eyes and bearing.

Another command from Captain Dawson.

"Forward at a gallop . . . ho!"

And as if in a single motion the 7th Cavalry took off, racing across the field.

"There they are, Johnny. I'd put my 7th up against the greatest horsemen in history, from Alexander's Companions, to Caesar's battalions, to the hordes of Genghis Kahn, or the British Lancers—anytime, anywhere. The best cavalrymen in the world!"

"You sure can be proud of them, and it's obvious they're proud of you, Colonel, but have you ever seen the Comanche ride? *They've* been called 'the greatest light cavalry in the world.' And then there's the Sioux and the Cheyenne . . ."

"I'd lead my 7th against any of them."

"Against *all* of them?"

"They're at peace, but no matter what happens, the regiment will live on. The 7th is already a legend."

"And so is its commander." Yuma smiled.

"I don't know about that, Johnny."

"A lot of people do."

"But there's a lot more to be done. Come on, I'll show you around."

Custer escorted Yuma, pointing out some of the nearly eighty wooden structures, the post office, telegraph office, seven officers' quarters, scouts' quarters, cavalry stables, quartermaster storehouse, guardhouse, bakery, granary, and hospital.

"We haul in our water supply from the rollin' river Missouri, while beef, as you know, is supplied by contract with men like Tom Riker."

"Yes, I know. After he paid us, Mr. Riker asked me to come up with him on his next drive."

"And are you?"

"Don't think so, Autie. Had enough of trailing herd, at least for a while."

"And what haven't you had enough of, as yet?"

"That I don't know."

"Well, I got an idea about that." Custer smiled. "We'll talk about it in more comfortable surroundings. Come over to the house for supper tonight."

The Custer house was comfortable, one of the most comfortable and pleasant dwellings of the string of dwellings on the Western frontier forts—and the presence of Libbie Custer made it even more pleasant. She was the perfect chatelaine, vivacious, informal, yet dignified and charming.

After the best meal Johnny Yuma had had since he could remember, the three of them, Libbie, Autie, and Yuma, repaired to the parlor for coffee and dessert.

"Johnny"—Libbie smiled—"George has told me so much about you. He considers you one of his best friends, and I hope you and I will also be the best of friends."

"That won't be hard, ma'am, and he's a lucky man."

"Well, we've both been lucky," she said. "We've got everything we've always hoped for so far." Libbie looked at her husband. "Of course, it would be more than nice someday to have one or two other little Auties just like him running around."

"What about you, Johnny?" Custer changed the conversation. "You still want to be a writer? Still keeping that journal?"

"Well, as someone I met once suggested"—Yuma smiled—"I'm still scribbling."

"And," Libbie said, "hasn't a good-looking young fella like you met someone—someone to . . ."

"Like I said, ma'am, your husband's a lucky man, but I . . ."

"Hell, Johnny, just because you get married doesn't mean you'll just sit and vegetate. Look at Libbie and me; we've got plenty of action—besides, some of the best writers in the world are married."

"Yeah, but I'm not one of the best writers, not nearly."

"A good woman might help you along the way, like Libbie has helped . . ."

"I think"—Libbie rose—"you two gentlemen have enough to catch up on without female interruption." She leaned over and kissed her husband. "See you later, George . . . and Johnny, I hope to see you a lot more."

"Yes, ma'am." Johnny rose. "And so do I, while I'm here."

"That's what I want to talk to you about, Johnny," Custer said after Libbie left. "About you staying here."

"To do what?"

"Well, ol' California Joe is out of commission for a while with that bum leg, can't ride. Riker said you're a good scout. The 7th can use you, and so can I."

"I didn't come up here to fight Indians." He touched the eagle claw on the thong around his neck. "I'm a blood brother to some of them."

"You wouldn't just be fighting them, except for the hostiles. We're here to do what we can to help keep the peace, what there is of it. To enforce the treaties on both sides.

"Look, Johnny, I'm a soldier, but you're not, and don't have to be. Every soldier has to carry out every order handed down to him or the army would end up in chaos and defeat. There are some orders I don't necessarily approve of—and there are some things I do that they don't approve of. But a direct order I carry out directly," Custer smiled an enigmatic smile, ". . . in my own way."

"Like at Gettysburg?"

Custer shrugged, still smiling.

"Besides." Custer was saving something for last. "You want to write. Up here you'll have plenty to write about that you couldn't write about anyplace else. Think about that, my bucko."

CHAPTER 59

"Bucko." Johnny Yuma did think about that.

But first he thought about his friend George Custer with his wife, Libbie, and how, ironically, they had everything they ever hoped for—except children. And how he himself did not have a wife, but did have a son . . . a son who did not know him as a father.

Then he thought about Custer's words. "You want to write. Up here you'll have plenty to write about that you could never write about anyplace else . . ."

He had witnessed other historic events, some of which he could never write about—what happened to Grant, Custer, and him at Vicksburg and Appomattox—but this was an opportunity to witness, and even participate in, the making of history on the Western frontier with the legendary

7th and his friend, the commander Colonel George Armstrong Custer.

And then there were the words of Elmer Dodson, "You can't write about it, unless you've lived it."

The choice was uncontestable, at least for the time being.

Yuma did have plenty to write about. He didn't wear a uniform, but a red scarf circled his neck as he rode with, and ahead of, Custer, Dawson, Queen's Own, along with the other white and Indian scouts of the 7th Cavalry—at Fort Wallace, where Custer corrected "the gross neglect and mismanagement" of the Commissary Department, "which subjected officers, men, and the Indians to needless privations"—following Indian trails and attacking hostiles who held white women captive—the cholera epidemic at Fort Harker, where the 7th delivered, after a blistering forced march, lifesaving drugs that quelled the sickness—at Big Creek, repelling an Indian uprising against a railroad construction crew and providing ambulances to carry the wounded to hospitals—maintaining the treaties through meetings with the leaders of the larger, more powerful tribes.

One meeting in particular which Yuma attended with Custer and Dawson, a meeting that included Sitting Bull and Crazy Horse. Yuma listened and later wrote about in his journal—words of caution and warning to Custer.

Although Custer did not ordinarily smoke, he made an exception when he parleyed with the important tribal chiefs who considered pipe smoking "Big Medicine."

"Yellow Hair," Sitting Bull said to Custer, "you have been true and fair with our tribes. But if the Black Hills Treaty is violated by the whites, no number of soldiers, not even led by you, can stop what will happen. A remembered fight to the death—many deaths because of the land which is ours by treaty and since the beginning of time. Yellow Hair, do not be there."

"I give you my word; I will abide by the treaty," Custer said.

"We know that is true," Crazy Horse added. "If not for you I might still be in white man's prison, or dead. I will always remember and be grateful. But the Black Hills have a bigger meaning to us than you, or any white man, can understand."

"I know that." Custer nodded.

"But do those who are in command of you?" Crazy Horse asked.

Custer could not answer truthfully.

Johnny Yuma was more than satisfied with his stay with Custer and the 7th Cavalry.

Then came the massacre—and Washita.

CHAPTER 60

"Give me eighty men and I'll ride through the whole Sioux Nation," Captain William Fetterman had boasted.

Some Sioux Indians, including a young war chief named Red Cloud, thought otherwise.

Captain William Fetterman, an ex–Civil War officer, who harbored a deep disdain for Indians, had previously ignored the letter and spirit of tribal treaties, now came too close, much too close, to the Black Hills and made the last mistake of his career and life.

Fetterman was lured out of the safety of Fort Kearny when Red Cloud feigned a decoy attack on a wood train. He rode out with seventy-nine other troopers to repel the attackers, who promptly retreated. When Fetterman gave chase the trap was sprung by Red Cloud and two thousand warriors.

The soldiers bravely, but futilely, fought to the last man—the last two men—against the onrushing warriors.

Fetterman and another survivor, Captain Fred Brown—rather than be captured and tortured—pointed their pistols directly at each other's head and simultaneously fired point-blank.

MASSACRE! MASSACRE!—CAPTAIN FETTERMAN, ALL HIS TROOPS ANNIHILATED—FETTERMAN AMBUSHED!—SAVAGES ATTACK, MASSACRE U.S. ARMY!—OUTRAGE, DEMAND VENGEANCE!

The newspapers trumpeted and unashamedly exaggerated—utilizing every known epithet to describe the Indian attackers, and at the same time gave verbal ammunition to those who needed no excuse to pursue expansion of the Western Territory and crush tribal resistance.

The United States Army and its reputation—its honor—were questioned and challenged.

Two U.S. Army officers responded to the challenge. General William Tecumseh Sherman and General Philip H. Sheridan.

Sherman wrote to President U.S. Grant—

No better time could possibly be chosen than the present for destroying or humbling those bands that have outrageously violated their treaties . . . I will

*urge General Sheridan to push his measures for
the utter destruction and subjugation of all those
outside the reservation in a hostile attitude, until
they are obliterated or beg for mercy.*

Sheridan concurred—

*The more we can kill this year, the less we'll have to
kill next year . . . Their attempts at civilization are
simply ridiculous. We have tried kindness, until it
is construed as weakness. Now we must deal with
them on their own terms.*

Custer's attitude toward Indians was quite
different—he thought it was stupid and fool-
hardy of Fetterman to taunt them and then be
caught in a feather-headed ambush. But Custer
was a soldier first, and his first duty was to carry
out orders.

Privately, both Sherman and Sheridan thought
that Grant, their former general, had gone somewhat soft. His Civil War strategy was to kill the
enemy and destroy their ability to fight back by
destroying their provisions and possessions. Up
to now he had given no such order against what
Sherman and Sheridan considered the present,
more savage enemy.

Privately, Grant believed that the Indian cause
was far more justified than the Confederate, but
concluded that the West must be made safe. He

couched his command to his two Western generals by instructing "Do what you have to, to protect our citizens from further attacks."

That's all that Sherman and Sheridan needed . . . that, and Custer.

CHAPTER 61

"Autie," General Sheridan said, "the reputation and honor of the U.S. Army is at stake. We've got to hit 'em back and hit 'em hard. Hit 'em where they least expect. Where and when they think it can't be done."

Chief Black Kettle, who had been defeated at Sand Creek, could not hold back his young warriors. They had robbed, raped, captured, murdered, and mutilated with repeated regularity all summer and fall, and now had repaired to their winter camp along the Washita, secure in the knowledge that the army could not conduct a winter campaign against them in such adverse fighting conditions.

"That's where you come in, Autie," Sheridan continued. "Where and when it can't be done. You and the 7th. You've got to show those red devils what the U.S. Army *can* do—and show 'em in a way they won't forget."

Custer had sat silent, just listening.

"Is this with the full knowledge of General . . . of President Grant?"

"President Grant has left it up to us, Sherman and me. Autie, you've seen what these red devils have done, beyond our imagination, if we hadn't seen it. It must stop, Autie. It must stop! And the next step to stopping it is up to you."

Sheridan removed a sheath of papers from a briefcase.

"Your assignment. Signed by me and approved by Sherman." Sheridan reached out his right hand.

"Good luck."

Custer grasped it.

"Thanks, Phil . . . and Merry Christmas."

"Libbie, I've got to carry out an order. One way or another you'll hear about it. I can't tell you now, but . . ."

"I don't want to hear or know about anything . . . but this, 'Custer Boy.'"

She fell into his arms and kissed him tenderly.

Colonel George Armstrong Custer in command of the 7th, with Captain Adam Dawson, Queen's Own at his side, and with the scouts including Johnny Yuma and California Joe, blasted through snowbound flats, bounded over frozen banks and treacherous gullies toward the lodges of Black Kettle's band.

The men of the 7th looked down at the snow-blanketed compound.

"Well," Custer said to the scouts, "you got us here when they said it couldn't be done. Now it's up to us."

"They don't have much of a chance." Yuma pointed below.

"No, they don't. Not much of a chance to do to the 7th what they did all summer and fall."

Suddenly against the frigid dawn, a wall of gold fire ascended, then hung fire . . . the brightest and most beautiful of morning stars.

Custer had been tabbed with numerous nicknames including—"Boy General," "Curly," "Cinnamon," and "Yellow Hair."

This morning, and after Washita, he was titled yet another byname . . . "Son of Morning Star."

"Charge!" Custer roared.

With startling savagery, guns erupted and cavalry blades slashed red. Custer leading the 7th Cavalry, scarlet scarves crusted with white snow, would let no one get ahead of him in the charge. Half-awake Indians, men and women, streamed out of their shelters, to be torn by bullets and blades, trampled by icy iron hooves. Washita became a human abattoir.

The sound and smell of slaughter, of screams and curses, coursed across bloody blotches of snow catching twisting bodies as they fell and shivered and died.

Johnny Yuma, in spite of the obscuring snow, smoke, and din, did his utmost to avoid targeting women and children. Most of the troopers, who had lost family members or other loved ones to Indian raids, had no such compunction. The troopers fired at anything mortal not wearing a blue uniform or a red scarf.

The troopers had never seen and done anything like it. And, like it or not, they did it. The killing included anything that moved, warriors, women, children, horses, and mules . . . until no warrior was left standing and Custer gave the order to cease firing and spared hundreds of women and children who had clustered against a southern slope.

Inside what was left of the lodges the troopers found albums, letters, and remnants of Bibles, evidence of Indian raids on homesteads.

Black Kettle was dead along with the young braves who would fight no more . . . forever.

Mawissa, Black Kettle's sister, offered Custer the hand of Princess Meyotai, a young Indian girl, in marriage as a token of peace. Custer respectfully declined.

But Autie gratefully received and accepted the letter sent to him by his commander, General Philip H. Sheridan.

The Battle of Washita River is the most complete and successful of all our battles, and was fought in such unfavorable weather and circumstances as to reflect the highest credit on your self and regiment.

"Was she beautiful?" Libbie later asked her husband.

"Was who beautiful?"

"The Indian princess who was offered to you?"

"Yes, she was." Custer smiled. "So beautiful . . . that I couldn't wait to get back to you, Custer Girl."

Chapter 62

But the devastation at Washita had destroyed something more, not in Custer, but in Johnny Yuma.

Yuma no longer had the stomach, nor conscience, for killing, not even of savage Indians. He had seen and done enough. Too much. He had made up his mind that Washita was his last campaign with Autie.

And just as compelling, maybe even more so, Yuma had received a telegraph from Elmer Dodson, to whom he had been sending pages of his journal.

Johnny Yuma told Custer he was leaving. Autie didn't want to believe it.

"It's not over yet, Johnny."

"It is for me."

"Listen, Johnny, someday the white man and red man can live in peace like the North and South. But now I'm convinced we've got to defeat them first, like we did you Rebs. They're the enemy now, like the Confederates were, and you know some of those Rebs were my close friends at the Point and after, like you and me. We fought for the Union and against slavery. Some of the Indian ways are worse, much worse than the South. They've got slaves, too. They buy, sell, trade, and steal women and children like horses. They've got to understand that all that has to change. But believe me, Johnny, I know my Indians. They talk peace, Sitting Bull, Crazy Horse, and the rest. But as Patrick Henry said, 'There is no peace.'"

"I realize that."

"The railroads are coming through. The Indians don't like that. More of their territory will have to be given up. I'm afraid of what will happen. Already there're rumors of gold in the Black Hills. The Indians won't like that either—but some whites are already licking their chops and sharpening pickaxes. Mark my words; they'll all unite. Sioux, Cheyenne, Kiowa, Arapaho, all the rest, all riding together for one last battle, and I'll be there."

"I know you will, Autie."

"And after that who knows where that last battle will lead to? After that, maybe I can quit soldiering."

"And do what?"

Custer just shrugged.

"You thinking of running for president after Grant?"

"Might be something." Custer smiled. "Other soldiers did. Washington, Jackson, Harrison, and our friend."

"I'll vote for you, Autie." Yuma smiled. "But . . ."

"Please, Johnny." Libbie had been listening and

spoke for the first time as she held Custer's hand. "You've brought George even more luck and . . ."

"It's all right, dear," Custer said and pointed to the red scarf around Yuma's neck. "As long as Johnny has that red scarf I'll be looking for him to come back."

"I don't think so," Yuma said and he handed Custer the telegraph from Dodson.

Both Custer and Libbie read it.

JOHNNY COME HOME——ROSEMARY NEEDS YOU.
SO DOES JED.
DODSON

"Rosemary," Libbie said, "is that the girl . . ." Libbie didn't finish.

Yuma just nodded.

"Who's Jed?" Custer asked.

"He's . . . my son," Johnny said.

CHAPTER 63

Johnny Yuma started on the long way home.

And so did Custer. But not because he wanted to.

Later there were various versions of what had happened, but few ever knew what actually happened.

One of those few was Elizabeth Bacon Custer. Before, during, and after their married life, Libbie kept a diary. Unfortunately, portions of that diary were destroyed by fire, but certain sections regarding what happened, had been preserved, and are herein quoted.

> *The winter was particularly severe. Many were afflicted, bed-ridden and worse . . .*

> *Doctors were in short supply and overworked . . .*

> *My dear friend Mary Springton was very ill at Fort Riley. The doctor had diagnosed pneumonia, compounded by fever.*

Mary had been my bridesmaid back in Monroe. And before that, a childhood friend, as close as a sister which I never had.

In spite of my husband's trepidation, I rode in an ambulance to do what I could to help . . . in spite of his trepidation—and our little secret.

My presence was of great comfort to Mary. I was at her bedside nearly day and night as the doctor had numerous other patients who desperately needed his attention.

As Mary's condition improved, my own weakened. I became fatigued, suffered dizziness and fever .

Of course, when the doctor arrived he became duly alarmed, ordered me to bed and did what he could to alleviate the malaise.

Doctor Morton was further alarmed when during my delirium I spoke of our little secret, *my pregnancy, and called out my husband's name, time and again.*

He sent word by telegraph to Colonel Custer telling him that I had fallen ill and repeatedly spoke of him during the delirium.

George had been ordered to Fort Hays for an important meeting and was preparing to depart when he received the message.

(Note: this part of the diary was indistinct due to fire. The account resumes on another page.)

In defiance of the order, my beloved husband made a mad dash to join me miles away at Fort Riley.

During my trauma, it seemed to me I heard his voice and felt his presence. Somehow I sensed that he was near.

When I regained consciousness he was there holding my hand as he had been for a long time, without rest, without sleep.

As I looked up, he smiled and kissed me. I felt his strength, his love.

"You're back, Libbie. You're back and I'm here with you."

"George, I'm sorry. We lost our son. The doctor says I can't have another baby."

He smiled, kissed me again, and said, "It doesn't matter, Libbie, nothing matters—as long as we've got each other."

Chapter 64

But it did matter.

There were those officers, jealous of Custer's "glory-grabbing," of that "dandified young buck"—who wanted to get rid of him and this was their opportunity. Charges were brought against Lieutenant Colonel George Armstrong Custer by Major General Hancock, Colonel Andrew Smith, and Captain Robert West for abandoning his post—and pending court-martial proceedings, he was penalized a year's pay.

Yesterday's hero is today's target.

Custer was required to leave the 7th, return to Monroe, and await his court-martial.

No one was more pleased than the recalcitrant Indians who had fought against him. The longer Custer was away, the better.

It was only through General H. Sheridan's intervention that Custer's army career was suspended, not ended. Sheridan had no choice but to allow the court-martial to proceed.

But Custer was determined that no matter what would come out of the court-martial, the fact of Libbie's pregnancy and the loss of their baby would not be revealed.

That was a private matter, and Custer intended to keep it private.

CHAPTER 65

"What's this about Custer and a court-martial?" President Ulysses Simpson Grant asked as he lit another cigar.

The toll of the presidency had left its mark on Grant. The lean, young body of boyhood, of the lad who had grown up in the health-giving air of the great outdoors, had gained weight, the sun-burnished face of youth had given way to a pale countenance. But the will and inner strength of the great Union general was still evident.

"He's unruly," Secretary of State Hamilton Fish responded.

"Is that so?"

"He's unruly," Fish continued, "uncooperative, and unpredictable."

"Is that right?"

"Custer's broken more rules . . ."

"And won more battles."

"Mr. President, he . . ."

"Reminds me of me."

"But . . ."

"But do you know how many times I was almost relieved of command? Do you know what it is for a soldier, a man of war, to be deprived of that command? If it weren't for President Lincoln, I . . ."

"With all due respect, Mr. President, we have more urgent matters . . ."

"Not to Custer." Grant drew smoke from his cigar.

"Mr. President . . ."

"All right. All right for now, what urgent matters are on the docket?"

"First of all, the Cuban situation. We received a coded communiqué from our ambassador in Spain that . . ."

CHAPTER 66

George Armstrong Custer had once again become a commander without a command.

As he and Libbie left Fort Lincoln in a carriage the band played "Garryowen."

Captain Adam Dawson, Queen's Own, and many of the troops stood at attention with unashamed moist eyes and saluted.

"You'll be back, Autie," Dawson had said to him. "This is the army's biggest mistake since the war ended. If you go to trial . . ."

"Not *if*." Autie smiled.

"We'll be there. A lot of us, to speak in your behalf."

"You can be certain of that," Queen's Own added. "If they bust you, they'll have to bust a lot more of us."

"Thanks, my friends, but we all may have gray hair by the time they get around to a trial."

"We may have *no* hair, dear boy," Queen's Own

added. "I can almost hear those war drums starting to beat."

"Adam. Queen's Own. Take care of the 7th."

Back in Monroe, the commander without a command, the warrior without a war, dedicated most of his time to doing everything he could to assist in Libbie's recovery after her ordeal at Fort Hays and the long journey home.

But she was more concerned about his "recovery."

CHAPTER 67

It was at first light when Julia opened the door that adjoined their bedroom to Grant's private study.

A lit cigar in one hand and a pen in the other, he looked up from his desk and managed a smile.

"Good morning, Julia."

"Ulys, you've been up since the middle of the night. What in heaven's name are you doing?"

"Remembering." Grant drew from the cigar in one hand and held up the pen with the other. "And writing a couple of letters."

"May I ask to whom? Or is that a state secret?"

"No, Julia, letters to a couple of soldiers."

"Generals Sherman and Sheridan?"

"No. Two other soldiers. If it weren't for them, it all might have ended . . . at Vicksburg."

CHAPTER 68

From Fort Abraham Lincoln it was a long land voyage; first on horseback, then railroad, stage-coach and in San Angelo Johnny Yuma bought a deep-chested buckskin and saddle.

He still wore the eagle claw, the Rebel cap and Confederate belt buckle; the red scarf of the 7th was folded into his saddlebag.

He had telegraphed Elmer Dodson at the *Bulletin* that he would be back to Mason City on Wednesday night so that no one would know he had come back.

As Yuma rode in through the dark night he noticed that the building that housed Tompkins Supply Store had been badly damaged and boarded up. He could make out a sign.

CLOSED UNTIL
FURTHER NOTICE

"I wanted to hear it from you first, Mr. Dodson. What's happened?"

Dodson was somewhat grayer, a mite more wrinkled and bent, but his mind and wit were as keen as ever.

"Have some coffee with some bracer in it, John. I'll make it short, but not sweet. It started with a skunk named Jim Gettings and his gang. I think Gettings is wanted in a couple territories but not around here—not yet. Gary had supplied the mine with a big shipment of dynamite and other necessities. The owner, Sam Cooper, came into town with a bunch of his men and paid off Gary just before dark. Ten thousand dollars."

"Ten!"

"I said it was a big shipment. Anyhow, Gettings had evidently staked out the whole setup. Gary put the money into that big safe of his at the store—until the bank opened in the morning—and went home.

"Deep into the night Gettings and some of his men broke in with some of their own dynamite, which they evidently didn't know enough about, set the fuse, and ducked. The dynamite blew half the place apart, but not the safe. Also woke up half the town. Gettings had no more chance at the safe. They started to vamoose.

"Gary Tompkins got there first with his rifle and Jess Evans wasn't far behind. Guns went off on both sides. One of Gettings' men got wounded, but they made it to their saddles while firing back. That's when Gary got it."

"Got it?"

"John, Gary Tompkins is dead."

"Dead," Yuma barely muttered.

"Just before he died, Jess heard him whisper 'Gettings.' Gary was the only one close enough to identify him. It was too damn dark, and that won't stand up in any court. Gettings has an alibi. They were all at a cathouse miles away. Some alibi, but it'll hold up."

"You mean he's still here? Gettings."

"He's an arrogant bastard. For all I know he's still got designs on that ten thousand and more that's in the bank."

"Did you tell Rosemary that you telegraphed me?"

"No, John. I didn't know how you wanted to handle that—when and if, you ever got here. It's a far piece from the Dakotas to here."

"From hell to sunrise wouldn't be too far."

"I knew that, John. What're you going to do?"

"First, I'm going to see Rosemary."

She fell into his arms and sobbed.

"Oh, Johnny . . ."

"Rosemary, no matter how much I love you . . . I wouldn't want it to be like this."

"He was a good man, Johnny, he . . ."

"Don't say anything more, Rosemary, not now. Have you told Jed . . . about us?"

"No, he still thinks Gary . . ."

"Keep it that way. But I would like to say hello."
Yuma looked toward Sheriff Jess Evans, who stood
by Jed not too far away.

She nodded, looked toward the two of them, and
motioned.

"Jed, this is Mr. Yuma," Rosemary said. "Do you
remember him?"

The young boy hesitated, and tried to smile.

"Hello, Mr. Yuma. I remember."

"So do I, Jed. So do I."

Yuma and Jess Evans walked down the street past
the boarded-up building of Tompkins Supply Store.

"What're you gonna do, Johnny?"

"I'm going to ask Mr. Dodson a question."

I ACCUSE!

The banner of the special edition of the *Bulletin*
blared, and in bold type the rest followed on the
only page—

**JIM GETTINGS, I, JOHNNY YUMA, ACCUSE
YOU AND YOUR GANG**
**Of the Attempted Robbery and the Events
That Followed,
Including the Murder of Gary Tompkins.**

THERE IS IN THE OFFICE OF THE *Bulletin*

A

$5,000 REWARD

FOR YOUR

ARREST AND CONVICTION.

WE NOW HAVE EVIDENCE

OF YOUR

GUILT.

MORE TO FOLLOW IN THE NEXT SPECIAL EDITION

OF THE

Bulletin

Hundreds of copies were posted and distributed in and around Mason City and vicinity—including a certain cathouse.

"Very good, John. I couldn't have written it better myself," Dodson said. "That ought to get his attention."

It did . . . and Jim Gettings had an answer.

"There isn't gonna be any next edition of the *Bulletin*."

Once again Gettings and his men waited until it was dark and quiet in Mason City. There was only a solitary lamp lit in the *Bulletin* office outlining the solitary figure of Johnny Yuma as he moved across the shadowy room.

From the street hoofbeats, then gunshots as the riders thundered into town toward the office. Glass shattered and wood splintered.

But Gettings had not reckoned on Yuma and on Sheriff Jess Evans, who was hidden behind the press. And most of all he hadn't reckoned on a dozen citizens, friends of Gary Tompkins, whom Evans had deputized. Citizens with rifles behind posts and barrels on the unlit streets.

As bullets tore into the *Bulletin* office, bullets from all flanks, and from inside the office, tore into the attackers.

From inside Yuma thumbed his Colt in rapid succession. A horse and rider buckled and fell to the ground. The horse staggered up to its feet. The rider didn't.

When Yuma's Colt was empty he picked up the scattergun, pulled back both hammers, and squeezed once, twice, into the swirling horsemen in the street.

First Jim Gettings, then another rider fell, both dead.

Crossfire ripped into the whirling attackers. Two more were wounded, one fired back desperately, but both managed to flee.

Inside, Jess Evans' gun dropped to the floor and he grasped his arm with his left hand.

Yuma ran to him.

"Jess, are you all right?"

"Hell, no. Dirty bastards winged me."

"Winged you, hell." Elmer Dodson was descending the stairs carrying an ancient pistol, cocked. He pointed at the shot-up printing press. "The dirty bastards plugged my press."

CHAPTER 69

President Ulysses Simpson Grant entered the bedroom. It was early morning—ten years since that night at the shack near Vicksburg—weeks after Grant had written and sent the letters and something else to Custer and Yuma. Late as it was, Grant was surprised to see his wife awake in bed reading by lamplight.

"Julia, you're up late."

"Well, I'm not exactly *up*. But you certainly are—at, what is it—past three in the morning. Ulys, you look . . . pensive . . . Are you all right?"

"Julia . . ."

"Yes, Ulys?"

Grant took a step closer and smiled.

"I have a confession to make, Mrs. Grant."

"What is it, Mr. President?"

"While I was downstairs I had a glass of whiskey."

"Alone?"

"Not exactly. With those two soldiers I met at Vicksburg—I sent them each a letter and a flacon of whiskey to commemorate the occasion."

"That's very nice, Ulys. And now"—she patted the bed—"I think it's time we commemorate another occasion."

At the same time in Monroe, George Armstrong Custer was reading Grant's letter aloud.

"'. . . and so, on this, the tenth anniversary of Vicksburg, where Destiny brought the three of us together, take a swallow of this good whiskey first—and *then* read the last paragraph.'"

Custer did as Grant had ordered in the letter.

Libbie could not, nor did she try, to disguise her anxiety.

"What is it, George? What did he write in the last paragraph?"

Custer's eyes widened.

"He wrote . . . 'and, George, to hell with that court-martial. As commander-in-chief, I'm ordering you back to the 7th. Sincerely, U.S. Grant.'"

Libbie flew into Custer's arms and kissed him.

"Custer Boy, shall we go upstairs and start packing?"

"Upstairs, yes." Custer smiled. "Packing, no."

He lifted Libbie, cradled her in both arms, and started singing the words to the tune of "Garryowen."

"Our hearts so stout have got us fame,
For soon 'tis known from whence we came,
Where're we go they dread the name,
Of Garryowen in glory."

". . . well, go on, John." Elmer Dodson took a swig from his coffee cup. "What else does President Grant have to say?"

"Johnny." Rosemary touched Yuma's shoulder. "Are you sure you don't want to keep the rest of it to yourself?"

"Hell, no!" Jess Evans said, "I want to hear what Ol' Whiskers got to say."

"Well,"—Johnny nodded—"he says, I mean he wrote, 'After Appomattox, and as president, I continued to track you down, which wasn't easy. And as the tenth anniversary of Vicksburg approaches, I thought it was time you, Custer, and I had that drink together, not in heaven or hell, but someplace in between. Custer wanted command of the 7th again. He's got it. If there's anything I can do for you send me a telegraph.

"'Maybe it was fate, providence, or destiny that brought us together. Whatever it was, and though it's a creation big country—I hope our trails cross again. Custer, Grant, and Yuma—two Yanks and a Reb—three Americans. Sincerely, U.S. Grant.'"

"John, in all those pages you sent back you never wrote about meeting Grant."

"No, Mr. Dodson. Some things I didn't write about."

"It's a hell of a story. It'd make you famous. Maybe you'll write it . . . someday."

"Maybe." Yuma smiled. "Rosemary, would you like me to walk you home?"

"No, Johnny." She placed her hand around his arm. "Tonight you can *take* me home . . . to our son."

As they started to leave, Elmer Dodson had one more question.

"John, is there anything that you'd like President Grant to do for you?"

"He already has, Mr. Dodson, 'Two Yanks and a Reb—Three Americans.'"

A. J. Fenady Remembers the Duke

Mary Claire Kendall

That America craves strength in the face of increasing challenges and threats, within and without, makes John Wayne, who died in 1979, more relevant and beloved than ever.

Recently I spoke with author Andrew J. Fenady about "the Duke" to mark the 105th anniversary of his birth on May 26. I interviewed A.J. at his offices in Hollywood near Paramount Pictures. Writer-producer Fenady's long parade of credits consists of TV series, including *The Rebel, Branded, Hondo*, sixteen novels, seven stage plays, and many features including *The Sea Wolf* (1993), *The Man with Bogart's Face* (1980), and *Chisum* (1970).

While developing *Chisum*, Fenady spent much time in many places with the Duke during and between the filming of *Hellfighters, True Grit*, and *The Undefeated*. Fenady was with him the night Duke won his Oscar and the day Duke, along with friends, celebrated five years after his lung operation, when he was declared cancer free.

Before his Oscar win, Fenady said, "Duke tipped his hand while we were having a drink together at the bar: I said, 'Good luck tonight, Duke,' and he said, 'Well, McFenady, we gave it our best shot.' But, I could tell he was confident." And, sure enough, Fenady said smiling, "He let something slip on stage after he presented an award. Even though he was not scheduled to appear again unless he won for best actor, Duke nodded to the audience and said, 'I'll see you later.'"

Fenady "first bumped into Wayne—almost" shortly after arriving in Hollywood in the early 1950s, "still smelling of college." Fenady was tooling around Hollywood in his Oldsmobile looking at the front of the studios, the billboards, the gates—to Paramount, RKO, Universal, Twentieth Century–Fox, MGM—as he liked to do, wondering if he'd "ever be able to be inside one of those Camelots." As he was approaching the Barham Gate at Warner Brothers, he recounted:

All of a sudden, out of the gate and off the curb strides the biggest man—the biggest anything I've ever seen in my life—against the light. He had the red light, I had the green and he's striding across the street like he owns it and I slam on the brakes and twist the wheel and the cars behind me do the same and I stopped and I looked out, and recognizing it was John Wayne, put my head out the window. He turned around and said,

"Why you dumb bastard, why don't you learn how to drive that damn car?" I had a ready riposte—I wasn't going to take it. Not even from John Wayne. I nodded and said, "Yes, sir." He kept walking to the Mexican café across the street and flipped the Camel cigarette before making an entrance.

Years later, in Durango, while filming *Chisum*, Fenady said he told Wayne this story: "Duke looked at me, smiled, and said, 'Oh, were *you* that dumb bastard?' as if he remembered."

Fenady formally met Wayne at Paramount where Wayne was filming *Hatari!* and Fenady was working on the *Rebel* TV series (1959–1961). Fenady had hired a "cutter" (now called an editor), Otho Lovering, who had worked on many of Wayne's films, including *Stagecoach*, *The Long Voyage Home*, and later, *The Alamo* and *McClintock*.

One day, sitting in his office, as usual with his door open, Fenady said, "I hear Otho's voice: 'Hey Andy. There's someone out here who wants to come in and say hello. Is it OK?' I said, 'Bring him in, that's what doors are for.' So, in comes skinny, little Otho and there filling the whole damn doorway is the Duke. And he comes over and he sticks his hand out and shakes hands and then Otho says to Duke, 'Look. See, that's what I was telling you about.'"

Otho was pointing to a blown-up publicity photo

from *Hondo* that went all the way from the ceiling to the floor of Fenady's office.

"*Hondo*. That's one of my favorite pictures," Duke said. "The rights to *Hondo* come back to me in a couple of years." After that, Fenady said, "Duke would stop by *The Rebel* dailies or the set grinning, and say, 'I might want to get into this television business myself some day.' A couple of years later, after becoming pals and working out with Duke's son, Michael, at the gym, all the stars lined up. "I'd made a deal with MGM," Fenady said, "and remembering Duke's comment, 'the rights come back to me,' I worked out a deal, developed, wrote, and produced the series *Hondo*, in partnership with MGM and Batjac [Duke's production company]."

Working for John Wayne, Fenady said, meant *achievement*. "You were top of the world. You worked with and moved with the best." During World War II, he said, Duke got a bum rap because he didn't join up: "First off, Duke was thirty-five years old with a wife, four kids, and a studio to support." He tried time and again to join John Ford's naval unit but his request was blocked by Herbert Yates at Republic for just "one more picture"—a war picture like *Flying Tigers*, *Fighting Seabees*, *Back to Bataan*. "Duke's visits and efforts for the troops, like Bob Hope's," said Fenady, "continued years after, in Korea and Vietnam."

The story of how *Chisum* came about will be told in Fenady's book, tentatively titled, *Big Enough for*

John Wayne . . . and Me. Though, he did offer a couple of gems for this interview:

Cigar Smoke

When I went to talk to Duke about *Chisum,* he said, "Okay, McFenady"—he always called me McFenady—"let's hear about Uncle John." Well, I knew he knew about Chisum because he called him Uncle John. I said, "Look, Duke, do you mind if I light up a cigar and smoke?" John Wayne had had a lung operation and his smoking was *verboten.* He looked at me and said, "Not if you blow the smoke in my direction." And then, when we were going to do the picture, Duke says, "Hey, McFenady, you know, when I'm up there, up on that horse (on the mountain), looking down and in a couple of other places, have Chisum smoke a cigar." His son, Michael, and I both cleared our throats, but it was useless to protest. There was no such word as *verboten* for the Duke. Chisum smoked and so did the Duke, but Duke smoked those expensive Cuban cigars in the picture . . . and so did I on the set."

Commemorativo Tequila Versus Gordon's Gin

Duke introduced me to salsa. He put it on everything—breakfast, lunch, dinner; whatever he had, he doused with salsa. He tried to introduce me to Commemorativo tequila, which was his drink. I stuck with Gordon's gin largely because I liked the taste of it and also because it was Ernest Hemingway's favorite drink. I figured what the hell, neither Hemingway nor I was going to drink anything with a worm in it . . . not even with salsa."

The film business has changed a lot since *Chisum.* In spite of what John Chisum, played by Wayne, says, change has not always been "for the better."

"Duke," Fenady said, "used to use the phrase 'when ours was a small business.'" Fenady said Columbia Studios in the 1930s and early 1940s budgeted just $17 million, with which they made fifty-three pictures, three or four for $1 million, whereas the others cost around $300,000. "It *was* a small business," he said, "and it was largely owned by and controlled by first-generation immigrants who came here to succeed, who loved this business. For them it wasn't a corporation, it was their studio, their home, it was their life." By contrast, today, "you don't know who to go to talk to for an okay. In the old days I've gotten okays by talking to one person at a studio. Today you can't do that . . . There aren't any Warners, Mayers, Cohns, Fords, and Capras. It's all mathematics."

Asked what memories well up inside him on the anniversary of Wayne's birth and death, Fenady said, his voice cracking ever so slightly, "I don't need any anniversaries to remember him . . . There's not a day that goes by that I don't remember him."

Nonetheless, two days later, on the anniversary of the Duke's birth, when I asked, "Do you remember how you heard the news on the day of Duke's death?" he said:

> I remember vividly. I got a phone call in the afternoon from a good friend of mine, Ted Thackrey, a reporter at the *L.A. Times.* "A.J.," he said, "we're not supposed to release this story for another two hours, but I know you'd want to know. Duke just bought the farm."
>
> The next day while we were shooting *The Man with Bogart's Face,* and just before noon, I asked for silence on the set and had the effects man toll a bell nine times for John Wayne, then said, "Duke beat the count—he got up and made it to the Big Sky." And during the day a lot of the radio stations kept playing the theme from *The High and the Mighty.*

Over three decades later, John Wayne remains indelibly imprinted in America's consciousness. The further out from his death, the more popular he is, ranking as "America's favorite movie star" as recently as January 2012 according to a Harris poll—a position he's held since the early 1990s.

Wayne—playing the "good guy," reassuringly leading and trouncing the "bad guys"—remains larger than life.

Why is this so?

Why is it the Duke forever commands that special corner of America's collective mind, where we desire nothing more than the Old West values he epitomized, where good and evil are clear cut?

The answer, Fenady said, lies in Wayne's philosophy, which was simple: "There's only one defense: Strength. Stay strong." "There comes a time," Fenady said, "when you find out you can't do business with Hitler. You can't do business with Stalin. You can't do business with L.G. Murphy—and some other current dictators." All the westerns Fenady worked on—*The Rebel, Hondo, Chisum,* he said, "had something in common: "Those fellows were pushed and pushed and pushed and finally they had been pushed enough and that's when Duke says, as in *Chisum,* 'Break out the Winchesters.' That's the way that he looked at it."

Critics of "the Old West" ushered in "New Hollywood"—the landmark 1967 film *Bonnie and Clyde* that glorified "bad guy" Western outlaws and outcasts, serving as the vanguard. in his 1995 off-the-cuff remarks accepting the prestigious Golden Boot Award,* Fenady responded to "those

---

*The Golden Boot Awards dinner, held for twenty-five years from 1983 to 2007, benefited the Motion Picture and Television Home and Hospital, which Mary Pickford, "the woman who made Hollywood," founded to help those in the film industry when they fell on hard times. The Motion Picture and Television Fund sponsors it. Having itself fallen on hard times, in 2009, the fund announced plans to close the home and hospital. Though, it was saved, its finances remain precarious. The night in 1995 that A. J. Fenady received the Golden Boot, he was joined by Claire Trevor and Burt Lancaster (in memoriam) among other stars.

righteous revisionists of the West who take such great delight in doing everything they can to demean, defame, defile, and pervert anyone who ever wore a badge or uniform, any man or woman who ever moved West":

> To those critics I would say, "Where would you have had the pilgrims and the pioneers stop?" At Plymouth Rock? Manhattan? The Allegheny and Monongahela? The Shenandoah? The Ohio? The Mississippi? The Missouri? The Red River? The Colorado? Where would you have had them draw the line and say, "This is far enough."
>
> Me? I'm glad they kept coming west. Otherwise California wouldn't be the thirty-first state. There wouldn't be a Hollywood. We wouldn't be here tonight and I would not have had the privilege and pleasure of meeting and working with people like John Wayne and so many others.
>
> It's easy for the critics to look back and say, "They could have done it differently—they could have been kinder and gentler"—well, maybe so; but the wonder is that they did it at all. And a lot of them died a not-so-kind-and-gentle death in the doing. On all sides the paths of glory led to the grave. And there was guilt and glory enough to go around on all sides—but for the most part, right was done,

and it was done right—and that's how the West was won!

"Instead of finding the heroic aspect of a character," Fenady said, "the Arthur Penns and Bob Altmans did everything to denigrate and downgrade the heroes, the Custers, the Hickocks, and the Buffalo Bills. They figured that was the way to get the attention of the young revolutionaries—hippies—of the time."

Ah, but Wayne *was* kinder and gentler, captured in the story of when Wayne met Fenady's wife, Mary Frances, mother of their six children. When Duke saw her wearing an elephant pin, he assumed it was because she was a Republican. But she made a slight correction, telling him, "It's a talisman from my husband, lest I forget him when he's away shooting a film. *Elephants never forget.*" Years later, when the Fenadys were having dinner at Chasen's with Michael Wayne and his wife, Gretchen—godparents to their youngest child—Michael reached into his pocket and pulled out a small elephant key chain.

"J.W.," Michael said, "asked me to give this to Mary Frances, 'so she won't forget him.'"

But, then, who could ever forget the Duke?

About the Author

Andrew J. Fenady was born in Toledo, Ohio, in 1928. A veteran writer and producer in Hollywood, Fenady created and produced *The Rebel* (1959–1961) for television, starring Nick Adams. The top-rated show lasted three seasons and the Fenady-penned theme song, "Johnny Yuma," became a No. 1 hit for Johnny Cash. He wrote and produced the 1970 John Wayne hit *Chisum* and the popular TV western series *Hondo* and *Branded*. His other credits include the adaptation of Jack London's *The Sea Wolf*, with Charles Bronson and Christopher Reeve, and the western feature *Ride Beyond Vengeance*, which starred Chuck Connors.

His acclaimed western novels include *Big Ike, Riders to Moon Rock, The Trespassers,* and *The Summer of Jack London.*

Fenady presently lives in Los Angeles and has been honored with the Golden Boot Award, the Silver Spur Award, and the Owen Wister Award for his lifetime contribution to westerns.

THE FIRST MOUNTAIN MAN SERIES BY
WILLIAM W. JOHNSTONE

Available Wherever Books Are Sold!

Visit our website at **www.kensingtonbooks.com**

THE LAST GUNFIGHTER SERIES BY
WILLIAM W. JOHNSTONE